Safehouse

Safehouse

JAMES ADLEY

Published under licence by Brown Dog Books and
The Self-Publishing Partnership Ltd, 10b Greenway Farm, Bath Rd,
Wick, nr. Bath BS30 5RL

www.selfpublishingpartnership.co.uk

ISBN printed book: 978-1-83952-582-7
ISBN e-book: 978-1-83952-583-4

Cover design by Jason Anscomb
Internal design by Andrew Easton

Printed and bound in the UK

This book is printed on FSC(R)® certified paper

DEDICATION

For my wife, Jude, with love and thanks
for your insight, wisdom and
constant encouragement

Part I

Chapter One

The Sussex Countryside, 1950.

Dragonflies and painted lady butterflies shimmered or swept by silently, mesmerised in the hot air. Two friends aged seventeen, on the threshold of adulthood but pausing for one final summer, asking time to stand still, reluctant to leave the languid riverbank. Eleanor had long dark brown hair, eyes beyond her years, a healthy, slightly freckled face. Sally's blonde hair came from her father, the essence of Mediterranean beauty from her mother, and she carried it all with a self-assured vibrancy that local boys found irresistible.

The friends sat cross-legged, watching the river as an occasional fish disturbed the surface, and talked and talked. Sally had stayed with Eleanor at their Sussex farm every summer for many years. It had become an always and forever, it had never been different, and in the winding-lane sanctity of a wonderful childhood was the unspoken promise that it would never change.

As the years went by, their conversations changed. By 1950 they inhabited that pivotal space between the past and the future, the cherished and the anticipated. And how the world was changing!

Frippery and gossip had been replaced by nascent feminism. Why shouldn't women do this and that?

Eleanor was in full flow.

'It's not about progress or votes or 'Can we attain this or that?' It's a right. I mean if we had a Bill of Rights like *they* do, my first amendment would say 'Men shall grant women nothing as equality is not theirs to offer. Women have the inalienable right to do just *everything...*'

'Think that wording went a bit awry there, El! Started well though!'

Then, as the sun climbed, the High Talk usually changed to delicious gossip. This mid-morning, Sally was bemoaning, berating and, according to Eleanor, *bleating.*

'Why must we be the cleverest? Midway would be fine, but no, we have to be in a school where we find ourselves on our own because we like academia, we like working, and we might want to talk about something other than boys.'

'Not much mind,' Sally said, imitating their classmate Phoebe from Norfolk.

'Oh no, not much mind,' agreed Eleanor. 'But there's a place for Catullus and Ovid before cigs behind the gym.'

They stripped off, flung themselves into the river, splashed around, complained about the hard, muddy riverbank as usual, and then dried off in the sun. They ate their sandwiches in the copse and fell asleep listening to the bees and enjoying the fragrant jasmine and lavender.

Eleanor lay in a reverie, the willowy place before sleep, and remembered the conversation that had brought them to their annual riverbank summer.

Sally and Eleanor hadn't been particularly close friends. It was the end of the spring term, and the class was alive with chatter about upcoming Easter breaks, walks, family events and parties.

'We'll meet on Hampstead Heath, near Kenwood House,' Felicity was reminding Alice, as she jumped up and down on her wooden chair excitedly.

Evelyn and Rita lived near Richmond Park.

'Saturday mornings at the Rex, sherbet lemons, afternoons in the park.' Dierdre's dress was filthy as usual from her time at the potter's wheel.

'Hey, Terracotta', Melissa called from the back row. 'How're you going to survive without your clay?'

'Don't be daft,' Dierdre retorted, in an affected upper-class voice. 'Do you honestly think I don't have a pottery room at home?'

There were just two girls who remained silent during these exultant late-term exchanges. It was unlikely that the children were aware of their withdrawal from the conversation, so absorbed were they in their own holiday predictions. The first time it occurred to Sally that she was not alone in having little to say about her upcoming holiday was when they both left the room.

Sally, with her apparent self-assurance, always left Eleanor feeling envious and inadequate.

Then, as they were walking down the corridor, Sally said, 'You're not looking forward to the holidays either, are you?'

'Is it that obvious?'

'Yes, every end of term, you never talk about Christmas or summer. Nothing. You just stay silent. And the sad thing is, so do I'.

Later at lunchtime break in the spinney, Sally was twiddling a daisy in her hand.

'I have to turn nature and flowers into my friends, that's how bad it is. My parents work for the Catalucian Government. They're important people, but they don't have much time for me!'

Looking down at the grass, as if she couldn't bear the honesty, Eleanor said, 'I adore my parents, but my father has a farm in the middle of nowhere. Hardly anyone comes to see us and they're always doing something with the cows or sheep. I know they'd like to do more with me, but it never changes.' Then suddenly, a flash of inspiration came to her. She jumped up. 'I know, I know. Why don't you come and stay with me in the summer holidays?'

Annoying things called *arrangements* had to be made, but then five years earlier, the wonderful riverbank summers had begun.

As four o' clock approached, they walked up the path, watched the procession of the cows as they wandered in for milking, and found themselves, yet again, watching Jerms bale the hay. They couldn't say if he was improving, but his upper body filled them with longing. When they had imbibed as much of Jerms' charms as they could without the total embarrassment of discovery, they walked across the yard and lay on the cane couches in the cool of the farmhouse lounge, reading.

As they sat quietly, their reading was interrupted by thoughts and reflections. There had been an unspoken acquiescence, a resignation – not entirely melancholy, it must be said; they both knew this would be the last of their long-grass summers. Their adolescence was reaching adulthood, and by next summer they would hopefully be at different universities of their choice.

How would they stay close as they followed their different paths? They had spent two holidays each year apart; Sally flew to Catalucia to be with her parents at Christmas and Easter. They both attended

St Brendan's Catholic girls' school, Sally as a boarder and Eleanor as a day girl. The future was less certain, and their relationship had perhaps relied too much on the rhythms of the year.

In the cool, dark lounge, Eleanor sat up. 'How should we mark our valedictory summer?'

'I've been wondering that too. Neither of us have kind of wanted to speak about it.'

'Well, now I have, we can enjoy the last week, and think about how we'll keep in touch.'

They knew their relationship would change; that there was an inevitability to it. But neither could foresee the dramatic contrast between the elegiac memory of the tranquil riverbank and the turbulent tides to come.

They arrived at the Greyhound pub with make-up and carefully selected summer dresses, intended to convey an entirely false nonchalance about their appearance.

They walked through the old, beamed saloon, where farmers and farmhands were relaxing after an exhausting day in the fields. One or two smoked pipes, and the general conversation was one of thanks, the weather had been wet enough in spring and dry enough the last few weeks for good combining. As the girls reached the small narrow skittle alley at the back of the pub, the brown wooden skittles had been set up and the RAF boys were ready to greet them. Eleanor and Sally preferred them in uniform, with their razor-sharp trouser creases and open-neck Fighter Boy jackets.

Douglas and Martin were from RAF Ringmer.

'We're the ambassadors of the RAF in the Greyhound,' Doug said cheerfully.

'If all ambassadors looked like they do,' Sally said to Eleanor, 'there'd be peace on earth.'

Safehouse

Sally was drinking even more than usual. She was standing so close to Martin; her breasts were nearly touching him and his eyes were devouring her. The skittles were soon forgotten as somebody played the piano. Jerms had come over to Eleanor and they joined a few couples dancing in an area of the pub where the tables had been cleared. The farmers were sitting outside, and Eleanor felt Jerms' strong muscular chest leaning against her. Jerms and Douglas and a few other RAF guys brought some chairs together, and soon they were all laughing and joking; as the drink took effect, the flirting became more obvious. Eleanor and Jerms left together, and he kissed her by a field gate. He started to touch her breasts, and Eleanor pushed him back gently.

'You know Jerms, we've always been friends. I'm leaving in a week. Let's leave as friends too. What do you think?'

Jerms reluctantly agreed.

It was late August and the bright June nights were long gone. It was dark as Jerms walked away, looking the slightest bit disconsolate, but Eleanor knew he'd have forgotten it all by tomorrow.

Eleanor saw Sally walk away from the pub, back towards the farmhouse. She caught up, expecting her to be giggly, slightly drunk and full of gossip. Sally looked at her, didn't smile and mumbled something about having drunk too much.

'Have to get to bed.'

She was straightening her skirt and doing something Eleanor couldn't see clearly with her T-shirt. When they arrived at the farmyard, Sally seemed unsure about what she wanted to do.

'I could go to bed, or maybe I'll sit a while by the milking shed and just watch the moon. Night, Eleanor.'

'Sally,' Eleanor said quietly, 'what's the matter?'

'Not that much. Martin didn't get what he wanted. I didn't get what I wanted either.'

Contemplative, quietly spoken and melancholy; not words Eleanor would have used to describe her summer friend.

'Did he–?'

'He didn't do much.'

Then she said the words that should have set Eleanor's alarm bells ringing, if only she had thought about it that night.

'He's an RAF pilot. I'm a schoolgirl who drank too much. Nothing happened really, El. My bra was off, we fumbled, I stood up. It never really happened.'

It was so ambiguous. What was it that didn't happen? Was it something Sally wanted to happen? Eleanor couldn't be sure. It was only later, much later, that Eleanor realised what Sally had meant. Nobody would believe her; nobody would take her side in an argument about a fumble in a wheat field. Everyone had seen Sally get drunk every night. She'd even asked boys to buy her secret drinks when the bar staff had been told not to serve her anymore.

Sally stood up, and unsteadily, in the dark of that August night, made her way into the farmhouse and up to bed.

The next morning Sally was up quite early. She was talking to Myra, Eleanor's mother, recently returned from a physicists' convention in London.

'I'll get the midday train to Waterloo. I can't thank you enough for another amazing summer.'

Eleanor wasn't listening to the words. It was as if Sally's demeanour had been subjected to a surgical operation. Her shoulders were low, her head was stooped, her eyes had lost their lustre and sparkle. The music had changed from major to minor in a matter of hours.

'But Sally, we've still got a week.'

Sally beckoned to Eleanor and they walked into the yard,

where Jerms could be seen in the distance, cycling towards the house.

'The magic's gone, El. I'm sorry. I want to remember the incredible days, but today wouldn't be another of those.'

'It's about last night, Sally, isn't it? Let's sit down by the stile and talk about it.'

'You know what, El, we could talk all day, and I'd still be telling myself what a silly, stupid girl I am. A tart is what they call me, at the airbase.'

'How dare they! I'll speak to that squadron leader.'

'No. You'll not speak to any squadron leader, El, because they're right. 'Sally gets her top off,' they say. 'If you're lucky, maybe a bit more. Not Eleanor. Oh no, she's decent and proper.'

'I can't spend time with you now I know what they think. We'll keep in touch. We'll stay friends forever, El. But I need distance, time until we meet again, to be with people who think of me differently. Maybe I need to think of myself differently. I don't know. But I have to leave. Mum and Dad get back into London tomorrow, so I'll stay at the house in Victoria tonight.'

Eleanor moved to hug her friend. And they did hug, but there are hugs that mean it and hugs that don't. It didn't.

Chapter Two

Museum of Fine Arts, Boston, USA. 13 April 1950

Adrienne's Easter holiday was nearing its end, and soon she would return for her final semester. After graduating the previous year from Girton College, Cambridge, with a first-class honours degree in History, she had won a Fulbright Scholarship to study at Harvard University. She was admiring Edward Hopper's *Summer Evening*, depicting a young couple standing on a porch. She walked back a few paces to improve her view.

'Together, but lonely.'

She turned and saw a tall man – *older*, she thought, *than her* – also looking at the picture.

'Perhaps they're just quiet,' Adrienne said.

'The evening light accentuates their pain,' the man replied.

'Not certain about that. It provides opportunity for the porch to be lit,' Adrienne said.

The man turned to her. 'I'm Howard Goldberg.'

'I don't usually have conversations with strangers.'

'Me neither, but then I don't know many girls who can talk intelligently about Edward Hopper.'

'And you're the arbiter of talking intelligently?'

'Let's look at another picture,' Howard said.

They both looked in awe at *Gas*, which depicted a lonely, isolated petrol station, in the early evening, on an empty road. The attendant was standing by the pumps.

She turned to him. 'I'm Adrienne Franck. Why're you in Boston?'

'I work for Sotheby's in London. They've sent me here to see the retrospective and meet Mr Hopper when he gets out of hospital.'

'You're going to meet Edward Hopper?'

'Actually, I met him in Maine last year, when we sold some pictures for him. And yes, I'm hoping to see him again in the next few days. And you?'

They were sitting on a bench, surrounded by Hopper paintings.

'I'm a Fulbright scholar at Harvard, working on a thesis about conflict resolution in international relations.'

'Isn't Henry Kissinger there? The one that wrote about Metternich?'

'Yes, I study with him.'

They continued to work their way around the exhibition, discussing each of Hopper's artworks.

'Do you think you might have dinner with me after we've finished looking at the exhibition?' Howard asked, his voice conspicuously public school.

'No, I don't think so,' Adrienne said. 'But once I've called Sotheby's in London, I'd be happy to meet you tomorrow evening.'

'That would be lovely. Do you know Parker's Restaurant in School Street?'

'I don't, but I'll see you outside.'

'Actually, the restaurant's inside the Omni Hotel, so I'll meet you near reception, at 7.30.'

As Adrienne made her way back to her hotel, she was surprised by her own excitement. She rarely found men either interesting or attractive, but during the short time that she'd spent with Howard, she had to admit she thought he could be both.

The following morning, she called Sotheby's in Bond Street, and asked to speak to Howard Goldberg.

A voice that might have come from Clarence House answered the phone. 'I'm awfully sorry, Mr Goldberg's in America at present. Can I leave a message?'

'Could you ask him to call Adrienne Franck, please?' She gave her number.

'Certainly, Miss Franck.'

The old, traditional restaurant had a yellow-tiled floor, a row of chandeliers through the centre of the ceiling, and comfortable red leather chairs.

Adrienne and Howard were enjoying their conversation, and they were making the most of the opportunity afforded by dining opposite each other, as they were able to look at each other, rather than glimpse or secretly gaze. Adrienne thought Howard's face was strong, open and honest, with a broad, slightly quizzical smile.

Howard just enjoyed looking at Adrienne. He loved her face and her smile, without noticing any individual features.

Once they'd ordered, they indulged in the joy of discovery. Somehow, everything seemed interesting. Howard had always been fascinated by politics, and it was clear that Adrienne had firm views about art. Finding an attractive person, genuinely interested in the other's passions, was something to savour, along with the lobster bisque, which also told a story. Howard's name was Goldberg, so it was clear he was Jewish. He was fairly certain that Adrienne was Jewish too.

Adrienne helped immediately. 'I see you're as *frum* as me!'

'Frum' referred to the extent to which a Jew was observant and adhered to the traditions and dietary laws. An observant Jew would not eat in a non-kosher restaurant, and anyone who kept the dietary laws would not eat pork or shellfish. Ordering lobster bisque was proof that they were non-Orthodox Jews, while saying nothing about the importance they attached to other aspects of Judaism: history, learning, synagogue, culture or Zionism, or indeed, the question as to whether they had some relationship with the Almighty.

'How did you get into art ... into Sotheby's?' Adrienne asked

'My law degree told me I never wanted to look at a legal book again. Ever since I was in my early teens, when my friends watched Betty Grable at the Rex, I loved looking at Cézanne, Manet and the Dutch masters. Then I saw an advert in the *Evening News* for a junior position at Sotheby's.'

'You must've done well to be sent to interview Hopper,' Adrienne said.

'When you absolutely love something, it's pretty easy to excel at it. I look at friends and their work and, well ... I'm lucky. Your turn!'

'I read History at Girton, Cambridge. Did well...'

'You mean you got a first?'

'Actually, yes.'

'Better than well, then. Sorry, carry on.'

The main courses arrived on big white plates: a huge steak for Howard, and lemon sole for Adrienne.

Adrienne continued. 'My dissertation caused quite a stir, and next thing I heard, my professor had circulated it to the UK Foreign Office and the US State Department. I was astounded, I can tell you.'

'So, what was its central point?'

'Never ask an academic a question like that if you don't want an answer!'

'What about if I do?' He smiled and Adrienne thought she hadn't enjoyed herself this much since her dad had bought her the *Encyclopaedia Britannica*.

'If you do, I'll tell you,' she said. 'When I decided to study History, it meant I couldn't study my other love, Psychology. But then I began thinking about the relationship between states, and I realised the principles applying to individual needs might also apply to nation states. I hadn't met Henry Kissinger then, but he agrees with me about the principle, though we disagree about many other issues.'

'I'm interested in psychology too,' Howard said, 'but more the psychology of art and artists.'

As the conversation continued, they realised this was something special. They both knew it without hesitation. Far too quickly the coffee came, and the dinner was almost over.

'So, what are your plans?' Adrienne heard herself saying.

'Tomorrow I'm interviewing Edward Hopper, then I have one free day before I go back to London. Have you ever been to the Maine coast, to York and Ogunquit?'

'No, I've never heard of them.'

'Well, there's a lovely beach and lighthouses. How'd you like to spend the day out there before I go home?'

Adrienne looked up at him and smiled. 'Howard, I'd love to.'

Maine Coast

Sitting next to Howard as he drove the Chevy, Adrienne was drunk with happiness. She'd thought about how quickly her feelings had developed for Howard, how she'd only seen him twice, how she felt like a teenager. She didn't care.

Maybe you just have to grab your chance of happiness when you see it, she thought, as she waited for Howard to pick her up. It was a sunny and windy day. They drove from Boston, through New Hampshire to the Maine coast; Howard kept to the coastal road until they passed the Portsmouth lighthouse, where they stopped and took in some wonderful sea air and the stunning view. Later they stopped briefly at York Harbour and looked at the boats and the clapboard houses. They held hands for the first time as they wandered along the road, and sat on a bench looking out to sea.

'If it wasn't for Mr Hopper, I wouldn't be here with you, looking out to sea,' Howard said.

'Well, you'd better thank Edward Hopper then, hadn't you?' she said, and smiled at him.

They went back to the car with its lovely smell of new leather and drove towards Ogunquit, where they walked down to the huge beach.

They began to walk into the wind, just where the tidal point made the sand damp. The wide vista, the huge bay, the sky curving like a light-blue dome, the feeling of space with the waves crashing on the beach were all perfect for their mood.

Howard wondered if his feelings might be racing ahead of Adrienne's. Adrienne wasn't worried about anything; she was just enjoying the walk, the day and the attraction.

'Everything in America's so optimistic,' she said. 'The shops are full of things we've not seen for years, the waitresses smile, the people seem happy. It couldn't be more different to London really, could it?'

'I'm afraid my views on all of that aren't very fashionable,' Howard said.

'Thank God for that! Who wants to be fashionable? I don't.'

They walked towards a café just above the beach, which advertised soda pops, popcorn, and pancakes and syrup. It had a red and white ring outside with the words, 'Beach Café' and 'In here, it's always sunny!' written around the edge.

They ordered pancakes with ice cream and syrup. Howard soon had ice cream on his upper lip, like a 4-year-old.

'So, what are these *unfashionable views*?' she asked.

'It's springtime and sunny, we're on a beach, and you want to talk politics?'

'I'm an academic! Give me a lovely beach, an interesting guy with ice cream all over his face, a view like that,' she pointed out to sea, 'and then top it all by having a chat that's not about the film at the drive-in!'

'Okay. Well, you're right. This side of the Pond people seem much happier and definitely more confident, and it's not hard to know why.'

'Really?'

Howard stopped spooning the pancakes and wiped his lip. 'Americans believe in success, not failure. While we're busy feather-bedding people, encouraging them to do nothing, paying them unemployment benefit, for God's sake, giving them free health care, the Americans exude success and excellence. They want people to do well, get on, make money, raise a family, buy a car, a house in the suburbs. We've got mealy mouthed socialists like Bevan and Cripps whining about Welsh valleys and slums.'

'You're right about one thing,' she said

'Only one?'

'Your views aren't fashionable. But you're also lucky.'

'Because?'

'You're with a girl who agrees with everything you just said. I look at Harvard and it's got a similar ethos to Cambridge, but Cambridge might as well be an island back home. Here, everyone believes in competition, in winning at sport, leading the class, being the best. That's why they're doing so well under Ike.'

There was a brief silence, except for the wind rattling the window. They could just hear the sea, as the tide was going out. Some children ran across the sand with a kite. The café was empty and the world had slowed down. Adrienne reached across the wooden table and took Howard's hand.

'Seems special to me,' she said, looking straight at Howard.

'It is special. Just a shame I'm going home tomorrow.' They leant in towards each other across the table.

'We can write and I'm going back in the summer. Maybe they'll find some more artists for you to interview.'

Before they left the beach, they found a sheltered spot with sand dunes and cliffs. Howard put his arm around Adrienne and they kissed and held each other. They stood arm in arm looking out to sea, and then, reluctantly, made their way back to the car and drove back towards Boston. They were as sure as they could be that this happy day would stay long in their memories.

They were right.

Chapter Three

Autumn 1950. Recovery

Eleanor was preparing for her upcoming start at university. She would be staying on the campus in Hove, studying Society and History. As she filled in forms and prepared clothes, she felt a pervading fear for Sally. On the third day after Sally's sudden departure, the phone had rung in the hall and Eleanor answered it.

'Oh, I'm glad you've answered the phone, El.' Eleanor instantly recognised Sally's mother. 'I want to talk to you about Sally.'

'Is she alright?'

'No, she's not alright. What happened before she came back to London? Something did.'

In the split second before she replied Eleanor realised how careful she had to be.

'Yes, she did seem a bit serious the morning she left the farm,' Eleanor said, avoiding the question. She had no idea what Sally had told her parents, if anything at all.

'This isn't really the time for half-answers like that. Sally stays in bed half the day, and yesterday she said she might not go to university yet.'

'I'll come to London immediately.'

'I suggested that. She says you've spent the summer together and she doesn't want to speak to you at the moment. If you're worrying about confidences … well, I'm worried about my daughter. So, let's talk, shall we?'

'I'll come to London,' Eleanor repeated.

On the journey to London, Eleanor's mind wandered to the wonderful farmyard days that would never return.

She met Sally's mother in Russell Square, the leaves beginning to turn. The tables were less busy, and there was a feeling in the air of endings rather than beginnings. It seemed right.

Maria's husband was an ambassador in Catalucia. Her aristocratic face and coiffured hair spoke of intellect and reason, self-discipline and calm. Today that calm was in retreat.

'I said goodbye to a happy, laughing Sally, and now I'm living with a different person.' She enunciated each word, so as to exhibit her pain and anger, even if she was uncertain about the direction in which the anger should be directed. 'So, if you know what happened in between, please just tell me.'

Eleanor wasn't surprised at what Maria had told her. She'd seen the change herself. Confidentiality seemed less important than Sally's welfare.

'Mrs Garcia…' Eleanor was quickly interrupted.

'Just so you know, I'm aware my daughter's no saint.'

Hesitantly, Eleanor related the events of that evening.

'How dishevelled did she look when you saw her?'

'It was dark. She straightened her top, but she was dressed. What's Sally told you?' Eleanor asked.

'Nothing really. She said it was the last summer by the river, she's going to stop drinking, and something about how she's just a very stupid girl.' Maria paused. 'Do you think she was raped?'

'Oh no, I don't think so,' Eleanor replied.

'You see, I think she may have been. But she won't speak about it, or anything else.'

'She has to go to university, Mrs Garcia! She has to, after all that work.'

Maria sat up in her chair, back straight, face ridden with anxiety. Her speech was staccato, her words clear and direct.

'Right now, Eleanor, I'm worried for my daughter and her wellbeing. If she doesn't spend this year learning about demography and imperialism, so be it. I want my daughter back. Help me.'

'But you said she won't see me.'

'She said she won't *speak* to you. Come with me back to the house.'

They walked back to the house without speaking. The first chill of autumn and the thought of seeing Sally merged into a cocktail of melancholy. They walked through the gates of the large official residence. The door was opened by a uniformed policeman. The grand hallway led up winding stairs to a landing with a light-beige carpet and ornate French settees. They walked through an unmarked door into the private quarters.

The room was tidy. The books were neatly on the shelves, and Sally was sitting up in bed, reading. As they walked into the room, Sally turned to face them and acknowledged their presence. There was perhaps the slightest glimpse of pleasure at seeing Eleanor, and then she continued reading as if she was alone.

Sally's mother left the room and Eleanor brought a chair near to her friend's bed. She sat there and held out her hand to touch Sally's arm. The joyful sparkling eyes, the carefree happiness that Eleanor loved was gone.

'Want to tell me anything? Want to talk?'

'I don't want to talk at all, to my mother, to you, or to anybody. I just want to stay in bed and read.'

There was a silence: grim and barren. Before Eleanor could say anymore, Sally looked at her, and began to weep.

'But I want you to stay here. I don't want you to leave me. I just want you to sit with me; I'm not making any plans or answering questions.'

Eleanor couldn't say how long she stayed in Sally's room. A woman came in and asked if they'd like an omelette for lunch; Eleanor said she would, and Sally didn't reply. Intermittently, Eleanor stood up and walked around the room, or looked out of the large window at the street below, where expensive cars vied for parking spaces.

Sometime during the afternoon, Eleanor was done.

'We can stay like this for a few days, but you can't throw your life away! It's hard enough for women to get to university. Allowing a man to change your mind just lets him win.'

Sally was not interested in debate. All the spark, the articulate tirades of the summer had disappeared. How should she deal with silence? Eleanor was young but she was intelligent. She recognised trauma, and she knew that Sally needed treatment from someone with professional expertise.

'Sally,' she said quietly. 'I'm going downstairs for a minute. I'll be back.'

She left the room and walked into the small lounge across from Sally's bedroom. She picked up the house phone and asked if Mrs Garcia could come up.

Sally's mother came into the room, hoping for a breakthrough, but looking at Eleanor, it was clear no progress had been made.

'She needs help from someone who knows what they're doing,' Eleanor said.

As she spoke, myriad thoughts entered her mind. Should she have known what Sally was doing? The Garcias had placed Sally in her family's care. Had that trust been betrayed?

Her feelings were not spared.

'It appears that you will be going to university and getting on with your life, while my daughter languishes hopelessly in her bedroom. I intend to find out what happened in your British countryside. This idyllic paradise that I've heard about every year seems to have produced what you find in that bedroom.'

Maria stopped talking and realised that perhaps she had been too severe on the teenager sitting opposite her. She didn't retract what she'd said, but she continued in a slightly less aggressive tone.

'That this happened near your farm does not make you responsible. It could even be said, knowing my daughter's propensity to get drunk and to flirt disgustingly, that I should not have allowed her to go to Sussex this year. I can't pretend my thoughts are clear, and my husband blames me completely.

We'll have to let a doctor see her, but neither of us have any faith in so-called psychiatrists, who dig up your past and ruin your future.'

Without warning, Maria's composure collapsed, and she wept on the velvet chair. Eleanor went over to her and knelt at her feet.

'Maybe we could help her together. I'm going to university, but I can get the train up to London often. I can spend time with Sally. Our love will help her recover.'

Maria nodded in agreement.

'But that still leaves the culprit. My husband and I have many contacts who will make sure they penetrate the secrecy surrounding your boys in the Sussex Royal Air Force!'

As autumn took hold, the mists and fogs of London shrouded the grand house in London. Sally gradually left her bedroom more often, ate a little more, and spoke reluctantly to the investigators who came to the house. The sessions were short. Each dealt with one part of the evening, so that Sally could describe the time in the pub before she had left by the back door with Martin. Soon a picture had been established. The married couple who owned the pub clearly had no time for Sally. Mrs Cooper described her as 'often drunk and rather flirty'. Her husband was less inhibited and said she was, 'a tart, throwing herself at the boys'.

Sally's parents talked long into the night about justice. They knew that Martin had done something for which he did not have consent. They also knew that their daughter had behaved without any dignity or restraint.

Sally's mother was clear: Martin should be brought to justice in a court. Her father was equally adamant that 'The reputation of this family and its presence on the international stage is not going to be diminished by testimony from our ill-disciplined daughter'.

And what did Sally want? She wanted to avoid descriptions of what had happened in the long grass and had no intention of giving evidence in court. In any event, no physical examination had taken place immediately after the alleged assault, there were plenty of people prepared to testify about Sally's behaviour, and in the climate of post-war Britain, the prospects for a successful prosecution of a Royal Air Force pilot were negligible.

Eleanor started university. Looking around the lecture hall she saw just one other girl amid all the confident, entitled boys. She'd never planned to go to the same university as Sally, yet Sally's absence cast its spell over the excitement of her first student term. She threw herself into her studies and spent many hours in the campus library. She loved the seminars, in which she could offer a feminine perspective on social and historical events. Some of the boys appeared to wonder why she was there at all – what good was it for a girl to go to university when she should be looking for a husband? Happily, there were boys with more progressive opinions, and she encountered left-wing views she'd never heard before.

One evening, her mother, Myra, spoke to her about her work away from the farm. She worked at the Faraday Institute, in Brighton, where she was an eminent physicist.

'What do you think of your country?' she asked her.

'What kind of question is that?'

'Possibly the most important of all questions, Eleanor, when it seems we have enemies all around us.'

'Well, it's quite an easy question to answer,' Eleanor said. 'I love it completely. I love its countryside and its cities, the fact that you can say more or less what you like, that we vote for our government. I've had a childhood deep in the Sussex countryside and I've loved it.'

Myra sat down next to Eleanor, and they hugged. Myra was swimming in a sea of love. Love and pride are a potent cocktail and in Eleanor, Myra had found both.

'What a wonderful answer. I know parents who'd love an answer like that.'

'Well, you got one.' Eleanor revelled in the opportunity to confirm her patriotism.

'I'm going to tell you something that proves how much I trust you. I am a physicist, but I also do other work to help this country that means so much to us.'

'You mean the work you do for the Intelligence Services.'

'You know?'

'How stupid do you think I am? I live here you know. I don't know exactly what you do, but I always assumed it was connected to your physics research.'

'I didn't realise you knew. There are people at the big universities indoctrinated by Communism and they'd like to betray our secrets. I play a very small part in trying to identify who they are, so other people can stop them.'

'I've heard some fairly silly views at university,' Eleanor said, 'but I just think they're young people and they're entitled to rebel.'

'I completely agree,' Myra said. 'It's when they take those views into adulthood and try to harm us that it gets serious.'

Eleanor didn't make too much of her mother's additional activities; they were linked to her work as a physicist, which was shrouded in mystery. It added to the admiration she had for her mother.

As winter approached, Eleanor visited Sally more often and coaxed her into going on shopping trips.

Sally was a more serious version of her previous self. She rarely laughed, never drank alcohol, and appeared to have very little purpose, but she was making progress. She still liked being in her bedroom with Eleanor. They sat quietly, cocooned in the huge residence, as the rush of Christmas spirit spread around them.

Chapter Four

At Harvard, Adrienne was taught by one of the twentieth century's most charismatic professors, McGeorge Bundy. His upbringing was so privileged it came the closest America offered to being aristocratic; he attended the most famous schools, graduated from Yale, and then became a senior lecturer at Harvard. Despite his background, he was not pompous, and was keen to recognise talent. In Adrienne Franck, he had identified a precocious intellect and an outstanding academic.

McGeorge was very popular with the Harvard students and liked to offer his views on their likely careers and skillsets as he saw them. One of McGeorge's favourite walks took him from Harvard to the Mount Auburn Cemetery, where he could think about issues that were so much wider than the minutiae of upcoming academia.

One afternoon in the late spring of 1950, McGeorge and Adrienne were walking near the Washington Tower in Mount Auburn Park. He'd asked if he could talk to her about her views on British Foreign policy, and about her controversial dissertation. They admired the extraordinary views of Boston and the summit of Wachusett Mountain.

'When you return to England, I'd like to keep in touch. I've greatly valued our exchanges, Ms Franck, and I think you have quite a future ahead of you.'

Adrienne was beyond flattered and was light-headed with delight as she told him she would be very happy to do so.

When Adrienne returned to her room she sat in a chair and, just for a moment, savoured the writing on the envelope. Then she ripped it open.

> *Dear Adrienne,*
>
> *I've been very busy working since my return, but I find I think about you at the oddest times. When I'm so busy and everyone wants me, and I'm in danger of missing a valuation deadline, I have quick visions of walking on the beach or sitting at dinner with you.*
>
> *It'll soon be May, and you'll be home for good late June, so lots to look forward to.*
>
> *I've just seen a new Rothko, and you'll not be surprised when I tell you it's much like the last one. It's untitled, of course; just lines of colour progressing up (or down!) the page. I'm sorry – I like modern art more than most, but I struggle with Mark Rothko.*
>
> *One of my colleagues just came back from the Institute of Art in Chicago, and he said the Tribune in Chicago ran a piece about how Harvard was full of communist-sympathising Reds. They ought to try living, with Attlee as PM!*
>
> *I'm hoping to buy a small house near Ravenscourt Park. It's £2,000, but with a loan and some help from my parents, I should manage it. Hopefully you'll visit me there often.*
>
> *Where will you live when you come back to the UK?*
>
> *How's your course going, despite all those Reds?*

Must go. My parents want me to go for Shabbat.
Lots of love
Howard x

A cloud stole the final evening rays from the settee cushions. She had been thrilled to receive Howard's letter, had hurried to read it, but a ravenous man could not be relied upon to offer a critique of a gourmet meal. She could now linger over the aftermath, luxuriate in the hopes that it generated, and perhaps subject it to some independent analysis.

'Stupid woman!' she said. An ingress of unfamiliar feelings rose within her. Her instinct was to fall back on the familiar, the intellectual.

She thought about their dinner, allowed herself to enjoy the vision of Howard's smile and his obvious attraction to her. The absent friend was fear. It seemed they were both heading towards something rather wonderful.

She would draft a response.

She turned on the lamp by her desk, and thought how lovely it was to be able to write to a man she already admired. Putting the top of her fountain pen on the base, she began to write.

Dear Howard,
It was lovely to receive your letter. Thinking about sitting in a beach café with you on a sunny day in Ogunquit would only hinder my efforts during rigorous academic discussion, so it's best avoided!

Yes, we had a lovely time, and I'm looking forward to seeing your house if you buy it.

The claim in the Chicago Tribune is so ridiculous, I don't want to use a letter to you to respond to it!

I'm not certain yet where I'll live. It depends where I work. It's not easy for women to find work advising the Government, and I'm not at all sure that I want to work within the Foreign Office.

Shabbat passes me by here, despite many opportunities to join the laughter of the long white tablecloth. Do you have siblings? I don't. Pick a symphony, any symphony, and tell me why you like it.

Write again soon.
Until then,
With love
Adrienne x

She took out another page of writing paper. She wasn't a poet, it had never interested her, but she liked the idea of writing another letter: one she couldn't send. It was like lying in the warmest bath, with no time limit, then drying in the *softest* towel.

My Darling Howard,
I seem to have fallen in love with you. Can you believe it? I've been on dates with people where I forced myself out the door to see them again and came back with a feeling of nothingness, of time wasted. People with no interest in me, or not much of a brain at all. And now, after meeting you only a very few times, look at me! I think of you all day. Apparently, I'm not the most boring academic since Thomas Hobbes, after all! I have feelings and dreams too.

Here I am in the most prestigious university in the world, and I'm actually counting down the days until I

come back to England.
I can't wait to hold you and more,
Your Adrienne

She loved writing it, then she tore it up and put in the bin.

June 1951. The Britannia

It seemed as if the entire ship's company was on the deck, watching Southampton Dock come closer. On this eastbound Atlantic crossing, there was no Statue of Liberty or Manhattan skyline to look forward to, but Adrienne was about to be reunited with Howard. The dockside approached, and soon she would leave the ship and embark on her new life.

Howard waited at the ocean terminal, opened the previous year; an Art Deco design, with an interior finished in blond burr wood. He had arrived early, having taken the train from London, and as *The Britannia* grew larger, he sensed his new life was approaching the quayside.

The train from London had given him an opportunity to think about the last few years. It was true, he'd progressed at Sotheby's, but as the train left Waterloo and wound its way through dreary, bomb-damaged south London, his thoughts had been dominated by two women.

He'd met Rachael at Christie's three years earlier, at an interview before he'd joined Sotheby's. She had short blond hair, a seductive smile, and a voice that he could hear, even now, as the noisy train travelled southwards. They'd agreed to meet for coffee after their interviews and to Howard's dismay, he'd been captivated by her. He wasn't seventeen, he was twenty-three, and had hoped he might have grown up. It turned out that Rachael liked parties and had no interest whatever in going steady with Howard. He had discovered this very early in their relationship, when he'd found her in a coat cupboard with another man; and yet, like the black-and-white road sign, there seemed to be no limit to her ability to hurt him.

There was always a moment when she wanted him, when she looked at him and knew with total certainty he would soon be in her arms – usually when he was forming a relationship with another girl. His friends had grown weary of his inability to escape her malign magnetism. They watched with a resigned, mild disappointment as yet another lovely girl walked out of his life, and for just one or two days, Rachael walked back into it.

One Sunday morning, about a year before, his sister Mandy had called him, and they had gone for a walk on Hampstead Heath. The rhododendrons were in full bloom and the April sun had surprising warmth as they walked slowly.

'It really has to stop, Howard. I'm sure you know that,' Mandy said.

There was no point in his asking what she was talking about. They both knew the reason for this walk.

'Our family has always believed in dignity, Howard. You learned it on the cricket square at Oakingham, and you saw it when Mum died. We hold our head high, Howard; we don't demean ourselves in the ditch with a tramp. Last Shabbat you mentioned something about opportunities in the American department at Sotheby's.'

'I did.'

She turned to him as they approached a muddy area. 'Just take it, whatever it is. Go away, Howard, please, and don't speak to her again.'

Strangely, it had worked; whether because even he could see the damage Rachael was causing him, or because it was so rare that his sister spoke to him about such things, he didn't know. Whichever it was, he had not spoken to Rachael again.

The train stopped at Epsom, and soon the open fields of Surrey became the gorse-covered sandstone of Hampshire.

After the anguish of Rachael, his thoughts turned to Adrienne. Somehow, he knew he could rely upon her, trust her, and his heart, which had been bounced around like a basketball by Rachael, would at last be in safe hands. Mandy would have called Adrienne's letters 'sensible', and they certainly weren't salacious or flirty. Adrienne had infused warmth into her words, while holding back a little. He liked that. It was clear she liked him, and, to his relief, he realised that dignity had returned to his life.

People walked down the gangplank, and he spotted her as she approached the Passport Office. Soon she walked into the terminal, and they were holding each other in a loving embrace.

Chapter Five

Eleanor and Sally were sitting in Sally's bedroom, where Eleanor had witnessed so much of Sally's painfully slow recovery.

'I can't imagine leading a normal life,' Sally said. Eleanor didn't interrupt her. 'I don't want a boy's hands on my thigh, and I'm not losing myself to anyone. That psych man who wanted me to talk about my parents and my early childhood and all that, he didn't make me better at all. You know who's made me better, don't you El? Just you. That's all, just you. Love isn't about boys or marriage or anything like that, it's about you. And before you say it, I know it might not always be like this. But right now, I like it being like this. No pressure, no pain. *Eleanor's coming at the weekend*, and that's fine with me.'

Despite the occasional glimpses of the younger, naive Sally – a bout of laughter, or a sentence that seemed likely to become gossip – for much of the time, Sally remained withdrawn and morose. No progress had been made with the investigation. In fact, it had stopped.

'I'm going to see the man in Hamptons about a temp job,' Sally said, one Saturday afternoon.

'That's great, Sal,' Eleanor said.

Then Sally spoke about the university course she would start the following year, but her sentences so often drifted from a spark of enthusiasm into a quieter, less confident tone, as if she felt undeserving of recovery; she shouldn't allow herself to be happy. Martin, the RAF pilot, had stolen her frivolity and youth, and instead of the riverbank Sally becoming a confident, hopeful young woman, she had hidden herself in a shell, from which she was just beginning to emerge into the greyest of London winters.

They ambled through Leicester Square, shaking off its post war blues and entering into the spirit of Christmas. Finally, they headed down Piccadilly and into their favourite bookshop, Hatchards.

When Eleanor first regained consciousness, she experienced the usual mental turmoil: *Where am I? What happened?* Her legs were held upwards in some contraption, but she could move her toes and her fingers, which for some reason gave her some level of reassurance.

The senior nurse on the ward, the formidable Sister Elliott, noticed that Eleanor was trying to sit up. She came over, and in the manner of someone for whom pragmatism had long ago replaced empathy, she tried to offer reassurance.

'You're in hospital. I'll get the doctor to come and see you soon. You're a lucky young lady. Your injuries could have been much worse.'

Lucky? What a strange word to use. Eleanor's mind travelled backwards like someone rewinding a cine-film projector. What was the last thing she could remember? She'd been at Sally's house, then they'd been walking in London, and … Sally! Was she in a ward? Was she hurt too? Where was she?

Mr Straker-Nelson had operated on Eleanor. He came to her bedside, white coat open to reveal a tailored grey, wool suit. She remembered every detail of his appearance that day, and would be able to describe it decades later, as if she'd been given a picture as a leaving present. He wore a tie with red-and-black stripes, with a yellow pattern on the black. She agreed with her mother when she later described a 'puffed-up Harley-Street face'. He was imbued with a kind of medical aristocracy, English public school, that had been nurtured in the hospital wards, where he was deferred to as if he were some kind of deity. He was tall, with swept-back grey hair and deep-set eyes. He had large hands, manicured nails and an aura of authority.

He sat next to Eleanor's bed, offering a concession to modern views on bedside manner. 'All went remarkably well, Miss Kennedy. Your fractures will mend well, and provided you do the exercises, you should be good as new.' He paused. 'I do have something to tell you though.'

Later, she couldn't remember exactly what he'd said.

'Terrible wounds ... lacerations ... would have had no life ... merciful ... not seen anything like it since the field hospital ...'

'What's a field hospital?' she asked, her mind seizing on the first concrete thing it heard.

'A war hospital. Your friend was killed by a bomb.' The doctor sighed. 'I suppose nobody thought to tell you. You were both victims of a terrorist bomb.'

As if through a mist, Eleanor realised that Sally had been murdered by people who knew nothing about her, had no idea about their friendship, her struggles after the assault, or the first signs of her recovery.

The surgeon was still speaking when Eleanor's well burst, and she sobbed. As if on cue, a nurse appeared and Mr Straker-Nelson left the room; in his eyes, his mission was accomplished.

The physical recovery went as planned. The abscess of anguish festered.

One afternoon, at about two o'clock, when the ward was already lit by garish strip lights, Eleanor saw Sally's mother talking to Sister Elliott.

In the preceding few days, as she'd lain in bed, with a newly admitted amputee crying out opposite her, she had tried to sieve her thoughts about Mrs Garcia visiting. Eleanor feared she would have to cope with Maria's emotions, when right now the only person in this equation she really cared about was herself. She had never really understood Sally's mother. Why, for instance, she had left her daughter with another family every summer? But as Sally's mother approached, the cacophony of noise that passed for a debate within her mind evacuated as Maria's collapse became apparent. Eleanor had lost a dear beloved friend. She had lost her only daughter.

Words were unimportant. It was an agony of intermingled grief and tears. Whatever reserve Sally's mother may have possessed had dissolved. Two kindred travellers trudged through the bleak winter forest with no welcoming cottage in sight. Before Maria left, they fell silent, and holding hands, shared the enormity of Sally's murder.

After a strange Christmas in hospital with her parents at her bedside, Eleanor returned to the Sussex farm to recuperate. Her father was not good at illness, his own or other people's, and he mouthed platitudes about how well she had been looked after, and how she would soon be back to normal. He seemed unable to talk about Sally's death at all, other than irregular mumbles of 'bad business' or 'Hope they get those bastards.' Despite his history of emotional constipation, Eleanor was surprised at how unaffected he appeared. *He's so upset he can't cope, so he's brushing it under the carpet*, she thought.

He threw himself back into his work – farm management, ploughing his fields, the milking schedule – his normality that passed for his 'therapy'.

Her mother, Myra, was the natural velvet blanket upon which to fall. Eleanor had a need to understand what had happened and how she felt about it, and, as there was literally nothing she couldn't talk to her mother about, they sat through the dark evenings by the log fire in the beamed lounge, surrounded by grey fields, frozen trees, leaden skies and a lake of love.

'The difference,' Eleanor was saying, 'is the finality. I might recover, probably will in time, but I'll never see Sally again. I won't be at her wedding, will never see her children, never argue with her. She was always there. She was a certainty.'

Their sadness coexisted and melded, parallel rivers joining and flowing towards an estuary as one.

Eleanor also learned how strong she could be. She didn't collapse or lie in bed. She wasn't outwardly distraught, but she needed to understand what had happened to her and Sally that afternoon outside Hatchards.

It was reminiscent of the saying 'Nature abhors a vacuum'. As the grief receded over the months, the anger grew, and her changing emotion assembled around a set of questions.

What right did those people have to take Sally's life, to rob them of beautiful Sal?

Who were they? And how was it possible for them to do that?'

It was then, as the conversations with her mother continued, that the first seeds were planted, suggesting that Eleanor could have some small part in protecting the country she loved and perhaps, in this way, achieve something more satisfying than indefinite anger.

The days became brighter, the magnolia tree in the farmyard filled with heavenly blossom, and some semblance of warmth could be found among the silage smells of the farmyard. Eleanor and Myra went on long walks. The Faraday Institute had been sympathetic to Myra's request for a six-month sabbatical.

'I saw one of your strange contacts here yesterday,' Eleanor said, as they turned a corner into a road, its hedgerows showing early shoots.

'Oh, Sam's not strange. Actually, he came to talk about you.'

Eleanor was surprised, but she had wanted to speak to an MI5 contact, so her face shone as she replied.

'Me? Why?' Eleanor's face registered her surprise.

'We know more about the rogue gang that detonated the bomb,' Myra said.

'Who's *we*?' asked Eleanor.

Myra nodded thoughtfully. 'Yes, that's the important question.'

'Now I'm really lost.'

'Sam works for MI5 and, as you know, I help them now and then. So *we* in this instance could mean me, Sam and MI5. Or it could mean something else altogether.'

'Have you been reading *Alice in Wonderland* again?' Eleanor asked.

Myra smiled. 'I'm proud of my family's Irish origins. I love the country, the yearning for freedom, its strength during unspeakable oppression. But like we've said before, Irish freedom can't come at the price of innocent lives.'

'I'd have thought that pretty simplistic before what happened,' Eleanor said.

'The group that killed Sally aren't Irish patriots,' Myra said. 'They think they are, but they're just thugs and criminals. Sally was someone they didn't care about. Anyway, as I was saying, what I mean is the *we* could include you at some stage. You've told me how much you love this country. Now you've seen, all too clearly, what carnage our enemies can cause.'

In years gone by, they might have walked towards the Greyhound pub, but now, without so much as a glance passing between them, they took a different road, walking towards Lewes.

'But what can I do?' Eleanor asked.

'It doesn't work like that. There may be nothing for you to do immediately, but Sam and his colleagues would like to know if they can call on you in the future, if they think you can help.'

Eleanor turned and looked at her mother as they approached a stile.

'They can definitely count on me!' she said. 'I'd love to avenge Sally's death and I'd certainly do anything to stop other people going through what we've been through the last six months. So, you can tell your Mr Sam that *we* includes me.'

In the country lane, springtime, a hint of raindrops, an isolated place, far from Piccadilly, they were seemingly protected from enemies of all kinds. Yet catastrophe had found its way into their lives and although the riverbank was a few miles down the road, the days of youth and naivety were far away. Eleanor would continue her studies at university, and it would be many years before she was called upon to play a part in her country's protection. As they returned to the farm, they both silently acknowledged the seriousness of the conversation. They knew it would have implications for the future, but knowing it is different to experiencing it, and for Eleanor, like so many who agreed to be part of intelligence work, the decision would change her life in ways that neither she nor her mother could possibly envisage.

Chapter Six

Cavendish Square, London. September 1951.

Paul Fleming was a junior minister for foreign affairs in Churchill's Government. He'd been contacted by his American friend, McGeorge Bundy, one evening when he was relaxing in his mews house in Chelsea. Soon McGeorge was extolling the virtues of his student, Adrienne Franck.

'Take her on before anyone else does,' McGeorge had said. 'One of the brightest brains I've seen.'

'To do what?' Fleming had asked

'Set up an organisation like our Brookings Institution.'

'We've got one,' said Fleming. 'It's called Chatham House'

'Pretty unlikely they'll take on a woman for anything important, and anyway, it's time for new thinking. Just don't let her go near the Foreign Office, Paul. Keep her close. She'll be a huge asset to the Tories, you'll see.'

It wasn't often that Paul received a call like that from an American foreign policy expert, and he called Adrienne on the phone number McGeorge had given him. And so it was that Adrienne came to be sitting in his office, last refurbished in about 1910, on the corner of Cavendish Square and Harley Street.

'You made quite a name for yourself in the States it seems,' Fleming said. 'The Tory Party and this room have a lot in common.'

Adrienne was wondering when she would be asked a question

or have an opportunity to speak.

'Why's that?' she asked.

'They both need new ideas and modernising.'

'You've not asked me here for my interior-design skills, so what part do you envisage for me?' Adrienne asked.

'We want people who aren't afraid to offer new ideas, even if they're controversial. Your thesis on psychology and diplomacy … that's the kind of thing we want. Also, we want young people. We might even want women!'

'In practical terms, what would you like me to do?'

'We're setting up an independent right-facing, foreign-affairs body. Separate from the Foreign Office. We want you to be its academic director.'

'I've never been a director of anything.'

'Exactly. It's perfect. You'd report to the Director General, a young MP for Bexley, recently resigned from the Civil Service – Oxford graduate, bright man called Edward Heath. If you could start straightaway, that'd be perfect, as we need a new analysis of our relationship with America.'

'Small job then.' Adrienne felt able to joke.

Paul Fleming smiled. 'And if you could also spruce up this room, that'd be good; it's your office now, if you want the job. This is Edward Heath's business card. Yours would look much the same.' It read:

FUTURE WORLD

Innovative Strategies. Conservative Values.
Edward Heath MP, Director General

The job seemed to have been tailor-made for her.

Safehouse

The Compleat Angler Hotel, Marlow

The beautiful blue metal bridge that crossed the Thames induced indecent levels of nostalgia as it approached the hotel buildings in their glorious setting. And there, with its riverbank lawn bathed in evening light, was the Compleat Angler. As Adrienne and Howard turned into the car park, the man in a straw boater greeted them as if he'd known them for a lifetime, and through an arch, the lawn and the river could be glimpsed like an overture. The hotel never changed and had stood serene through political turbulence, family squabbles, and worse, as the slow waters of the Thames lapped its lawn.

Howard and Adrienne, Pimm's in hand, walked along the manicured riverbank, admiring the boats. Adrienne struggled slightly in her stilettos. Howard was entranced by the elegance of her turquoise chiffon dress, and the sun caressed them as they wandered arm in arm, their happiness complete.

Later, after their delicious dinner, they walked outside again, this time into the warm evening. There were hints of lavender and jasmine in the air, and on the edge of the rose garden, Howard went down on one knee.

'Adrienne, I love you with all my heart. Will you marry me?'

Adrienne was not surprised by the proposal, but she was thrilled.

'Oh, Howard, yes, *yes*, I'd love to. I love you so much!'

As they walked back through the French doors into the dining room, Howard signalled to the head waiter, and they were each given a glass of champagne. Then Monsieur Beaumard called the restaurant to order, his voice rich with a strong French accent.

'Ladies and Gentlemen, I'm so sorry to interrupt your evening, but I have some special and very happy news. Please could you be upstanding and congratulate Adrienne and Howard, who have become engaged just this evening!'

Applause rang out through the restaurant. Almost in unison, the guests stood up, raised their glasses and said: 'Adrienne and Howard!'

December 1951

Adrienne, now Academic Director of Future World, asserted in her reports to Bundy that psychology was the key to understanding international policy disputes. Quoting again from her thesis, she repeated her truism: 'the constituent part of every nation state is human beings.'

Just before he set out to play the organ in St Martin-in-the-Fields' afternoon Carol Concert, Edward Heath finished reading Adrienne's first major report. He called Paul Fleming.

'Exactly what we wanted, Paul. Controversial, outward-looking, brilliant and realistic.'

Then he called Adrienne, intending to ask her how soon they could meet.

As the phone rang and rang at Adrienne's West London home, and Edward Heath's call remained unanswered, Adrienne awaited Dr Pattison's return to his consulting room with fear and dread. He sat down and began to speak. Her worst fears were confirmed. She was pregnant.

As she travelled to meet Howard, she was devastated, and the fact that he would be pleased infuriated her even further. It wouldn't affect his career one jot. He could carry on investing in art, taking foreign trips and building up his business.

Meanwhile, and for the foreseeable future, her career, on the verge of extraordinary advancements, was either about to be massively curtailed or over.

They were sitting in Howard's flat in Chiswick.

'Wouldn't it be great to get married at Caxton Hall?' Howard said.

'You're joking! Do you honestly think you're going to avoid a shul wedding?' Adrienne's parents would insist they were married in their synagogue, by their rabbi.

'Hmm, s'pose so,' grumbled Howard.

'Just think who you're marrying and how much above your station!' she joked. 'Then remember your life carries on without a hitch, whereas I will have to stay at home and change nappies.'

'Look, I agree it's unfair. I'm not happy about it either.'

'Know what I'm so happy about?' she said.

'What's that?' he asked, lighting a Corona.

'You're the most useless liar I've ever met. Don't play poker and never even think of negotiating with the Russians.'

'What you mean?'

'You're as happy as Larry that your pretty young bride-to-be has to curtail her career to look after your baby.'

Howard had a strong sense of justice and shared Adrienne's resentment. Her contribution to the country, her career and her intellect would be lost because their love had produced a baby. He was no Betty Freidan, but the unfairness shone like a porch light on a winter's night.

He held Adrienne on the couch and surprised her with a promise. 'As soon as I'm able to, I'd like to do my share of childcare.'

Adrienne was surprised at this almost revolutionary thought, which just increased her love for Howard and soon they were caressing each other and more in the certain knowledge that they loved each other totally.

March 1952, Ravenscourt Park

The messages of congratulation, read out at the wedding, highlighted the incongruity of Adrienne's situation. The longest was from her erstwhile professor McGeorge Bundy, but the brightest academics and statesmen at the forefront of foreign policy, Henry Kissinger, Dean Acheson, George Kennan and Edward Heath, all sent telegrams. Howard smashed the glass under the Chuppah, they cut the cake, hoped nobody would ask about her insistence that she not be held up in a chair, the best man's speech was only mildly embarrassing, and before long, the wedding was over.

Her parents were as delighted as they could possibly be. Howard's parents seemed happy. The cars drove away, they went up to their hotel suite, made love and went to sleep.

Some days later, as she sat on a bench in Ravenscourt Park, she reflected on the disaster that had befallen her.

'And make no mistake,' she said aloud to the crocuses, 'this is a disaster!'

She wasn't sure she wanted children at all. Howard had worn a condom and they'd tried to avoid the most fertile time of the month, and it had all failed.

But must her career stop? As she walked around the playing field and heard the distant shouts of school children from Latymer or St Paul's, she was desolate and angry. She resolved to continue to work for Future World, even if much of her work was carried out at home. She would insist on having a nanny, and then whatever help she needed. The strangest part was that she had no time for women who theorised about inequality or inequality of opportunity. She thought women best advocated their abilities by achievement and intellect, not by complaining or seeking some kind of radical social change. She had led by example. And what good had it done? The conception that started the life of her child was in danger of ending her life as she had envisaged it. But she would not allow that to happen.

One evening some weeks later, over dinner in their house in Chiswick, Howard and Adrienne were chatting.

'I'm forced to keep some strange company,' he said.

'Forced?' she asked, bemused.

'There's a group that meet in Soho in Dean Street. They're all very talented – their work will be worth a fortune one day, especially Francis Bacon and Lucian Freud. I'm buying their art quite cheaply now, at between £150 and £400.'

Adrienne nearly choked

'Did you say *quite cheaply*? That's a fortune, darling!'

'Nonsense,' Howard said. Then he paused as if he was about to launch into a speech. 'I do have something to tell you.'

'Well?'

'I went to a clearance sale a couple of weeks ago. I don't think I told you.' He smiled mischievously.

'You know perfectly well, darling, that you didn't tell me.'

'It was on my recent trip to Holland. I like visiting towns where artists grew up or began their careers. I saw an advert in an Amsterdam paper for a clearance sale in a village called Schipluiden, and thought I'd go, as I knew a rather famous artist lived and worked there.'

'You're teasing me now, aren't you.'

'Definitely, but it's worth it, just wait.' Howard drank some claret, put it down as carefully as a white-gloved referee putting a snooker ball on a spot, and continued.

'I thought it would be an auction, but it was chaotic. I looked through a few boxes. It was freezing in the hall, no heating, and I was about to go when I saw something.

'Before I tell you about it, just a bit of background. In 1672 the artist had a financial disaster and his fellow artists assumed he'd stop painting with ultramarine. But what they didn't know was that he had a patron, Pieter van Ruijven, so he was able to carry on painting just as gorgeously.

At the bottom of a box I saw something that reminded me of *Lady Seated at a Virginal*.'

'No! You're not about to tell me you found a Vermeer. Oh my god, Howard!'

'I wasn't at all sure, but I thought it was an extraordinary painting, and I was in Schipluiden, after all, which is where, as you've guessed, Vermeer lived for a while. Anyway, I tried to look nonchalant and disinterested, and picked up quite a lot of other worthless clutter, and then went to pay. I haggled them down to about £30 for the lot.'

He turned to Adrienne, looking suitably pompous, for the announcement that would change their lives. 'Well, my darling, what I have to tell you is that the Isabella Stewart Gardner Museum in Boston, um ...'

He paused. The room fell silent.

'They've confirmed it's an original Vermeer painted in 1660.'

Howard couldn't think of a single previous occasion when Adrienne had been speechless. But now he watched as she put her knife and fork down, wiped her mouth with a linen napkin, and just sat looking at some imaginary far-flung horizon.

'That's the other thing: Sotheby's have put a reserve price on it of £3 million.'

Adrienne was thinking. She'd been sure this man could never

keep a secret. *Open book*, she'd thought. Yet for three weeks he'd kept this entire story to himself. How could he?

'If you're wondering why I didn't tell you before …'

'Well, you know … just a *bit.*'

'It's so life changing I just couldn't say anything until I knew for certain it was genuine. They told me last Friday, and I heard the reserve price today.'

Howard stood up, uncovered an ice bucket and opened a bottle of Moët & Chandon champagne. Adrienne ran over to him, the reserve of the Harvard intellectual completely disappeared.

'I honestly can't believe it – £3 million, Howard! We'll be rich.'

Any voyeurs in the park would have seen a usually quite staid couple dancing around their own lounge.

Chapter Seven

'I work for the Government.'

Daniel was sleeping in his cot. The nanny was having her afternoon off. Thank goodness! Nurse Ethel seemed to want to bake Daniel in the nursery, insisting on a temperature that Adrienne refused to maintain. Now, the house was so quiet she could hear the clock tick in the lounge. Howard was in Nice, discussing Picasso. She was alone in Chiswick as the light faded in the late afternoon, preparing a paper on Britain's future relations with France and Germany, and for the first time, she was suggesting that these relationships might actually be more important for Britain than the so-called 'Special Relationship' with the United States. She looked up from her typewriter, put her head in her hands and groaned as she thought about her excruciating morning.

The local church offered a group for women with young babies. It was a symptom of her abject loneliness that she had even considered going. What was happening to her decision-making skills?

They had sat in a circle in the youth hall, their prams in front of them. With a growing sense of alarm, she realised they were going to be asked to say a few words about themselves. After all, soon they were going to be the best of friends. Adrienne thought about her spring walk in Massachusetts with Professor Bundy, needing to pretend to be anywhere other than where she was at that moment.

'I was a dinner lady at our Lady of Lourdes Secondary,' said one woman.

'I was a secretary in Hammersmith. I don't miss the commute or the wandering hands!' another said.

The youngest woman was attractive and fashion-conscious. 'I was hoping to be a model,' she said. 'Got on a few agency lists, and then ...'

Adrienne panicked. What was she going to say? *I advise governments on international relations strategy?*

'I worked for the Government,' she said.

'That's what those new traffic wardens say,' whispered one of the other women.

Everyone mingled, had coffee, talked about their baby's weight. Adrienne couldn't say what other topics came up, because she was in a trance, a dream of utter unreality.

Soon she made her excuses and left.

She walked up her garden path, opened her front door, lifted Daniel out of his pram and held him up with outstretched arms as the mothers had done that morning. She loved him, he was her son, but she resented everything about him. She knew he was blameless, innocent in every way. Society was to blame for her interrupted, perhaps even discontinued, career. But the utterly dependent bundle that needed her attention all day and much of the night made her angry. She shouldn't be angry, but she was. She shouldn't resent him, but she did. The logical Adrienne, the fierce intellectual of the lecture hall, where was she? Smothered in nappies, prams, ironing, shopping and boredom.

While Daniel slept that afternoon, Adrienne saw the clock hand turn to ten past three. She had never looked at a clock before, except to ensure her infamous punctuality at meetings and lectures, but now she realised that only her work gave her any link to the outside world and the realities of international politics.

As the days and weeks went by Adrienne's only comforts were the papers she wrote in the early hours of the morning. She succumbed to the introspection and self-analysis of the prisoner in solitary confinement.

There were some constants.

She didn't want to talk to people with whom she had nothing in common. The flower arrangers' gossip, the hairdresser telling her how lovely it was that Mr Churchill had been to see the new queen, the coalman talking about the Ruskies: all these filled her with contempt for the people discussing subjects about which they knew nothing.

She made no effort to be friendly with any of the mothers at the toddler group. Not that they wanted anything to do with 'the stuck-up snob in the posh clothes and pearls.' There was a mutual feeling of dislike between their group of fifteen and her group of one.

There were also variables: when would Daniel go to nursery and where? When would Howard next be home? Much to the disgust of Daniel's grandmothers, she had made no attempt to breastfeed. She had no wish to increase Daniel's dependence on her, as it was already at an unbearable level.

In March she heard Dean Acheson, the US Secretary of State, on the BBC Home Service, denying American use of germ warfare in Indochina. Hearing Dean's voice discussing a matter of huge importance at first lifted her spirits, and then smashed them on the rocks of desolation as she realised that she could only play the smallest part in these vital debates. She had become addicted to the radio, her lifeline to reality.

Safehouse

August Bank Holiday, 1953

The painting had been sold, and their money worries were well and truly at an end. They had bought a house in Regent's Park at the end of Cumberland Terrace.

They were walking near their home. Daniel was in his pushchair. The park greeted the holiday with wonderful weather, and the queue for the boats was longer than ever. They bought a fourpenny cornet and held hands as they walked. Despite the problems caused by the unexpected child, Adrienne and Howard's happiness just grew. They admired each other more and loved each other in a way that was rare indeed.

Admiration was important. Howard had always loved the idea of being with a woman who had intellect and views on the issues of the day. As Adrienne's happiness increased, it seemed to Howard that so did her beauty, and he was always proud to walk with her through the park.

Adrienne loved hearing about Howard's art forays, and their greatest delight when he returned from a trip was to ensure Daniel had been bathed and put to bed, that nanny was at hand, and then retreat to their bedroom to make love and to talk.

Adrienne had just completed an important piece of work that had come to the attention of Harold Macmillan, concerning the possibility that Britain might want to join the group which was forging closer ties within Western Europe. She asserted that a country that had been helped by Britain might not want to see itself as being in debt, and maybe France was most likely to object to Britain's membership of some future union. She had been surprised by her ability to continue her work and their combined financial resources soon made further help available. Adrienne met with Edward Heath as often as she could, and their friendship and mutual respect grew.

And what of Daniel? What were her feelings for him? Parents often say that their children are their overriding priority. She loved Daniel, but there were too many times when she saw him as an obstacle to her work. Howard loved talking about his son, about his hopes that he would captain the Oakingham First Eleven as he himself had done. Only half-joking, he speculated that Daniel would be a future Tory MP. Adrienne knew she had a problem with her son. She had known it early in Daniel's life and it worsened as each year passed. She loved Daniel, she enjoyed holding him and greeting him, gurgling in his cot in the morning, but she was not besotted by him nor consumed by her love for her child. When she looked at other mothers, she knew she must appear aloof. She wasn't, but Daniel was never the most important person in her life, and she was honest enough and had sufficient self-awareness to admit it. Neither of them could foresee the consequences of this ominous combination. Neither of them had the empathy that might allow them actually to listen to what their son wanted or needed.

Indeed, the irony was not lost on those who analysed Daniel's life. His mother was an expert in the psychology of nation states, but utterly lacking when it came to the relationship that should have been the most important in her life: that between herself and her son.

Daniel's fourth birthday

As Daniel walked through the gate to join other children for his first day at a private nursery, Adrienne's delight contrasted starkly with the tearful parents walking back to their cars in the quiet West London crescent.

What's the matter with them? she asked herself. *Don't they want to get on with their lives?*

At breakfast, Howard asked Daniel if he was looking forward to playing with other children. The question had not occurred to Adrienne. She had spent four years, as she saw it, trying to combine work and (albeit minimal) childcare, and now the question as to whether her son viewed nursery with happy anticipation or not, did not exist in her stream of consciousness.

The thought that never entered Adrienne's head, the insufficient interest in her son, was like a spore-forming bacteria. As Adrienne had learned in Higher Cert biology: spores are a dormant form of vegetative bacteria. They are highly resistant to physical and chemical influences.

Spring 1957
Howard and Adrienne were walking hand in hand in Regent's Park. As they stopped to look at the birds and geese, by the beautiful pond, Howard turned to her.

'Let's change lots of things!'

'Just like that?' Adrienne asked. She was used to Howard's impulsiveness, but she was wondering where this chat was going.

'Yes, just like that.'

He hesitated.

'And?' Adrienne asked, holding both his hands as she stood in front of him on the pathway.

'I'm quite tired of so much travel.'

'First-class transatlantic must be hard!' she said playfully,

'It's not, but I'd like to stay home more.'

'Oh, haven't we *gotten* so American? Stay home more!'

He ignored her, and she saw he had a slight frown. The greying sideburns made him look intellectual and distinguished.

'It's a three-part plan,' he said. 'We get more child help, which we can certainly afford; I stay home more; and you go back full-time to doing what you like most this side of the bedroom – working!'

She let go of his hands and whooped with joy.

'That's the best plan I've heard for years.'

St John's Wood Primary School, London
Howard and Daniel walked hand in hand through the gates and up the steps into the old house, and then the teacher led Daniel, upper lip trembling, into the classroom. As Howard walked back to the school gate, he watched the other new parents huddle and then arrange to meet at a local café. Any sense of isolation he may have felt was drowned by a sense of relief as he welcomed a few hours of peace while Daniel was drawing, counting and learning his alphabet. He walked up Avenue Road, looking at the remaining yellow ochre leaves. He had a nanny and an au pair. He had food that had been pre-cooked, ready for him to heat up and give Daniel at the times shown on the list. Daniel was no longer a baby. Howard was full of wonder for the women who, with no help whatsoever, took their children to school or even worse, looked after toddlers.

How many men realised that the world of work, which they complained about incessantly, was like a holiday in the Algarve compared with the monotony and exhaustion that was the everyday experience of looking after young children?

But he also recognised new feelings. Spending time with his son had elicited a bond that might never have formed otherwise. He had a newfound love for his son, born of contact and time, not distance and aspiration.

Adrienne had been quite justifiably furious at the cavalry charge of reservists who had suddenly shown their face when she announced she was going back to work. People, who had apparently been entirely occupied, found time to come to their Regent's Park home to 'Give Howard a break'.

'A break from what?' she exclaimed. 'He'll have Anne every morning and Agneta most days! He hasn't started yet! How come he needs a break, but I never needed any help when Daniel was keeping me awake all night or had a fever, or–?' Exasperation made her speechless.

Her mother-in-law, Julia, sat in the kitchen, the weekend before Adrienne was due to return to work.

'It's not normal, you know. Of course, Howard will need help. He's never done any of this before. It's very boring for a man, you know.'

'Not boring at all for a woman, of course.'

'You know perfectly well what I mean, Adrienne, so don't pretend you don't. Men go out to work and women look after children.'

'Not in this house! We've agreed to do things a little differently, as you may have noticed.'

'What I've noticed,' Julia said, 'is that my lovely son is so keen to save his marriage that he's sacrificed his career for yours! Of course he pretends otherwise, but we all know the truth, don't we?'

And so it went on. Her own parents were little different. The school called the house to make sure Adrienne was 'well', and St John's Wood High Street was sprayed with the bullets of gossip about the strange goings on at Cumberland Terrace.

At the end of the first week, Howard invited his own parents and his in-laws for Saturday tea. The tea was prepared by Anne, with bridge rolls and patisserie from Home & Colonial on the

High Street. He told Adrienne to meet a friend.

When they were all assembled around the dining table, tucking into smoked-roe bridge rolls, he cleared his throat.

'Look, there are some things I need to say to you, just to get them clear. I want to spend more time with Daniel and I can afford it. I've been very successful investing in the artists you said were worthless, and when I came back from New York a few months ago I told Adrienne I wanted her to go back to work.'

Julia snorted. 'You don't honestly expect anyone to believe that, do you?'

'Mother,' Howard said, 'I will try say this respectfully, but the way I feel right now I'll probably fail. You are not and never have been privy to the private conversations between me and my wife. You had the infernal nerve to tell Adrienne I'd sacrificed my career for hers. Nothing could be further from the truth. I want to spend time with my son, and I'm enjoying it. Is it hard work? Of course. But to put it bluntly, if you ever say anything like that again to my wife, you'll be lucky to see your grandchild grow up at all.'

Julia turned to her husband, Harry. 'He never used to speak to us like that.'

Adrienne's father, Giles, had a diplomatic demeanour and a soft public-school voice.

'Let's all agree, the change in childcare's been a bit of a shock to us all. It's not how it's normally done. We never wanted Adrienne to go to university, let alone get a first-class honours degree and just carry on studying. It's not normal, but there it is.'

'What I think,' Julia said,' is that the reputation of this family is more important than Adrienne's hurry to go back to work. Do you have any idea what people are saying?'

'Mum, I'm going to tell you something. When I see exhibitions for artists like Andy Warhol or Rauschenberg. I laugh to myself about the tittle-tattle gossip that started when people first saw their art. It was 'worthless, shocking, vulgar'. Now, suddenly Sotheby's are making thousands from them, and they're trying to say they knew how popular they'd be all along!

I didn't listen to gossip then, so do you honestly think I care one jot what people say about me now? Look, I'm not interested in changing your Stone-Age attitudes. You can all think what you want. What matters to me isn't what you say, but how Adrienne and I react to it. We're just going to ignore what you say and get on with life. Clear?'

Julia and Harry decided they didn't have time for the gateau.

Giles and Victoria stayed a bit longer, but still struggled with what their daughter was doing.

'She'll change her mind and see sense, you'll see,' Victoria said, as she put on her coat.

Chapter Eight

Myra

Eleanor had been an outstanding student with original ideas on established texts. She refused to be daunted by the supposed eminence of authors or lecturers, and in seminars she stood out like a beacon. Her views came from what was gradually being described as a feminist perspective, and as her contacts with American feminists grew, she was certain that this was the area in which she would specialise. As she completed her doctorate, the heads of department at Hove University were keen to retain her talent and offered her a place on their staff with time for research. She was thrilled.

In November 1960, the election of President Kennedy seemed to offer new hope to progressives, and there was optimism in the air.

On a particularly cold and grey afternoon, the faculty administrator interrupted an undergraduate seminar that Eleanor was taking.

She took the phone call. It was her mother. Her father had suffered a huge heart attack and was fighting for his life in Sussex County Hospital. She apologised to her students and drove her Mini along the sea front in a howling gale towards the hospital. Her father had always been bright and cheerful, even when he'd been complaining about Jerms or the crop, but of himself and his emotions he'd offered nothing. *How strange*, she thought, *not to know your father, other than as breakfast-time cook and hard-*

working farmer. And as she approached the hospital, she realised that her fear and trepidation wasn't about her father at all. It was about her mother. What would she do if her husband died? How would she cope?

As Eleanor walked into the hospital and asked where her father had been taken to, she saw her mother walking towards her. Her face said everything. Her father was gone.

In the days and weeks that followed, Myra and Eleanor had many discussions, but they agreed that the farm must be sold. Her father had had a good life-assurance plan through the Farmer's Union, and Myra would continue to work at the Faraday Institute for a further year before taking her pension.

By early 1961, Myra had moved into a cottage in Barcombe, a beautiful Sussex village. Working in Hove, Eleanor stayed with her mother most weekends. Their long country walks and wonderful conversation became a constant and cherished part of their lives, and the relationship between Myra and the adult daughter of whom she was so proud flourished like the meadows and copses of the Sussex countryside.

Hove University, Vice Chancellor's office. 1961
Charles Crawford had recently refurbished his office. It had a rosewood desk and shelving, and books he considered suitable for the house of learning in which he had the honour to be Vice Chancellor: Churchill's *A History of the English-Speaking Peoples* and his histories of the Second World War, Rustichello da Pisa's *The Travels of Marco Polo*, Virgil's *Aeneid* and the works of Macaulay.

He sat behind his desk, with its gold cigarette lighter, and looked at the woman seated on one of the two chairs facing him.

'Have you agreed to give this interview tomorrow?' he asked Eleanor.

She spoke in a soft voice that belied her strength. 'Yes, Dr Crawford. It's an opportunity to explain the power of peaceful protest.'

'I'm pleased,' he said.

'You are? I'm so surprised.'

'It's good to surprise people! I agree with your cause and your methods. If Hove University becomes the UK centre for peaceful feminist protest, that's fine with me.'

World View, BBC TV
Peter Clark opened the programme.

'Tonight on *World View* we welcome Dr Eleanor, whose recent book *Ending Patriarchy: The Power of Peaceful Protest* is this year's surprising success, especially given its catchy title!'

The audience laughed

'For the uninitiated, Dr Eleanor, tell us a little about the book.'

'Gladly. Last year, I met a remarkable man in Georgia, not well known as yet in Britain. His name is Martin Luther King. He's formed a Christian fellowship to mobilise people around the cause of civil rights in the Deep South segregation states. His serenity and sense of justice inspired me. And, you know, women also suffer injustice and discrimination every day.'

'You're not suggesting that women in Britain are treated as badly as coloured people in Georgia, are you?'

'Our struggle's a different one: equally important, but because it seems less dramatic, it's harder to raise its profile. I want women to feel able to leave the kitchen, to progress in their careers and,' – she turned to the audience – 'I want equality of opportunity with men as an assumption, a starting point.'

'You've a long journey ahead,' Clark said, with a slightly cynical smile.

'Then I'd better get to it, hadn't I?' She smiled at the audience. 'What am I doing in this studio?'

Hove University, Department of Sociology
The modern lecture hall was filling up with undergraduates laughing, arguing, talking about the essays they had yet to start. Two lecturers walked in.

'Settle down, settle down,' Dr Mick O'Gorman said. He was tall and lean and his face seemed to have a constant frown until suddenly it broke into a wide beaming smile.

'As you know, because you've been mad enough to choose this module, we're going to look at conflict and social change. Behind those bland words we hope to show you some different perspectives on the connection between theorising and effecting radical changes in society.

Both your lecturers are interested in Ireland, but that's about all we have in common.'

Eleanor stood without a lectern. 'The paths to change I'm going to discuss will contrast totally with those being offered by Dr O'Gorman. I'm going to look at evolutionary change, by talking about influential historical figures who have taken society in a new direction without violence. Dr O'Gorman is going to discuss those who've advocated change by revolutionary means, and who, in some cases, have taken part in armed revolution.'

Dr O'Gorman nodded. 'And because this is such a huge subject, we're going to limit it in two ways. We're going to look at women and their struggle – what Dr Eleanor called in her book 'femalcipation' – and we're going to focus on Britain and

Ireland. We make no apologies for the fact that we're going to be controversial, raise hackles and upset your parents.'

The students laughed. Eleanor felt confident as she explained.

'There's only going to be one sin in this course: non-participation. You think we're lecturers. We're not. This is the only lecture you'll get.'

There was muttered conversation in the lecture hall.

'All the other sessions will be in much smaller seminar and tutorial groups, so there'll be no hiding place whatever. You're not at school. You're at university. We assume you've done the reading. We want your thinking, your views.'

'It's very nice but why'd you want to have lunch with me?' Eleanor asked.

'We're going to teach these fresh-faced kids, so we're a kind of unit within the faculty and I think it's important we know what we really think.'

'About what?'

'Roast beef. What do you think about routes to social change, feminism and Ireland?'

'Maybe we should have booked dinner too,' Eleanor said, smiling, as she put her napkin on her lap.

'Let's just pick a topic, talk and see where it leads,' Mick said.

'OK,' Eleanor said, picking up the offered baton. 'Attachment Theory. Since I published my book, I've been thinking about what John Bowlby wrote.'

'Not really my field, but I know a bit about his view: how we turn out depends how close to our mother's breast we stay and for how long.'

'Reasonable summary,' Eleanor said, 'but I'm worried it's going to be seen as some orthodox text, some default way forward.'

'How does breast-feeding affect feminism?'

'I'm sure you know that.'

'It's not my field, it's yours.'

'I think you'll find its everyone's. Bowlby claims to have scientific, biological proof of a correlation between the future outcomes of a child and the quality of the connection between baby and mother. Note, *mother*! Not parent. Whether he likes it or not, that's an anti-feminist statement. Whereas *bourgeois* Betty Friedan and *Krupskaya* Juliet Mitchell try get women out of the home into work, what does Bowlby do? He offers guilt, as if mothers don't suffer from it enough as things stand.'

'Yes, I see that. So, you don't like Bowlby and you don't like Attachment Theory. Can I play devil's advocate for a minute?'

'Go ahead.'

'Let's just consider the possibility Bowlby isn't a political man. He's conducted research with that woman he worked with, that Canadian woman …'

'You know the littlest bit more than you let on. You mean Mary Ainsworth.'

'That's her. She came up with that test.'

'The Strange Situation Procedure,' Eleanor said, wondering why Mick had pretended to be so ignorant on a subject he obviously knew a fair bit about.

'Anyway,' Mick continued, 'let's assume he did the empirical and statistically reliable research, then he published the results, which are very inconvenient for feminists, but does that make them worthless?'

'I've had that debate often. Let's leave Attachment Theory there for a while, and you pick a topic.'

'OK. Revolution. When we decided on which of us was going

to lecture on evolutionary and which revolutionary paths to social change, you immediately chose evolutionary.'

Eleanor leant back, looked out to sea and swept her hair back. Mick stared, knew he was staring and didn't seem to stop. Eleanor held his gaze, smiled and took a spoonful of ice cream.

'I suppose its natural. I'd rather lecture on my own chosen path.

Firstly, there're lots of radicals out there now. Juliet Mitchell's just waded in with her Marxist analysis. I met Sheila Rowbotham last month, and those two seem destined to compete for the most radical feminist backdrop.'

'You also get a better chance to keep your job.'

Mick was being provocative, but she met him head on.

'Well, there' s something to be said for that.'

The waiter brought the bill, they shared the cost and walked down to the front.

'Revolution?' she asked.

'I'm interested in ideological and revolutionary appropriation.'

'Go on.'

'It's when a person, or a group, infiltrates or becomes involved with a radical activist group, and then uses the group to further an alternative aim.

There's only one way the Brits will leave the island of Ireland, and it's not your pacifist protest that'll do that. It's war – always has been. Then, hopefully we'll turn the Irish war into a class war, and maybe even gentle Hove might feel the force of revolution one day. That's a thought, isn't it?'

As Eleanor took the bus home, she was quivering. She was working with a potential terrorist! As she stepped off the bus into the breezy sunshine, she thought: *This is my opportunity to talk to the Intelligence Services.*

The next weekend Sam from MI5 came to the house. He had a ruddy, whisky-laden complexion, deep frown lines, and hair that had been slicked back with too much grease. Eleanor spoke to him in Myra's study, her various awards adorning the wall.

'I'm glad we're having this conversation, Miss Kennedy. Your co-lecturer is of considerable interest to us.'

She didn't interrupt. He continued.

'We were pretty sure that the daughter of Myra Kennedy would be on our side, and even without that pedigree, your loss ...'

He seemed unsure of what to say next, so Eleanor stepped in.

'Sally's death makes me even more determined to stop terrorists. I think that's what you mean, Sam.'

'Indeed, it is.'

'What would you like me to do? He knows I don't support revolutionary change, so there's no point me appearing sympathetic to his cause.'

'We don't want you to do anything of the kind. We just want you to watch him for now, tell us about the people he meets. Just be our eyes and ears.'

Eleanor hadn't called Sam for some weeks. There had been nothing of interest to say, and her father's death had preoccupied her. But late one afternoon, when the students had left the faculty for the library or their halls, O'Gorman saw Eleanor in the administrator's office. He asked if they could chat.

'How would you feel if we gave our students a lecture from the horse's mouth, so to speak? Let them see what a revolutionary fighter looks like in the flesh?'

O'Gorman was actually suggesting that the Fenian militant Carrick Murphy, known to all simply as 'Carrick', should come to the mainland and address the students.

Eleanor tried not to look startled, and said she'd like to think about it. She called Sam from a noisy Brighton station.

'He's almost certainly on the mainland already,' Sam said, 'and we've missed him. I think O'Gorman's probably testing you. If their street contacts notice an increase in attempts to follow Carrick or to find him, then they'll know you're helping us. We'll have to handle this carefully. But thank you, Eleanor.'

Eleanor nodded fiercely. 'No thanks needed.'

Chapter Nine

My mother died last year

My mother died last year. As the frosts froze the air, the garden shrouded itself in mist and went to sleep, my mother surrendered to the winter wind.

I went to stay at Mother's cottage to look after her. There may be more beautiful places to live than Barcombe, but I don't know them. The Sussex countryside, the ambassador of nature in all its splendour, warms the heart and the hearth and sends jasmine breezes deep into your soul on a June evening.

None of this, not any of it, heals the loneliness, the yearnings or the sadness.

Unless you've been truly lonely, known days when you know you'll be noticed by nobody, wandered country lanes alone as the moon gradually replaces the setting sun in the last orange of dusk, felt the ache that overwhelms your being at the thought of other people leading happy, loved, laughing lives, you cannot know the terror that is loneliness.

On a Sunday in the late summer of 1961, the stifling still August air hung like an invisible mist, the lilies of the valley rustled a little in the courtyard outside our kitchen, the thirsty robin drank from the bird bath and welcome lemonade was on the table.

My mother, in her summer dress, her grey hair hanging on her shoulders.

'Eleanor darling, I found something on my body, in the bath last night, a little lump on my breast. I'm sure it's nothing but I'm going to show Dr Paisley tomorrow morning.'

Words that seemed no more than a rivulet, became a torrential wave of tests and clinics and eventually surgery at Sussex County. Dr Porter genuinely empathised with women going through the trauma, initiated the use of lumpectomies instead of full-scale mastectomy, and, unusually in my experience, he also understood how to talk to a patient.

My mother faced the horrors of radiotherapy and the exhaustion that followed. Most days I comforted myself with the notion that it was the treatment that caused her to feel so ill, and to make her lose weight until she became skeletal, but even I realised the truth when her body turned yellow, and she was diagnosed with secondary cancer in her liver.

Autumn was darker than it had ever been that year, and as I pulled the curtains in the lounge one late afternoon, I told myself that I was going to lose her, and I didn't believe it at all.

Mother the protector, the nurturer, the teacher, the one-person support network, began to fade and I became all these things. We brought her bed downstairs so she could watch the television and listen to the wireless in the lounge, and because, in truth, her legs could hardly carry her upstairs.

We talked.

'You'll be alright, darling. The house is yours. Daddy left me with an investment portfolio and Mr Henderson will manage it for you.'

Mr Henderson, who watched my breasts at least as closely as he watched the share markets. One thing I was quite clear about: Mr Henderson wasn't going to manage anything.

I had stopped contradicting mother, telling lies about how she was going to live. She deserved better than that. Then, and I can't remember how it began, we started to talk about Jesus.

Neither of us had a faith, except perhaps in humanity and the importance of political action, but we found common cause as people interested in the link between gender and peace in the world. She was a pacifist. We were both believers in the teachings of Jesus, and we often talked about the difference between reading his revolutionary words, like the Sermon on the Mount, and a faith in some omnipotent god. My mother expressed this view to the local vicar.

'I agree with a great deal of what Jesus said, but I want nothing to do with your Christianity. You see Vicar, Paul started the ruination of Jesus' teaching, and the Christian Church has spent 2,000 years distorting everything he said. So, no I'll not be wanting your blessing or your visits, though I appreciate the call.'

It was a phone call, but it would have been so good to watch Rev. Hitchin sitting at the table in his pretty vicarage, listening to what Mother had to say.

She winced in pain, her voice was quiet, she didn't eat very much, but she enjoyed the conversation.

'Peace is the only hope for humankind,' she said.

'I thought that was Physics,' I said.

'One of the few advantages of dying slowly, watching the curtains close on your life, is that you can think about the macro without worrying about the micro. The big picture.'

She looked at me, as I turned a lamp on in the bay window and looked again at my parents' wedding picture. She sank a little lower in her chair, a shadow of the mother I had loved for so long.

'Eleanor, I want to be serious for a moment.'

'Aren't Jesus and H- Bombs serious enough for you?'

'That's not what I mean, and you know it. Darling, I've very little

time remaining and I'm not sure I want a great deal more. You've been the daughter every mother prays for, from party girl to carer, though God knows I never wanted that.'

She coughed and her whole body shook.

'But I want you to make some promises to me. They're not hard to keep but they mean everything to me. I want you to really try to meet some friends, serious friends, with whom you can talk and discuss the world. I know some people at CND, and I'd really like you to meet them. And I don't want you to give up on relationships either. Will you promise to try?'

'The first, I will; the second, I'm less sure of. But I promise you this: I'll give it the serious thought it deserves, coming from the person I love more than anyone in the world.'

Then we were hugging and crying and laughing too at our emotions. As the fire crackled in the hearth, the darkness descended on the world outside, the two of us who loved each other as perhaps only a mother and daughter can, clung to each other and let our tears mingle in the saddest of all knowledge – we wouldn't be together by Christmas.

On 18 December she died. As I sat in the front pew in Barcombe church, I realised we were inconveniently holding back the hurricane of Christmas for a few sombre minutes. A rich life, full of love and experiences had been shrunk physically into a coffin and figuratively into a short eulogy, and then the few mourners left the church. I thanked the vicar, who seemed unmoved by the recent phone call, and as I walked through the porch into the deepening gloom, his words of comfort were scattered in the sky. I was alone.

As I returned to her home, I thought back to my school friends, and of course, Sally. She would have been here, by my side, my rock and my comforter. My anger grew as I thought of the hugs and

love that Sally and I could have given to each other on the joyous
occasions, and on a day like this, when I needed a friend more
than ever. But I was alone. Bereft, desolate and soulless on a winter
afternoon. I put the key in the lock, smelt the slightly musty hallway,
sat in a chair in the lounge, looked at the empty bed and sobbed.

Then I turned on some lights, switched on the TV and watched
Harold Macmillan talking about his friend President Kennedy.

I made some tea and put on the lamp by my bed. I thought about
the comfort of bed, tea and light, I listened to the snow hitting the
window and drifted off to sleep.

Spring 1962
Before the cock crows thrice

On a Sunday morning in March 1962, Eleanor awoke to the sound
of birds and the sun pouring through her curtained window.
The gloom of winter was over, but spring asked for hope, and
she struggled through her loneliness to answer the call. Winter
seemed more appropriate. She walked into Barcombe village, the
hedgerows bursting with buds, the warmer sun on her shoulders,
and thought about the promises she'd made to her mother.

Should she join the Campaign for Nuclear Disarmament? She
didn't believe the boys would give up their toys. She didn't much care
about nation states: whether Britain, America or Belgium had nuclear
weapons or ditched them was of no interest to her, except to the extent
it moved society in her chosen direction. Then there was the personal.
The cause was only partially helpful to peaceful feminist protest. It
brought some women to prominence, but it yet again highlighted
men's obsession with war. On a personal level, Eleanor thought this
would also be a good way of meeting like-minded people.

Eleanor knew she had a multifaceted personality. As she

gave lectures and taught students, she wore confidence and offered acerbic responses to silly questions. But the students and the interviewers, the critics and her fellow lecturers, would be astonished if they knew about the other Eleanor – the inhibited, introspective Eleanor, quite aloof, lacking social skills, unsure of herself in groups. She'd had relationships but had never lost herself to anyone, never allowed herself to be out of control, and it was obvious she emitted an aura, which said anything but 'Come and get me'.

When she returned home from her walk, passing the Royal Oak pub, the timid side of Eleanor left her feeling psychologically naked. She wondered if she would have the guts to go into the pub alone one day – her, Dr Eleanor, author, feminist, new TV darling!

As she walked into her empty house, she looked at the photo of her mother on the dresser. She gazed at it for a few minutes, placed a photo of Sally next to it, and then picked up the paper on which her mother had written the phone numbers of people she knew at CND. Looking at her mother's writing, something she'd written not so long ago, brought her closer to her mother, and yet it brought on the grief again. As Eleanor looked out of the window at the blossom on the magnolia tree, she thought about how much her mother had loved it. She'd regarded it as a herald of earthly renewal.

She thought about Christ's prediction about Peter: 'Before the cock crows twice, you will deny me thrice'. She was about to deny her mother one of her last wishes. She had no intention of joining CND.

Chapter Ten

Cumberland Terrace, St John's Wood. August 1962.

Daniel lay in the bath after his day at school, thinking about his age and the overwhelming fear that never seemed to leave him. As far back as he could remember, his night-time behaviour had hardly changed.

He remembered how when he was little, the latest mother substitute would give him supper, bathe him, read to him, and then turn off his bedroom light. His terror had set in immediately. Shapes at the window, goblins in the corner he couldn't see. His toy soldiers marched on the bed. But worst of all, he couldn't even begin to think about what might be *under* his bed. Even now as he came into the room on his own, he immediately looked under the bed, and only then could he be sure he needn't run straight out of the room.

Even if he could vaguely see the light in the hallway, that did not protect him from everything happening inside this room. He wondered what was pushing the curtains out. What was the face he could see through the dark?

As he washed, he tortured himself by drifting back to his younger days.

No, he couldn't stay in this room one second longer. He trembled with fear, freezing cold, not wanting to leave the bed, but then what choice did he have? Mummy had gone to some faraway place called 'Merica', and Daddy was buying more of those strange things he put on the wall. If he called out, nobody would hear him anyway.

What was that noise? It sounded like it came from the window. He took Bobby the bear, opened the door, walked out onto the landing, and sat by the stairs. The landing light was on. He could hear the TV somewhere. He decided to sit there until someone came to bed. Then he would have just the tiniest window to go to sleep before all the lights went out.

As he brought himself back to the present, he realised how little had changed. Either one of his parents, or more likely now, one of the home helps, would put him into bed, turn out his light and say goodnight. They were, even now, under the illusion that Daniel then went to sleep. After all these years, his nocturnal routine continued. He would still sit, usually sucking his thumb, on the landing, by the stairs. He heard all the adult news programmes – *This Week*, *World in Action* and *Panorama* – and became familiar with the newsreader, Andrew Gardener, as his voice floated up the stairs to the landing.

How could it be, he asked himself, at age 10, he was still so utterly terrified of the dark? Why had his parents never agreed to his constant requests for a lamp to remain lit in his room? Their response ranged from scorn to disinterest, and he just could not convince them of how the darkness was ruining his life.

The choice facing Daniel in that bath was clear. Did he hate his time at school more or less than the darkness? It was so easy to answer! There was nothing he hated more, nothing made him hate *himself* more, than his terror of the dark. So then, he thought, there is a simple answer. *I'm 10 and lots of boys at Hampstead Prep board at 10, even if they live locally. The boys sleep together in dormitories, so I won't be afraid of the dark.* His parents lived extraordinarily busy lives, and he was quite sure they'd be delighted if he boarded. He could imagine their response as it floated into the bathroom: 'Of course, darling. We're delighted you like your school that much.'

And so it was for the want of a bedroom lamp, Daniel became a boarder in Hampstead at a school he despised, and his friendless, lonely, school life began.

In the early 1960s, in the house at Cumberland Terrace, decisions were being made with lifelong ramifications. Adrienne and Howard, for all their apparent intelligence, lacked the most important parenting skill of all: the ability not only to listen, but to hear what their child was saying.

Indeed, it is possible that the disastrous events of the coming years might never have happened if only they had allowed their son to have a table lamp in his bedroom.

Although they followed their fascinating, fulfilling careers as they travelled around the world, they seemed utterly oblivious to Daniel's misery.

In later years, they were to claim he'd asked to go to boarding school. This, of course, absolved them from responsibility. Daniel had only himself to blame.

This was the version that assumed an orthodoxy, but it belied the truth. Howard had come to love his son with a new and unexpected profundity. He picked up Daniel from school, did his prep with him, and often supervised him at weekends while his wife scurried around the world. He felt an overpowering love that bore no relationship to the cold and undemonstrative father–son relationship that he had endured. Initially, Howard had assumed that his father's level of emotional constipation was the norm. But his closeness and familiarity with Daniel had allowed new shoots to spring up in the tree of paternal love. He looked forward to hearing about Daniel's day, watched him play football and shared his anguish at the lack of justice when he was brought off the pitch by the teacher. Their Saturday morning walks into Marylebone High Street led to lunches in cafes where he was proud to sit with Daniel. This was something new and unexpected.

So, he was shocked when Daniel asked to board. Why would he do that? Was it perhaps normal that he should want to be with his pals? (He'd never met a single boy that fitted that description). Maybe Daniel felt excluded by being a day boy. Adrienne was so thrilled by the idea she floated on air. He knew for certain her reaction was abnormal for a mother, but then, so many mothers waved off their children to boarding school. Somewhere deep inside, Howard had questions he couldn't formulate. Ironically, he wondered if he was being selfish. Maybe his reluctance was self-indulgent; he wanted Daniel to stay at home.

One evening, when Daniel was asleep and they were walking in Regent's Park, Howard asked Adrienne outright.

'Why do you think Daniel wants to board?'

'His friends board, he wants to be part of the gang.'

The answer, like the clothes coming off a man after a road accident, exposed the brutal reality that was Adrienne's ignorance of her son. It was clear to Howard that Daniel didn't have many friends at school, and he wasn't part of any gang.

'I don't think so,' Howard mused. 'There's something going on that we don't know, but for the life of me I can't fathom what it is.'

'If you oversold your art, like you overthink your son, we'd all be broke. He said he wants to board. We can afford it. He'll be with his friends and have the opportunity to make more. And I can stop feeling guilty when I'm not at home in the evenings.'

Howard's response could have been long and controversial. Indeed, it *should* have been. But there was no circumventing the simple truth: Daniel had asked to board.

His inability to articulate his concerns, and the Niagara Falls-like momentum spewing out of Adrienne, swept Howard away. And maybe she was right anyway.

But maybe she wasn't.

October 1962. The Cuban Missile Crisis in Sussex
Eleanor was preparing a late supper, with Richard Dimbleby and Ludovic Kennedy talking in the background on BBC's *Panorama*. The programme was interrupted by a newsflash and soon the viewers were looking at Richard Baker in the newsroom as he revealed that President Kennedy had broadcast to the American people about a build-up of Soviet missiles in Cuba.

She called her local friends and soon they were assembled at the Anchor Inn. The usual Saturday lunch-time group had been swelled by the news.

What did it mean?

Crisis in Washington
It seemed to Adrienne that Daniel had solved all her problems. There were still the school holidays and weekend exeats, but the daily drudge of planning a busy life around her child had ended. And even better, he had suggested the change himself.

Adrienne had little time to reflect on her parental good fortune, because a situation had developed which, if it were mishandled, might lead to thermonuclear war.

As she was offered a brandy by Ted Heath in her office at

Future World, the duty clerk brought in an urgent message from President Kennedy. A crisis was developing in the relationship between the United States and the Soviet Union. Intercontinental ballistic missiles had been photographed on the island of Cuba.

Bundy asked Adrienne to fly to Washington immediately. Adrienne spoke to Macmillan and he agreed. He had both a professional admiration for Adrienne and a growing personal friendship. It suited him well to be able to tell his wife, as she left the house for another dalliance with Bob Boothby, that he would be spending the evening in the company of the very glamorous Jewess, Adrienne Goldberg.

In the years since the Suez Crisis, Future World's thoughtful and restrained advice had been invaluable. Prime Minister Harold Macmillan was in no doubt as to the main source of that vital support: Adrienne. Now he wanted her to advise him from Washington, and it seemed President Kennedy's advisors would welcome her views too.

Sussex, The Anchor Inn
'They can blow up Mexico and Washington from Cuba. Can they reach us?' Ginny asked.

'It's not about that,' Eleanor said.

'I'd say it is,' Ginny said.

'No, what I mean,' Eleanor explained, 'is if the Soviets launch even one missile at America, we'll all be caught up in nuclear devastation, so it doesn't really matter whether the Cuban missiles can reach us or not.'

'Is that an argument for England keeping nuclear missiles or not?' Megan asked from behind the bar. Nuclear threat or not, Dave was still studying her chest closely as she pulled a pint, so at least some things hadn't changed.

'It's complicated and we don't really agree on that,' Eleanor said.

'If we're all blown to bits it won't matter much if we agree or not,' Megan said.

'We can all agree on that,' Ginny said. 'Let's buy *The Sketch* and *The Herald* tomorrow, get both sides and come back and chat about it.'

Later, at home with a cup of tea, she thought about the phone call she'd received as she was having breakfast.

'Eleanor Kennedy?'

'Who's calling?' she asked.

It was Sam from MI5.

'Please speak to Charles Crawford tomorrow. He's one of us'

Charles Crawford worked for MI5! That was a real surprise.

Before bed that night her mood was changeable; a mistral one minute and a glorious sunny day the next. This could be her opportunity to avenge Sally in some small way and make her mother proud, but village life was nurturing her recovery. It was calm and stable. She wanted to indulge her stability, her recovery for a little longer, before … well, who could say what might happen in the coming days.

She often listened to Alan Freeman on the light programme. The song being played was a new hit by Carole King: 'It Might as Well Rain Until September'.

'This song, bed-poppers, was written for Bobby Vee, but we like Carole King singing it, don't we?'

'We certainly do,' Eleanor said to the radio. She sang and danced around the kitchen, using a rolling pin as a microphone.

She was leaning on the Bendix twin tub and the top fell through. Carole King did not appear to notice.

Then she turned off the radio, ran to the Dansette, and put on last year's tune, one she'd listened to endlessly with Sally. Acker Bilk's tones flooded the kitchen with 'Stranger on the Shore'.

And that was the big mistake, because, when sitting at the kitchen table, Acker's soulful, elegiac playing reached into every part of her being, like the sea rushing into the moat of a childhood beach castle. Soon she was sobbing, and the river of sorrow threatened to engulf her. Her mother, Sally and the riverbank all flowed through her mind and body, as she headed for the rocks.

Later, Acker Bilk's even sadder 'Aria' blared from the lounge like a piece of funeral music in a church.

She closed the Dansette, walked into her lamp-lit bedroom, and realised she felt better.

'Thank you, Acker,' she said.

The next morning Eleanor's friends met for breakfast at the Anchor. The newspapers were frightening. It really seemed as if Kennedy's blockade, his response to Khrushchev's missiles, might lead to a nuclear holocaust. Events in another part of the world might reach their Sussex village and blow it apart. The *Sketch* headline 'Blockade' summed it up. If the Soviet ships heading to Cuba didn't turn around, the US Navy would board them, and that would mean war.

'I sense Kennedy might be a restraining hand,' Eleanor said.

She called Charles Crawford's secretary, and to her surprise, he had a slot to see her the next day.

Safehouse

Washington DC. White House Situation Room
Saturday, 27 October 1962. 10 am EST

Adrienne sent a note to JFK requesting a meeting to be attended only by Secretary of Defence Robert McNamara (RM), Special Assistant to the President, McGeorge Bundy (MCGB) and Robert Kennedy (RFK).

AG: Mr President, two days ago your resolve forced Khrushchev to blink and the ship turned back. It seems to me you're much more powerful now than you realise. Khrushchev's looking for a way out and I think we can give him one.

JFK: Continue, Adrienne.

AG: I think your brother should meet with Soviet Ambassador Dobrynin this evening, at the Justice Department in secret.

RM: And say what?

AG: There's a huge danger this whole thing will escalate out of control to nobody's advantage. That he (RFK) and Dobrynin can probably settle it together this evening, in secret. If Khrushchev agrees, no further missiles will be sent to Cuba, and the present ones will be evacuated within a UN certified period, then the USA will enter into UN-supervised talks with the intention of taking all the American Jupiter missiles off Turkey. Bringing in the UN allows both parties to seem reasonable, and neither appears to have unilaterally backed down. Khrushchev can say he got his Turkish *quid pro quo* and we get rid of the Cuban missiles and the crisis as well.

RM: Secret diplomacy, eh? Risky business.

AG: Thermonuclear war? Risky business too.

Later that evening, RFK met with Ambassador Dobrynin.

The following morning, Nikita Khrushchev went on Radio Moscow, with an announcement. 'I have sent a message to President Kennedy today. The Soviet Government has ordered the dismantling of weapons in Cuba, as well as their crating and return to the Soviet Union. In return, the USA, under United Nations supervision, will remove their Jupiter missiles from Turkey. The crisis is over.'

Hampstead Prep School

Daniel had spent his exeat at home with his father. His mother was away yet again. Now he was back at school, and they were showing a film for the boarders, *Twelve Days to Noon*, about a plot to blow up London. As the lights went down, Daniel wept silently. He was horribly homesick, and had only two requirements: a cuddle from his mum and a lamp in his bedroom.

A Year without Myra

She knew it was approaching. It was the mountain in her mind.

It had been the coldest autumn she could remember. The windows had been full of ice instead of condensation, and frost came early and smothered the garden in white. The late dahlias never stood a chance.

The spirits had conspired and tonight she was alone.

She lit a fire and sat in the chair she'd moved to the space where her mother's bed had been.

She put 'True Love Ways' on the Dansette.

'How Mother loved that song,' she whispered into the empty room.

Wasn't it just a day? She missed her each and every day, so why turn this upcoming day into such a monster? She could pretend it had been a different day, or try and ignore it altogether.

'Now, that's just ridiculous!' she said to herself. The fire began to take, the logs had the smallest of crackles, and the room had a hint of warmth.

She realised she just had to take it head on. It had been a year since her mother succumbed. Was there any language that could make her feel better? What was wrong with the words 'death' or 'dying'? She didn't like those words, and she could choose the words she wanted.

We just knew we were fine with each other, she thought. Her father had never been good at saying how he loved her, but she had never been in any doubt that he did.

And darling Mother, (that sounds good), she had an embrace like no other, a welcome smile full of love, light and delight.

When she'd called her mother, Eleanor knew she was the person her mother most wanted to hear from. All that was gone.

As the fire warmed the room, and she thought about the progress she'd made in a year, she knew her mother would have been pleased about the friends she'd made in the village, and proud that she was about to offer her help to MI5.

Chapter Eleven

Barrie O'Connell lived in a flat near Elgin Avenue in Maida Vale. London seemed to have come to a halt, with snow piled high on the pavements. Those foolish enough to try and drive a car found that vehicles slipped back down hills on thick ice or became stuck in huge snow drifts. In fashionable Park Lane, abandoned cars littered both sides of the dual carriageway, and as night fell and the frost hardened, lucky people turned on lamps and lit gas fires, happy to be away from the freezing night.

He walked the last few steps of his stairway and into the gloomy hallway, heading for a party that promised Christmas cheer and Irish camaraderie.

His thoughts sent him reeling back to a day many months before. He had come down the stairs into the same gloomy hall. There had been a letter addressed to him, pushed through the door. It was conspicuously short on small talk. As he walked out into the freezing street, the terror from that short note, and the horrific night that followed, continued to penetrate his body every bit as much as the Arctic winds.

The note had simply said: *We know you're seeing Lucinda. Do you know who the fuck she is?*

Safehouse

North London Tavern, Kilburn, London

Huge ceilings were covered in Christmas chains and holly and ivy. The Wolfe Tones were playing Fenian ballads. Eleanor's friend Tina was up singing and dancing the rebel songs.

Some girls were doing Irish dancing on a makeshift stage, and Eleanor saw a microphone being prepared. Tomás Mac Giolla, the new leader of Sinn Féin, walked on stage. The dancing stopped, the music went silent, and a huge cheer went up through the pub.

'Have you not seen the two men drinking together at that table?' she called.

Tina hadn't. Mac Giolla was speaking on the stage about uniting Ireland, avenging the English and arming the Falls Road and the Bogside.

'There you are, Eleanor. You asked me to bring them over, and here they are.'

The Wolfe Tones were back singing Republican songs, the revellers joining in the words, the Guinness flowed, and one of the men turned and smiled.

'Eleanor? Now, that could be an Irish name.'

'It could be. My mother's Irish, she came from Kinsale, but I grew up here. What's your name then?' she asked.

'Barrie O'Connell. Great to meet your lovely smile.'

The music changed to the number one on the hit parade. 'Return to Sender' blasted through the pub.

Without realising she'd agreed, she was jiving. He was a natural dancer and let Elvis take him through the steps, whereas she was spun and lifted and loved it all. He was tall and strong. Muscles bulged from his short T-shirt, he had a wonderful broad smile, and Eleanor felt radiant in the glow of his laughter.

Chapter Twelve

The only thing to fear is fear itself. (Franklin D. Roosevelt)

January 1964

Barrie worked in Leicestershire, managing his own company. He was an expert in 'technical aspects of sports pitches and drainage'. When Eleanor told him it sounded like a dry subject, he said it was the worst pun he'd ever heard.

Barrie told his small team he was taking the next day off work.

'You got leprosy?'

'Got a funeral?'

Barrie had not taken a single day's holiday in the last year as he built his business, struggled with the books, with staff, with customers and suppliers.

Peter, a soil expert, looked at Barrie, sitting quietly at his desk, and thought he'd solved the mystery.

'Ok, who is she?'

A chorus of bawdy comments followed, but secretly they were pleased. Barrie was a good boss who led by example and extraordinary hard work. He couldn't join in with the office banter about sport: he knew nothing about it.

'Strange,' Dave had said in the White Horse, as he raised a pint of Ruddles beer. 'He builds pitches for so many sports, but he knows nothing about any of them.'

'No need. Build 'em well, nobody cares,' said Peter.

As he drove towards Lewes, the woman he was thinking about was not Eleanor, but Lucinda. He could visualise her now: older than him, with swept-back hair, an aristocratic demeanour and rounded vowels. He had met her at Benenden School where he had been working on the design of an all-weather hockey pitch for the richest educational establishment for girls in England. She'd started talking to him as he came in from the building site.

One day she said to him: 'We don't have to talk here, you know. Let's have a drink one evening.'

I've been asked out by a woman, and a beautiful one at that, he'd thought. He met her at the George Inn at Robertsbridge, about twenty minutes from the school – far enough away from prying eyes, but just a short car journey.

Lucinda loved his rich Irish accent, huge hands and long flowing black hair.

'So, who am I sitting opposite?' he had asked. 'I want to know about you.'

'Men usually talk about themselves!'

'Not much point, it seems to me. I'll leave here none the wiser.'

'Well, I'm older than you by some measure, and I teach English A level to girls who actually want to learn about it.'

'So that's what you do, and you know what I do. That's a start. You'll know a good deal more about English literature than I do, but I'll wager you know a little less about Irish literature.'

'I wouldn't bet more than a sixpence,' she said. 'I'd hate an upper-class English woman to impoverish yet another Irish man!'

'Oh, you would, is that right? Have you been married, Lucinda?'

'Can we leave all that kind of thing for another time?'

'Of course we can.'

'I'd like to just enjoy the now and take it slowly,' Lucinda said.

'We can take it as slowly as the river runs upstream,' Barrie said.

When the children broke up for Christmas, Lucinda went to stay with her aunt in Fountain House, a block of flats near London's Marble Arch.

One cold evening in December, they'd enjoyed a Whisky Mac in the Elgin pub, and soon they were on their way back to Barrie's flat, up his stairs, through the door and into each other's arms.

Barrie remembered how he had laughed about the state of his flat and the gas fire that didn't always work, but they were immersed in each other, and the touch and the caress had replaced the cares of the night.

Since the day when he'd received that note through the door, Barrie had been consumed by fear.

It was as if he had an abscess which could not be treated and for which there were no painkillers. The first time he'd really masked the pain was the night he'd danced with Eleanor.

She was different in every way from Lucinda: *younger, slightly naive*, he thought.

If he controlled his own life, he had the power to change it and, to some extent, to choose his emotions. If the source of the fear was external and beyond control, what then?

Barrie brought himself back to the present and his upcoming rendezvous with the lovely Eleanor. He tried to concentrate on the future. Surely he should be optimistic about his business, and a possible new relationship. However hard he tried, Lucinda and his dank, dark hallway filled the car, as he travelled to Sussex.

Barrie and Eleanor sat in the bar of the pub in Lewes, talking about music and art.

She loved his sardonic humour; but it was 'the smile eclipse', as she described the way his smile consumed his face, that made her whole being drown in joy.

They began seeing each other every weekend. Sometimes they met in London, but when Barrie had more time, he came down to Barcombe and they enjoyed weekends together in the Sussex countryside.

Eleanor's seminars continued, filled with discussions about evolutionary feminists seeking peaceful change.

Charles Crawford, the Vice Chancellor, and many within the university, supported her courses against sometimes fierce opposition from conservative lecturers and faculty heads.

Meanwhile, whether in Barcombe or in his cottage in Rutland, Barrie could pretend he was far away from Maida Vale and, as he held Eleanor late at night, he found safety and some remission from the all-pervading fear.

But, as he knew all too well, remission is temporary.

July 1965, Hove
'Would you like to spend some holiday time at my cottage?' Barry asked.

'Don't go thinking you've got a house maid, you've no such thing!' Eleanor said with a smile. 'And there's one other thing I want agreed.'

'Didn't realise this was a negotiation,' Barrie said.

'Call it what you will.'

'And what is this other clause in the agreement?' he asked, without disguising his humorous scepticism.

'We have to be able to talk about things seriously when they matter.'

'Well, that's a deal-breaker if ever I heard one,' he retorted.

'And that response is exactly what I mean. What is it about you, Barrie? You just can't be serious with me, or anyone else for all I know.'

'Fair point. I've built up a successful engineering and building business, bought this cottage without a mortgage, and just laughed and joked my way through life, don't you see?'

'No, I don't see!' Eleanor's anger was growing. 'I don't want to lose our sense of fun or the good things we've got. I just need an occasional conversation.'

'Well, you drive a hard bargain.'

November 1965

Barrie was having a busy morning in his office, but there was one phone call he had to make that had nothing to do with the price negotiation for a new type of sand.

He called his school friend, Jeremy Taylor, a horse master, responsible for looking after horses in feature films. He had just finished work on *Carry on, Don't lose your Head* when David Lean called him and asked if he would help on his new epic in the desert about Lawrence of Arabia.

More importantly, Jeremy knew good inns and hotels.

'I'm thinking of making an honest woman of her,' Barrie said.

Jeremy and his wife had visited Barry's cottage in Empingham, a small Rutland village, a couple of weeks ago, and they had remarked on the change in the garden.

Now Jeremy was delighted. Barrie was thinking of marrying Eleanor.

'I should hope so!' Jeremy said. 'Lovely girl like that. More than you deserve.'

'Thanks for that,' Barrie replied. 'Listen, do you know a good place where I can propose to Eleanor, and also maybe have the wedding later in the year?'

'Actually, old boy,' Jeremy tried a fake Eton accent, 'I know just the job.'

'Knew you would.'

'Actually, I'm thinking of buying it.'

'Really. And what is this beautiful place you're about to ruin?'

'It's called the Inn for all Seasons, in the Cotswolds.'

Barrie told Eleanor there was a site he wanted to look at in the Cotswolds overnight, and asked if she'd like to come for the drive.

'You're just too good to me, Barrie, you know that. How could a girl refuse an offer like that?'

'Oh, and pack a posh frock,' he'd said.

Now, that is interesting, Eleanor thought. Should she tell Charles Crawford about the posh frock requirement? There couldn't be many reasons for it. Barrie was a useless liar.

What would MI5 think about her marrying the subject of their enquiries?

MI5 London

The Director General of MI5, Michael Frobisher, looked like a city lawyer, and with his sharp mind and gregarious nature, he could have been one. His office overlooked the Thames, and London, dressed for Christmas, lit up the darkening gloom. In Frobisher's office the atmosphere was convivial enough, a crackling fire in the grate, port in full flow and some excellent news.

'She thinks he's going to propose,' Crawford announced.

'She's obviously done her job well, then,' Sam replied.

'Question is,' Frobisher said, 'has she done it rather too well?

Divided loyalties are what I'm worried about.'

The Hove University Vice Chancellor was reassuring. 'I'd wager she knows where her loyalties are. She only has to think about her friend Sally; every now and then I introduce a few pieces of that jigsaw into our conversation. I'd say let her marry him. Can't stay closer than that, can you?'

January 1966

The wedding was over. The cold east winds of winter were sweeping into Rutland from the Urals, but Eleanor was as happy as she had ever been. She had secured a lecturing role at the university in Leicester, her seminars were amongst the most popular in the faculty, and this evening, a red winter sunset infused her with hope. She loved the sound of the roaring fire in the grate, the new lounge lamp offered cosier, more intimate light, and she lay on the settee, celebrating thoughts of the husband she adored.

Her meeting with Charles Crawford at Hove University seemed like another era.

'Barrie will be at the North London Tavern for the Christmas party. See if you can stay close to him, form some kind of relationship,' he'd said.

She was partly in denial about her MI5 role, and then occasionally, reality slipped into her mind and filled her with foreboding.

She relished the new opportunity at Leicester University, and her life seemed set fair, except that it was like looking west during a summer picnic, seeing beautiful blue sky, while ignoring the black storm clouds gathering over the farmhouse to the east.

Safehouse

And the clouds were gathering. The joyous jive in Kilburn, romantic weekends in Barcombe, and the proposal that night in Oxfordshire: what did she think she was doing? She had been asked to stay close to Barrie; MI5 were interested in him. She hadn't lost him, but she had lost herself to him.

As Eleanor left the university, Barrie was driving from Uppingham to his Empingham home. He took a diversion and drove through the Rutland countryside to the church of St Peter and St Paul, a church he had found recently in the beautiful village of Wing. Barrie reckoned he could do with help from both saints.

He sat in a pew facing the relatively short white colonnades that populated the central portion of the chapel. He leant forward, his head in his hands, and thought back to that miserable night again, and the consequences seemed somehow primeval. The vicar walked in, took a book from a shelf, saw Barrie, and left him alone.

Barrie had loved his childhood in County Cork, but he had been glad to escape the 'family of fairies and Catholicism', as he called it, which had been stifling in its religious observance. The rigid routines of Christian life – confession, Mass, the solemnity of Good Friday and the superstitions– seemed to form as large a part of modern daily life as they had back in the mists of time.

But there was another reason for his delight at leaving the Emerald Isle. The apparently dormant desire for Ireland to be united, for the end of the British rule over the 'Six Counties' had been suppressed, but it was there in dreams and quiet, shared conversations. The inequalities in Northern Ireland were so blatant and so savage that only a people prepared to be enslaved like the Hebrews in Egypt could have suffered it without seeking change. Barrie wanted nothing to do with the paramilitaries, but he knew Sean, his brother, was committed to a united Ireland.

While the politicians talked, Sean's friends had a phrase that alarmed Barrie. They said, 'Enough of talking', and Barrie knew well what happened when talking stopped.

The Americans, who loved the artificial nostalgia of helping the Old Country, were happy to attend dinners where funds were raised for a plethora of honest causes. As the boats bobbed up and down off the coast of Sligo, the real nature of these causes became apparent. The waiting Republicans pulled box after box of Armalite AR-18s onto dry land. The 'Widow-makers', as they were known, had arrived safely.

As he sat in the church, trying to find a cocoon from the world outside, he visualised the letter in the darkened hallway again and those words: *We know you're seeing Lucinda. Do you know who the fuck she is?*

Barrie decided they were best described as 'godforsaken' but they had been just the prelude to the night of terror that followed.

Meet us at the end of Harman Close off Harman Drive in Cricklewood.

We mean no harm to O'Farrell.

Dierdre O'Farrell had been Barrie's neighbour in Cork. It was a common sign-off for Republicans: when they wanted to be sure you would attend a meeting, they inserted a threat. As Barrie knew, they meant it. But then he intended to meet them, so the threat lost its power.

As he'd walked through the crunching snow from the bus, which had yet again failed to climb the small incline up to Finchley Road from West End Lane, he thought about Lucinda, and how little he knew about her. If they knew more, then this could be an interesting evening. But then again, this wouldn't be interesting. It would be terrifying. These were people you didn't cross.

He'd walked down Farm Avenue into Harman Drive, thinking about the commuters who walked home with supper in their mind, babies to bath, a mortgage to pay. How he would have liked to have been such a man on this night. Instead, he had a rendezvous with the Republicans.

He'd walked to the end of the close, into some waste ground and felt a hand wrap around his mouth. Some steel had jabbed his back, and soon he was in a car.

The man in the driving seat faced forwards and began to speak. 'You've been a cheeky boy, Barrie, and we don't like the cheeky boys.'

He knew not to respond.

'Tell me, young Barrie of Cork, how do you think your mother put you through engineering college? Don't bother, we'll tell you. We paid for most of it.'

Now that shocked him. He knew his mother had scrimped and saved, and he had kept a job going near the college, but …

'And why do you think it was engineering? So, you can build roads and bridges, do you think? Oh no, sorry we forgot, so you can make bucketloads of money selling ditches to rich schools, that's why.' He'd turned to his comrades.

'Funny boy this Barrie, don't you think? The Six Counties are simmering with injustice and hatred, we're preparing the fight back, and what does he do? He leaves the country to go live in splendid Maida Vale! What a feckin' joke.

Hasn't occurred to you, has it, but we'll be suggesting some added ingredients to your supplier list. New vital ingredients in the ditch business!'

'But don't you worry your little head about any of it,' the man in the passenger seat had said.

'Do you know what a *sleeper* is, young Barrie, do you? Let me enlighten you. We want you to go on making lots of money, but one day – it could be many years from now – we'll pay a little social call on you. We'll come for the tea and the cucumber sandwiches, so we will. And when we do, we're sure your Republican spirit will not be wanting.'

'Oh yes,' the driver man said, 'the lovely Lucinda. You've been popping her cork all over West London. She's a teacher, as you know, but her father's a junior minister in the enemy government in London.'

'Ah you didn't know that! Well in future we'll tell you the posh ladies we want you to put your dipstick into. Let's just say, Lucinda isn't one of them.'

He was bundled out of the car and onto frozen ground. The car left the wasteland with a skid and drove slowly down Harman Close, before turning left into Harman Drive.

And if that had put terror into his heart and soul, the next letter that had been pushed through his doorway left him sprawled on the floor. The letter had read:

Benenden, Cranbrook TN17 4AA
Spring Term 1964
Dear Parent,
It is with great regret that we have to inform you that Lucinda Davenham was killed in a car crash just after Christmas. We know how shocked you will be. We have, of course sent condolences to her family.
This year, the A Level English will now be taught

by Victoria Spindleton whom you will know from her wonderful production of Emil and the Detectives in December ...

The Ache

Looking back, Eleanor couldn't determine when 'the ache' had begun. When did her yearning to have a baby begin to dominate her thoughts until it became an obsession? She couldn't say.

As she walked to the college in Leicester after parking her car, she watched the mothers and the babies in their Silver Cross prams.

She was not manic; she just knew as each day passed, and each time she made love to Barrie, that she needed his baby, as surely as anaemia needs iron.

A new shop had opened in Leicester called Mothercare. She found herself wandering around its aisles in her lunchtime, picking up muslin cloths and putting them to her face. She imagined pushing the prams and pushchairs. She looked in the shop windows at Ladybird children's wear and at the brown Start-Rite sandals, with their little bridge strap.

One day, after her last tutorial, she walked into Mothercare and bought some muslins, Johnson's baby powder, zinc and castor oil, and gripe water. As she took her basket to the till behind the counter, she imagined her baby at home, with Barrie looking after her. For some reason she always imagined a girl. She didn't care whether she had a boy or a girl, but in her longings and dreams it was always a girl.

If Barrie was away working, she walked in the fields around the Eye Brook Reservoir. She felt empathy with the frozen January fields, the petrified trees, and the emptiness of the water. She leant

Safehouse

against a gate, looked out at the water, and before she knew it, she was weeping. At 36, she knew it would be more difficult to conceive. But this was not a logical, reasoned response. It was a deep emotional yearning.

She stood by the gate, at Eye Brook, imagining holding her new-born, that unique and wonderful smell of a baby, just awoken from her sleep, and the baby powder; that fragrance that everyone remembers, like they remember roses or lavender.

Her daughter was on a playmat or in a playpen, smiling and making a gurgling noise. Eleanor was sitting in a blue wicker chair, with a drawer of course, breast-feeding her until, drunk, the baby slumped on Eleanor's chest with dribbles of milk on her nursing blouse.

Soon the room she'd renamed 'the nursery' at their home had a wicker chair and a teddy bear, with a key that played Brahms' 'Lullaby'.

Barrie was aware of the room and Eleanor's obsession, but he had two solid reasons for not mentioning it. Firstly, he had no idea how to raise the subject or what he would say, and so avoided this sort of emotional discussion at all costs. Secondly, he couldn't say it changed his life in any way, and if it brought Eleanor pleasure then he reckoned that was fair play.

Chapter Thirteen

A year later. January 1967

She was late.

Eleanor walked out of the surgery but could not remember doing so. She was flying through the air on a magic carpet.

She walked into a call box, lifted the receiver, put 4d in the slot and dialled the number.

'Barrie O'Connell Surfaces.' Eleanor pushed button A, so she could hear Rita the receptionist.

'Can I talk to Barrie?' she asked.

'Hello, Eleanor. Is everything alright?' Rita asked. Eleanor rarely called Barrie's workplace.

'Oh yes, all's fine. Is he there?'

'No, actually he's gone to see someone at Oakingham School about some project they're considering.'

Eleanor was disappointed but hoped she didn't show it.

'Is there a message?'

'No thanks, Rita. Really not urgent at all. I'll wait till he comes home.'

Eleanor decided it was better to be able to see Barrie's face, and not appropriate at all to have told him on the phone at work.

She went to work and smiled inwardly all day. On the bus home, she could hardly contain her excitement. As she saw Barrie's Zephyr in the driveway she rushed into the house, bumping into the half-opened front door, into the lounge and threw herself into Barrie's arms.

'And I've done what to deserve this greeting?' he asked, bemused.

'Oh, quite a bit, my darling, quite a bit. You've only got your wife pregnant!'

He swept her up in his arms, as only Barrie could, and carried her around the room and then gently put her on the sofa.

'Oh,' he said, smiling broadly, 'better be careful! None of that rampant sex now, you know.'

Eleanor had put a bottle of champagne in the fridge before she went to the doctor. Now she took two flutes, gave Barrie the bottle, and soon they were toasting new life and a future with a family. They cuddled on the settee, and then sleepily and happily made their way upstairs. Two happy, contented people, deeply in love.

The days were getting longer, and after work she was able to walk by the Eye Brook again. She watched the sun fall lower over the water. She watched the ducks, and then a sandpiper swoop low over the water.

As her mind travelled the journey of her last few years she walked around the reservoir, crying. Then she stopped and said out loud: 'The baby will change everything.'

As she walked on, she revelled in the image of her daughter coming down the stairs in a pretty party dress, her hair in bunches, as the doorbell rang and the first party guests arrived.

Barrie had been spending a lot of time at Oakingham School. It was exactly Barrie's speciality and it suited him that he could work so near to home. As he worked, he thought about Eleanor and her baby. She had started to talk to it as if it was already a living being. He had no idea if this was normal behaviour, but Eleanor appeared to have withdrawn emotionally from him in the past week or so, as if all her emotional energy was being channelled into her womb. He didn't resent this sudden change of mood. Rather, he was worried for Eleanor's own welfare. If she was projecting so much into her womb, what might she be like when the baby was born? What hopes and fears might she put upon this child? Barrie had no knowledge whatever in this area, and he half-laughed to himself. *Obstetric psychology*? No, his field was trenches and filters. Still, he worried about Eleanor talking to her baby in the garden.

Monday, 20 March
Barrie had gone to work. Eleanor walked downstairs for breakfast. She realised, to her relief, that she did not feel sick today.

As she sat at the breakfast table, she felt a mild pain in her back, and then some stomach cramps. She left the breakfast table, walked into the downstairs toilet, assuming she needed a bowel movement. As she lowered her knickers, she saw spots of blood and something congealed and bigger than blood.

The cramps in her abdomen increased and she reached for the phone and dialled 999.

After the Miscarriage
Nothing had prepared Barrie for the abject desolation that afflicted Eleanor as she returned home from hospital in Leicester.

Apparently, it had to be somebody's fault.

'Where're your tears? You're just full of sorrow, Barrie, aren't you?'

Eleanor's scathing derision was almost impossible to bear.

'I'm married to a fucking fridge, one of those even colder things. A freezer, that's right, Barrie. I'm married to a freezer.'

'What about my feelings?' he wanted to ask. 'What about my sadness?'

Yet something inside Barrie, some wisdom and calm of unknown origin told him this was her time and not his. It was her time to be angry, to hurt, to cry, and maybe his would come later. Was he really to be her punchbag? It seemed so, but Barrie's love for Eleanor had nothing to do with her ability to bear a child. Eleanor's feelings for herself, in stark contrast, seemed inextricably linked with her pregnancy and its loss. That was how he saw it. The irony of their relationship was her view of him as being incapable of demonstrative emotion, and yet in his own quiet way, he thought a great deal about her feelings. He decided that his role was just to love her, to take the hurt and the anguish and, like a water-treatment plant, send the hurt back to her, cleansed and full of love.

As the days passed, and Barrie returned to work, there was no sign of Eleanor improving. She'd been to see a priest, but now lay on the settee, with her head in a cushion, weeping, mumbling words of sorrow and loss, praying to herself. She rebuffed his attempts at physical embrace. He just sat with her in the evenings and hoped for some improvement where there was none.

She stopped talking. It seemed she'd regressed into some semi-comatose world. He spoke to her doctor, who told him, 'Give it time, Barrie.'

And then in early April, she seemed gradually to improve. One day, when he returned from work, she told him, still weeping, still in the depths of sadness, that she he'd spoken to the Samaritans in the last week and felt less alone.

'I don't mean you make me feel alone Barrie, I don't.'

He was sad she hadn't been able to speak to him, but if the Samaritans offered a glimmer of hope, that had to be a good thing. He loved her more than anyone he'd met in his life.

Recently, as Eleanor's anguish led to quiet evenings, it wasn't fear that infused Barrie's mind when he looked at her. No, the thought that the IRA might contact him didn't trigger fear anymore – now it was terror.

Some fears are imaginary and blown out of all proportion. And some are not.

Part II

Chapter Fourteen.

March 1967
Fairmead Boarding House, Oakingham School, Rutland

Extract from The New Boys' Fag Test
Minor punishments may be imposed by House Prefects.
These include sweeping the House Quad and Tish Calls.
A Tish is the cubicle where you sleep in a dormitory, and
a Tish Call is a requirement to take a piece of paper into
the Night Bursar at School House, leaving your Tish at
3 am.

Legs out of bed, freezing wooden floor, numbing cold and dark, no landing light, just solid dark, like 'no-way-through dark'. Daniel could hear other boys breathe and snore. The rest of the world was sleeping as he dressed, walked out of the dorm and down the staircase.

'At least I can't see it; it's brown and dark and the paint on the pipes is flaking and -' He could smell, suet, and boiled cabbage. 'It's freezing. Why *am* I doing this?'

Down the stairs, his stomach full of fear, he walked towards the graveyard, when all he wanted was to go back to bed.

'Pretend I'm wearing Dad's sheepskin coat, walking into St John's Wood High Street on a Saturday morning. Try to forget I'm walking at 3.05 am out of Fairmead House, over the crunchy gravel of the driveway.'

The noises were starting: tree noise, dark noise, cold noise. wind noise. He approached the graveyard, with danger behind every grave.

'I'm halfway past the graveyard, there's a streetlight ahead,' he thought in a desperate attempt at reassurance.

The wind was brutal and icy. The leaves were talking again around his feet.

His biggest question, as he fought the wind and the cold, was why he had to be out in the freezing cold, walking down that road past a graveyard.

Last Sunday morning, in his milk-smelly study, he had been thinking about what he could say to his mother from the phone box in the marketplace, so that somebody – anybody – would take him away from that school.

He had been in Tony Pritchard's study, actually believing he was with the cool crowd and nobody was rubbing their nose and calling him a 'Fucking Jew!'

Then suddenly, everybody had left the study. They had just run out and then he heard the noise. The noise that explained why he was walking down this freezing cold road. The *click*.

Petrified and paralysed he thought: 'You can't lock a study!' and then came the realisation that he was wrong. He visualised all the other boys, filing into House Tea in the order of their entrance mark.

He heard the roll call in the dining room.

'Goldberg?' The calling of his name was usually followed by much rubbing of noses and necks bent to imitate a Jew at prayer.

'Goldberg?'

'Where's Goldberg?' the house prefect asked, 'Does he have a leave pass or is he in the San?'

Nobody knew.

'While we wait, can I go to the bog?' he'd heard Pritchard ask, and as Daniel walked up the freezing hill, he could still feel Pritchard's betrayal.

The lock had turned and the study was open.

As he walked towards the Night Bursar's lodge, he thought back to an even lonelier walk than the Tish Call, even more frightening than the cemetery stone. He had walked alone into the bright dining room. Everyone was standing in a semi-circle.

There was a space across the room where he should have been standing, so, head down, with shame burning his bones, he had taken his place.

The laughing, nose-rubbing and sniggering came back to him like an echo in the night-time wind. The conversation had been seared into his consciousness and branded on his body. He would remember it for the rest of his life.

'Oh, Goldberg, kind of you to turn up! Been down the pub, have we?'

'No.'

'Perhaps you'd like to share with the rest of the house the nature of your pressing engagement?' The prefect was starting to enjoy himself.

'No.'

De Lacy muttered, 'Been in synagogue, Goldberg?' Everyone laughed.

'Well, perhaps you'd like to make a little Kosher Tish Call, maybe pick up some smoked salmon?'

The whole house responded with rowdy laughter.

The blessed, delicious streetlamps were comforting him as he opened the door to the lodge and handed the paper to the bursar, who grunted some indecipherable words.

Then to the school colonnade. The chapel clock sounded a single note. It was three thirty.

He was alone, on a bench with lights on in the square, and friendly rain drizzling down.

The luxury of the analysts with their vocabulary of 'Separation Anxiety' and 'Attachment Theory', or other adjectives that might describe 'desolation' or 'isolation', was unavailable to Daniel. Instead, he invented a world which he was able to understand, and which no other human being could snatch from him. His warm familiarities became the leaves, the cracks in the pavement, and often 'the Run'.

The Run was the most important part of his morning. As he walked from Fairmead House to his classes in the town, he tried to *run* past two or three pavement cracks before a car passed him. The success of this venture determined if his myriad worries would assert themselves or perhaps reduce a little. Goldberg's life was riddled with worries: cadets, sport, maths, and walking back to the house without appearing always to be alone.

He stared at the classroom block. Three floors of classrooms, the glass now darkened by the night, waving in and out of focus as the wind and the rain interrupted his view. He had learned the name of the master who held court in each classroom, top left to bottom right, during his fag test. As he sat, becoming increasingly wet and dishevelled, he imagined a different picture behind each glass; safer, without having to count worries every day in the shower; a bedroom, with wallpaper covered in yachts and lakes and cars; a fort on the carpet with soldiers lined up neatly, and the reserves scattered around the bedroom floor. Mostly, he thought of a lamp by the bedside. It wasn't his own bedroom; that wasn't a happy place at all. It was where he feared the next worry, the next separation, the next time all the lights went out in the house.

No, this was a friendly bedroom, where the lamp was always on, the carpet was red, the curtains blew backwards and forwards in the wind, and tomorrow brought only hopes and happiness, not fear and dread.

The next bedroom overlooked a bus stop on a busy road, with lots of laughing, happy children greeting him as he arrived. They were huddled together arranging the weekends, talking about the homework they'd done at home, and how they were all going with their dads to Stamford Bridge to see David Webb.

Goldberg brought his thoughts back to the colonnade. The rain fell, the noticeboards were distant with their lists of sporting fixtures and school events; he could pretend they had disappeared. Dangerman was nourished by negativity, fear and self-hatred, but now, as Goldberg sat alone in the rain, while the children with cosy home bedrooms were fast asleep, he allowed himself to feel safe for a few minutes more.

He stared at the windows of the empty classroom blocks, and then walked back to Fairmead.

Sport was over, and Daniel had a couple of hours before he had to return to Fairmead. A group of boys ran past the school fives' courts, and just behind the last buttress, in a small recess, was the school Buttery, a cafeteria where boys could buy cream slices, dandelion and burdock, eggs and chips, and similar fare. It was a place for boys in groups, and being on his own, Daniel avoided it. A little way past the Buttery was the music school. Daniel didn't play any musical instruments, but the kindly Head of Music spoke to him after a music class.

'There are records and record players in room 25, just past the last practice cubicle.'

Daniel was walking there now. He could see the boys laughing and joking in the Buttery, as he walked into the music school and into room 25. Most boys had stereo systems in their studies, so they had no need of this room, but Daniel liked it on many counts. It had a lovely view of the valley, stretching down from the town centre, and then up towards two boarding houses, his own and Lanchester. The valley was filled with chestnut trees and poplars, and he could gaze at the view without anyone challenging him to do something more useful.

A record had been left out on a desk: Brahms Piano Concerto No 2. A note had been left by the music master: *Listen to the third movement, and don't scratch the record.*

Daniel put the stylus carefully on the record, and sat on a chair, alone in the room.

Soon, a beautiful melodic cello filled the room.

'Thought this was supposed to be piano music' he reflected.

But he surrendered to that cello as it led him on a soulful journey. Soon, the piano and orchestra joined the cello, and for a few minutes of tranquil serenity, Daniel was not in Oakingham, he was not thinking about his Maths Prep, or the Cadet Force. He was doing something few listeners to music managed to do: he was listening in the way a blind man might touch. Every note, every change of melody, each new instrument took him in a different direction.

When the final movement had ended, and Daniel had returned the record to its sleeve, he took out his notepad and the fountain pen he had been given for his bar mitzvah.

He wrote:

> *Escape*
> *I like to be where the music takes me*
> *In the country lane that's green and free*
> *No refusals in phone boxes*

He couldn't find anything to rhyme with the last sentence, but liked the idea of writing words nobody else would see, so he put another record on the turntable, and as Leonard Cohen sang about Suzanne, he wondered if he would ever write words like that. How did Leonard think of those words?

The thought stayed with him as he walked back to Fairmead and ignored the taunts of the boys in the driveway. In his study, he turned for solace to the Psalms. He was never disappointed.

> Rescue me from the mire,
> do not let me sink;
> deliver me from those who hate me,
> from the deep waters.
> Do not let the floodwaters engulf me
> or the depths swallow me up
> or the pit close its mouth over me.
> Answer me, O Lord, out of the goodness of your love;
> in your great mercy turn to me.
> Do not hide your face from your servant;
> answer me quickly, for I am in trouble.

Safehouse

Come near and rescue me;
redeem me because of my foes.

Chapter Fifteen

The Cadet Force.

It was on the RAF Cadet Parade Ground where the quiet, kindly, thoughtful boy felt naked to the shrill east wind, exposed to the blitzkrieg of humiliation. The Oakingham parade ground was Goldberg's nemesis.

The preparation for the CCF was terrifying. He was never able to grasp how to attach a loose collar, so they invariably sloped or failed to appear at all. He could find absolutely no reason to wear spats on his lower legs but wear them he must. His beret, the signal for mocking and humiliation every week, was on the wrong part of his head wherever he put it.

De Lacy loved cadet Fridays – peak Goldberg-baiting time.

'Head covered, Goldberg? No prayer shawl?'

Goldberg never replied, he just continued polishing his boots.

Williams had been promoted from pilot officer to flying officer, although he had yet to see the inside of a Boeing, let alone a Harrier. He barked at Goldberg with his newfound authority, his Welsh lilt employing a sarcastic tone.

'Can't see your face in those boots, Goldberg. Don't want to see your face mind, but just remember, one minute late on parade, and you sweep the quad.'

The boys all left the changing room, laughing and joking, and

Goldberg headed for the parade ground, with one spat upside down, his collar threatening to fall off and his beret in his hand.

Walking up the road, towards the CCF he was met by a group from another house, who had recently taken to Goldberg-baiting.

'Couldn't choose who to walk with?'

'Spoilt for choice, eh?'

Goldberg carried on walking, crossed the road, through the alley way, past the Buttery, and up to the parade ground.

War was apparently imminent: everywhere there were RAF cadets and, today, the genuine article: RAF officers. RAF Parade Day had the aura of a grand military occasion. The officers from nearby RAF Cottesmore came to the school parade ground to assess how their money was being spent. Goldberg liked gallantry medals and he could see DFCs and a DSO, the ribbons pinned to the immaculate uniforms.

The Regimental Sergeant Major, borrowed from the Army Cadet Force, marched into the centre of the quad, as if he were addressing recruits being sent to the Western Front. He pushed out his chest, carried his cane under his arm, raised his head and assumed an air of the utmost self- importance. He bellowed out the language of Staccato parade ground.

'We are honoured to welcome Wing Commander Bonnington, Squadron Leader Digby-Douglas and Group Captain Haines. They have asked me if they can inspect you and they may ask you a question or two. Corps, atten-SHUN!'

The cadets brought their legs up to ninety degrees and down sharply, so their feet made a V shape.

The boys were in a semicircle, shoes gleaming, spats neatly polished; their RAF trousers all had razor-sharp creases.

The RAF officers slowly made their way around the circle. The parade ground was silent, apart from the rustling of a few leaves and a distant sound of marching feet, as the Army cadets went through their paces.

Group Captain Haines had a warm smile as he approached a cadet whose attire was unusually substandard. The CCF RSM followed the group captain and gave Goldberg a terror-inducing stare.

The group captain bent down. 'What do you think of the RAF Cadets, young man?'

When he thought about it afterwards, Goldberg had literally no idea how he came to respond as he did, but in a clear, sharp voice, that many of his fellow pupils had never heard before, he said: 'I think it's playing at soldiers and a total waste of time, SIR!'

There were sniggers and mutters from his fellow cadets, and the group captain was shocked for a moment, but he stayed facing the defiant cadet, and then to Goldberg's astonishment, Group Captain Haines' face lit up with a smile.

'Well, young man, there are more than a few in HQ who would agree with you totally! Thank you for being so frank.'

The Corp RSM moved the officers on and tried to pretend nothing untoward had happened.

Later, so much later, psychologists looking back at his life would put forward the possibility that it was 'reaction formation', a tendency to protect oneself from a behavioural response by acting in a strongly contrasting manner. They all agreed this was the first moment when the meek and beleaguered Daniel Goldberg first hinted at a different person within.

As he was once to comment: 'Psychologists were rather short on the ground in the Oakingham parade ground.'

The next morning, under the colonnade, a large white piece of paper pinned to the noticeboard read:

Dishonourable discharge from the CCF, RAF branch. Goldberg, M (FMd)

May 1967
Richard de Lacy's Study
A sign on the door read: *Eichmann's Study. In here it is always 20 January 1942 at the Wannsee Conference.*

Goldberg was returning alone to his study. The corridor was dark and cool, and he was just relieved the wretched cricket game was over. As usual, somebody had taken one of his pads from his cricket bag.

He walked past De Lacy's study.

'Get in here, Jew boy.'

De Lacy pulled Goldberg into the study and threw him across the floor. He landed painfully on De Lacy's tuck box. As he picked himself up, he wondered if he was fully conscious. Williams sat behind De Lacy's desk, wearing a black peaked cap with Gestapo insignia and round glasses. He spoke with a phony German accent, that could have been comical, but being in a study covered in Swastikas and Nazi memorabilia was terrifying, and Goldberg was falling from the bottom of one cesspit into another.

During the past few days, he had realised there was a new feeling to which he couldn't give a name, because he just wasn't sure what it was. As he fell on the tuck box, he glimpsed the reality, the truth of the new feeling: it was hunger. Hunger for warmth and support; for a loving embrace; for a landing light and a bedside lamp. He needed an end to dark corridors of despair, lonely walks and terrifying cricket matches. How much more of this could he really take? The feelings were too quick to be thoughts, they just flashed through him as he struggled up from the floor.

On the far wall was a huge picture of a Nuremberg rally with Hitler cast as the Roman Emperor in Speer's stadium.

'Do you know what a Jew is?' Williams asked. 'Do you know about your race? Men in the gutter counting the pfennigs they've taken from the poor?'

De Lacy's athletic build conformed with his Aryan views about life, and he consoled himself with the thought that Hitler also had dark hair. Speaking in an accent that was as incongruous as Andy Warhol's Campbell soup tins being inserted into Constable's 'Haywain', De Lacy began to read a text.

'Whatever you can do or dream you can begin it. Boldness has genius, power, and magic in it. Knowing is not enough; we must apply. Willing is not enough; we must do. None are more hopelessly enslaved than those who falsely believe they are free.'

'That,' said De Lacy, 'was written by one of the two great believers in Aryan purity and Teutonic infallibility. Goethe. It's just so true.'

'What are you talking about De Lacy? Can't you see how ridiculous you really look?'

The punch took him by surprise, but it occurred to him he would still have the bruise when his parents came at the weekend.

De Lacy put down one text and picked up another, as Goldberg propped himself up against the study wall.

'This, this is from the greatest of them all, Goldberg. Listen and despair. *I hold the Jewish race to be the born enemy of pure humanity and everything noble in it.*'

'Richard Wagner,' De Lacy continued. 'He saw it all coming, even before the god of all gods wrote his bible, *Mein Kampf.*'

Goldberg was only capable of whispering. 'The book about nothing, written by a house painter.'

He was trying, really trying, to stick up for himself, but more for his people, and for normal people: people who weren't trying to be renascent Nazis.

Williams seemed to be in another world, oblivious to the small study in an English boarding school in 1967. He spoke as if he were talking at Nuremberg in 1938.

'Snivelling, mumbling yiddo prayers, taking jobs from real Germans, living in smelly hovels, vell, Goldberg, ve have tidings of great joy for you – The Final Solution has begun.'

Goldberg looked at his persecutors, but he could think of nothing to say. He was sure he should be taking the fight to them. He was letting the Jews down.

De Lacy and Williams stood together in front of Goldberg, raised their hands in a Nazi salute and shouted 'Heil Hitler!' as if they were in a room full of supporters.

Goldberg stood up, dazed, his mind was racing, his stomach churning. Dread wracked his body and the sinister study threatened to envelope him. Somehow, he managed to cry out, 'I'm proud to be Jewish!'

De Lacy and Williams laughed loudly and hysterically. 'He's proud to be Jewish. Did you hear that? Like it's something to be proud of!'

They chanted: 'Goldberg's proud to be Jewish!'

Goldberg turned to face the window and then realised why the room was so dark.

Nothing that had happened, nothing in his life, with all its heartache and fear, could prepare him for what he saw. Across the window was a huge photo of a memorial. Not a memorial to honour dead soldiers or Nazis, but the newly opened room at Yad Vashem, in Jerusalem: the Israeli memorial to the slaughter of a people.

Here, in this study, it was being used for an all too different purpose. Just looking at the names cast in iron on the floor, made Goldberg shiver: Theresienstadt-Terezin, Treblinka, Dachau, Buchenwald, Sobibor, Mathausen, Sachsenhausen, Bergen-Belsen, Auschwitz Birkenau.

Williams and De Lacy looked at Goldberg's shocked, white face.

They stopped laughing, looked at each other and smiled.

'Important to have something to celebrate every day, don't you think?'

Chapter Sixteen.

The Changing Room, Fairmead Boarding House

Goldberg decided that he and the narrow corridor in his boarding house had become one and the same. It was bleak, brown and led only to places that increased his insecurity and misery. As the pupils walked into the driveway, they saw the house and garden with its middle-class air of normality and affluence. But this wasn't their entrance. The boys entered by a side door from the quad which opened into the corridor, and immediately on the right was a door with reinforced glass that opened into a changing room, no different from many other such rooms: pegs, showers, benches, mud and the odour of smelly boys.

As evening fell, it became disused. The allotted fag had cleaned it, swept it and placed the clothes left lying around in a pile for collection by boys who would have an extra fagging duty for untidiness. Then the lights were turned out and nobody was to be found there.

Nobody except Daniel. He turned on the lights and stood in front of the mirror by the window. As he looked at his reflection, he heard the strains of 'Penny Lane' from a boy's transistor radio, and then Emperor Rosko broadcasting from *The Duchy*, Radio Luxembourg, on 208 medium wave, and asked himself fundamental questions.

Who am I really? Why am I here? What is it about me that

other boys hate so much? And another question pushed its way through the queue of uncertainty, most evenings: *Why is it I feel some comfort, some protection surrounding me that I cannot see?*

He was still bereft and lonely beyond any description, yet within the silence of the changing room, Goldberg spoke words, and he was sure the words were heard somewhere.

The Psalms soothed him.

'I lift up my eyes to the hills, whence cometh my help? My help cometh from the Lord.'

And from his *Reform Jewish Prayer Book*, given to him on his bar mitzvah by Rabbi Michael Feldman, he read his favourite prayer.

> *We are loved by an unending love.*
> *We are supported by hands that uplift us*
> *even in the midst of a fall.*
> *We are loved by an unending love.*
> *Embraced, touched, soothed and counselled.*
> *We are loved by an unending love.*
> *Blessed are you, BELOVED ONE, who loves Your people*
> *Israel.*

The idea he might be loved, supported, heard or uplifted, was too fanciful for him. But in the saying, arose the yearning that one day, the words might have real meaning for him.

And so, all alone, sitting on the bench with the pegs behind him, he shut his eyes, clasped the prayer book, and said the words of the Shema.

Safehouse

Hear O Israel, The Lord is your God, The Lord is One.

Then, as usual, he shed a tear, wiped his eyes, and walked down the long and lonely corridor to his study.

De Lacy was on a path to self-destruction. Although he was hugely dangerous to Daniel and his wellbeing, he also seemed unconcerned about the effect of his outrageous behaviour on himself and his future. He was so consumed with the malign that his brain seemed to have no capacity to consider the future, or the direction in which he was heading. He wasn't actively ignoring implications; he was being swallowed up by the monster of savagery deep within him.

There were many reasons for De Lacy's total lack of empathy and brutality, but it was clear to anybody who cared enough to notice, that he was consumed by anti-Semitic hatred which, if left unchecked, would have devastating consequences. The problem for Oakingham was simple: very few people cared enough to notice.

5 June 1967. 12 Noon
The hours stretched out: a journey with no destination, a ship on the ocean where there were no ports. When Chapel ended and Daniel stayed in town because he wasn't going cycling with the gang, then he took refuge in the town of Oakingham and wandered aimlessly from shop window to window. He hoped and prayed to all the gods he'd heard of, and many he hadn't, that nobody saw him there alone, and then as he walked into an alley, he took comfort from his own aloneness. Aloneness: a state between solitude and loneliness.

He knew every paving stone and every shop window, all the normal people: families in cars; young boys in groups with a dermatological need who would keep Harley Street busy for centuries. A father dropped off his daughter for ballet; lovers walked hand in hand; other Oakingham boys rushed past. He walked to nowhere, but he wasn't in Fairmead House, watching the gang go out on their bikes together, or the other gang, the Sporties, play Fives, or the Arties who went into the art centre.

'For god's sake, one of these activities must suit you, Goldberg!'

Well, maybe they might, if they didn't involve being with people who hated him so much he'd never even given a second thought to how he felt about them. It's unimportant anyway because they hated him, so what he thought of them … well, he didn't want to think about that.

As the day faded, he thought back to his weekly 'reverse-charge' phone call to his parents from the smelly call box. Lately, he'd heard about parole, and how prisoners come before a panel of people to be told if they'd been granted the right to leave prison. His parents were the parole board that never granted parole, whatever he said, however he cried.

'Now, darling, the exeat's only two weeks away.'

'Well, darling, you must have some friends. It can't be as bad as you say.'

What about the school reports that Fraser sent home? 'Daniel has again appeared very lonely this year, and I so wish he could be on better terms with his contemporaries.' It was obvious to almost everyone he was shouting with a megaphone, 'TAKE HIM AWAY!' No, this was a pre-ordained parole board, so why call? Because he called.

Then, he walked later, sometimes much later, as the light faded, or it was supper time, or he'd had enough of being in Oakingham town. He walked slowly, with his head down facing the ground, past the graveyard, up the hill, until he reached the gravel in the House driveway. He heard it crunch and walked through the door to the gloomy brown corridor and ached with hope that he saw nobody until he shut his study door and could listen to music like Elgar or James Taylor, or that man he loved so much, Leonard Cohen.

But for some reason, he decided to listen to one of his closest friends, *BBC News*. Daniel was suddenly aware of Michael Elkins, the BBC correspondent in Jerusalem, saying something so astonishing that he felt a tinge of an emotion he'd never experienced before. Happiness.

'Less than 15 hours after the fighting began, at dawn this morning, there was every evidence that though fighting will continue, Israel has already won the war ... I may not now report where the Israeli armed forces stand, but the place names will be familiar to anyone who has read a good account of the first five days of the 1956 Sinai campaign. This time Israel has created the nearest thing to instant victory the modern world has seen ...'

He thought about all his recent reading on the Holocaust and the Jews of the ghetto, books he'd taken from the library.

The horrors of the gas chambers and the pogroms and the Pale of Settlement, when Jews had walked with their head facing the ground, or Moses Mendelssohn, who went through a gate reserved for Jews and cattle, into Berlin.

All the humiliated, downtrodden desperate Jews in line in the snow.

The huddled group saying erev Shabbat prayers in tiny rooms.

The bearded man, pushing his wheelbarrow up steep, heavy, clay soil for days on end.

Zelda walking with a yellow star, watching her family being thrown onto trucks and railway carriages meant for cattle.

And now Israel! Why had he never really heard about Israel before? Here were Jews winning, defeating others to save their country, elated and respected throughout the world.

He jumped up from his chair and wished he had some material emblem that he could wave, treasure and display.

He thought of the Israeli pilots in their uniforms and imagined them in their briefing room just before they climbed into their cockpits. He knew nothing of Israeli air-force ranks.

They'll forgive me, he thought.

Was Group Captain Aron Kaplan talking to each of them, one by one?

He was enjoying his fantasy.

'Flight Lieutenant Gidon, when you scream down that runway, when you dash into battle, when you fly really low over an Egyptian airfield, you're doing this for the family that never said goodbye; they just looked really deeply into each other's eyes with love and terror.'

'Squadron leader Dov Hyams, as you climb into your plane, and you're told 'You're good to go', will you yell out inside, 'This is for the freezing eighteenth-century Jews who could never be lawyers or doctors or humans, they could only be Jews, to be mocked and assaulted. Will you do it for them?'

'Pilot Officer Freedman, you're doing it for the man in Belsen who refused to eat on the day he thought it was Yom Kippur, and refused to do hard labour, so he stood outside in the snow in his striped rags, in a blizzard, freezing deep in his bones, sweating from Typhus fever, and prayed aloud, remembering his High Holy Day prayers – 'Selach Lanu, Mahal Lanu, Kaper Lanu.' Forgive me all my sins on this day of days. – just before he was picked up, thrown into a pit and shot. Will you do it for him?'

And now, as tears filled his eyes, his throat tightened, and he wept. The dam burst and the torrent of tears he'd held back so long, flooded the wretched study floor. He asked, out loud, not caring who heard him,

'Is there a pilot, who might have hurtled down that runway, and headed out to defend his country, his Jewish country, shouting, "And this is for Daniel!"'

Sunday afternoon, Oakingham town square
Goldberg opened the door to the red phone box that had been his weekly nemesis, his place of despair and loathing. He stepped inside and ignored the smell.

Shaking a little, he dialled 192.

Was this how it felt to phone a girl and ask her out?

'Directory Enquiries, how can I help?'

The first positive response he'd heard on this phone!

'Can I have the number for the Israeli embassy in London, please?'

She responded quickly, as if this was a regular request, and gave Goldberg the number.

He wrote it down on the yellow phone directory, and as a sign of defiance he added a Star of David.

Coins ready, he put them in the slot and dialled the number.

Fairmead House, Sunday afternoon.
Jeffrey Figgin was Head of House, house prefect and school prefect. He was tall and blonde, with a classic aristocratic demeanour, not hindered by his habit of wearing black-striped trousers, even on

weekdays. He walked down the narrow, dusty, gloomy corridor in Fairmead House as if he had been called to see Winston Churchill in the War Rooms. Opening the door to Goldberg's study he swept into the tiny room with a flourish.

'Smell in this study's disgusting. Do something about it!'

'What do you suggest?'

'Snivelling little creature: what a revolting, gutter living, flea-ridden race you really are. And by the way, what are you doing in this school?'

He wasn't expecting an answer, and the tirade continued.

'Spend some more time in your gutters!' He handed Goldberg a typewritten notice, left the study, and shut the door.

Goldberg sat at his desk and read it.

As punishment for dishonouring HM cadet force, and making disparaging comments to senior officers, you will be required to report at 14.00 hrs each Friday, to the builders engaged in building an all-weather hockey pitch on the Upper. Your duties will include, but not be limited to, digging trenches and disposing of waste matter. At present there are no suitable protective clothes available.

Wing Commander Snoddy (RAF Retired)

Figgin decided he would post the orders on the house noticeboard, as a deterrent to others who might be insubordinate.

In the years that followed, the consequences of this simple decision rippled like a shower of rain, flowing through cracks in paving stones; the shower became a rainstorm and the rivulets became a torrent.

Safehouse

Daniel wrote a letter to the Israeli ambassador

Fairmead, Oakingham Rutland
Dear Ambassador
I've decided I'd like to live in Israel. I'm so pleased you won the war.
I hate my school and people bully me here nonstop for being Jewish. That wouldn't happen in your country so that's where I want to live.
What do I do next?
Daniel Goldberg

Chapter Seventeen

The Upper, Oakingham

Rain swept across the huge playing field. A primeval scene, devoid of human warmth. Lifeless, scarred by cricket fields, the amphitheatre of humiliation and anguish. The poplar trees were far in the distance, their frantic dancing choreographed by the summer storm.

Goldberg was the sole walker on this playing field of despair. He fought against the wind and made his way towards the scene of his punishment: hard labour.

As he approached the far side of the field, he saw parallel trenches, now flooded with rainwater, and huge piles of covered sand. Near the hut was a patchwork of wildflowers, being punished for its bright presence by the assault of the rain. Like a reluctant explorer, equally disinterested in the journey and the destination, he trudged towards the site.

He knocked on the filthy hut door. A tall, broad-chested man with huge hands and long hair opened the door and looked at him with a wide smile.

'What you thinking of, knocking on this door? Does this look like a door worth the knocking?'

Goldberg walked hesitantly into the hut.

'I don't know, sir.'

The second man laughed so loudly he spilt his drink, a huge

jarring guffaw, and in a rich Irish accent he almost sang: 'I don't know, *sir*?'

They both looked at Goldberg's forlorn and uncertain face. The man who had opened the door beckoned him to a chair by the table.

'Sit yourself down, young man. What on god's earth are we going to do with you?'

'I'm here to help build the pitch.'

'Great stuff. Now firstly, what's your name?'

'Goldberg.'

'So, no, it isn't.'

'Sorry?'

'What's your first name? Why would you give us your surname? I'm Barrie and that lazy slouch would be Dermot.'

Dermot was sitting at the table looking at the rain through the window. His hair was caked in mud, his hands were dirty and stained, and in a lightly mocking voice he called out, 'O'Halloran's the name, but you can call me Dermot. Now what are we going to call you?'

'Daniel.'

'Well, Daniel, maybe you can help us. See, as we said before, and we've the habit of repeating ourselves, we've not the foggiest idea what we're gonna do with you every week. Not a clue.'

'I'm here to help build the pitch.'

'Wonderful. And what would you know about perforated pipes and sand slits?'

'Nothing.'

'Any experience in building projects?'

Goldberg decided it was safe to enter into the spirit of the conversation. 'Loads. About the same as you know about poetry.'

Barrie smiled.

'Sit down, Daniel. Now, that's an unfortunate thing you just said there now. Most unfortunate. See, I've been looking for someone to talk to about Yeats, Joyce and Seamus Heaney for years. And now, on a rainy day in June, along he comes, the self-confessed expert.'

Hardly drawing breath, he continued. 'What you did was offer me respect by calling me 'sir', then you looked at my hands and my face and then committed the sin of assumption, so you did, young Daniel.'

'I agree. I'm sorry.'

As the rain splattered against the window and an orchestra of needles poured down on the roof, Dermot continued the gentle mocking.

'That's the quickest apology by an Englishman to an Irishman since the Famine.'

Barrie brought a stool to the end of the table and put his hand under Daniel's chin. 'So, what did you do to be coming here every Friday?'

Barrie listened to Goldberg's story. He felt he was being offered a discourse about the Theory of Relativity, as it was so distant from his life experience that Daniel's words fell like rain into a lake of incomprehension.

'So, do you like being in this school?'

'No, I hate it.'

He expected a question about his parents, but none was forthcoming.

Instead, Barrie placed his hand on Goldberg's shoulder, leaned over him and in a voice as soft and warm as a rug by the fire, he said, 'Well, young Daniel, this can be your sanctuary then, can't it?'

And so it became.

Safehouse

Saturday, 1 July 1967

> *Embassy of Israel, London*
> *Dear Mr Goldberg*
> *Thank you for your letter, and your interest in living in Israel. I'm happy that you want to come to Israel, but this is something you will have to discuss with your dear parents first.*
>
> *I wish you well with your studies and hope one day I will have the opportunity of welcoming you to Eretz Yisrael.*
>
> *Shalom,*
> *Ariella*
> *Ambassador*

Goldberg's reply was read many times in the months and years ahead. It was actually very simple. He handwrote a copy:

> *Sunday, 2 July*
> *Dear Your Excellency Ms Ariella*
> *Although I'm a schoolboy and you are an ambassador theres [sic] quite a lot in your letter that is wrong.*
>
> *I won't be discussing my trip to Israel with my parents, and they aren't that dear to me at all.*
>
> *There won't be any studies, and I'm hoping to be in Israel very soon.*
>
> *Shalom*
> *Daniel Goldberg*

Hut on the Upper, second Friday in July, 5.30 pm
Barrie and Dermot walked slowly back to the hut from the site, sweating and swearing in the hot evening sun.

'Not much's feckin' changed then,' Dermot said.

'What?' Barrie asked.

'A young Englishman's sat in a cabin watching two Micks work till their hands bleed.'

'I only saw one Mick working myself,' Barrie said.

Barrie gave Daniel two sheets of paper. They'd agreed to swap a poem.

'Amazing what a thick Irish labourer reads these days.'

Daniel blushed and mumbled some words of apology. Dermot interjected.

'He's got thoughts above his station, that Barrie, you know. Won't be long he'll be stopping the *Racing Post* and be giving me the tips about who killed Julius Caesar.'

Daniel handed Barrie a poem.

Barrie and Daniel sat on wooden chairs, looking out at the hockey pitch site. In the distance, the first eleven was out-playing Marlborough, ahead by an innings. The hut was hot and smelt of cigarettes.

Barrie's hands bore evidence of the digging and lifting that had given him his livelihood all his working life. He had a weathered, tanned face, and long black dirty hair and his Irish accent came with a sardonic, quizzical eye.

Goldberg had white hands, as soft as velvet, and a public-school voice he would come to see as a stain that nothing could remove.

It was sadness, unspoken, and for many weeks, unmentionable, that bound them in almost surreal friendship.

'I've started writing some words of my own, but I'm not ready to show anyone yet.' Daniel told Barrie.

'Christ, we got feckin' Shakespeare in the hut.' Dermot scoffed and laughed. 'I'm a simple man earning a few bob so's I can buy a round. That's me. I'm off.' He picked up his *Daily Sketch* and a thermos flask and walked out. The hut shook gently as he slammed the door.

Daniel was used to Dermot.

'I've started reading W.H. Auden. There's one …' He paused uncertainly. 'I've probably got the meaning wrong.'

'But then you probably haven't,' Barrie replied. 'The meanings change as you read them more, but the first meaning's still a meaning.'

'Surely the poet knows the meaning?'

'Not at all! You hear music – Beethoven, The Beatles, whatever. As you hear it, it's yours. The ownership passes from them to us, or so it seems to me.'

'But they wrote it, they know what they meant.'

'Yes, but you heard it or read it, and know what it means to you.'

'But how'd you get into all this?' Daniel asked.

'Good one coming from you.' Barrie looked at Daniel. 'Why're you supposed to be building a hockey pitch, miles from home, when most boys are having their tea?'

Barrie realised how much he was enjoying this chat. Eleanor would've loved it too, and a wave of sadness settled on his soul, so he came back to the now.

'Your third reading might glean stuff you hadn't seen up until then, but what it meant the first time still matters. I don't think there's a wrong.'

They talked about the Auden poem, both enjoying the security, the total lack of humiliation or competition. It was as if they were having a delicious meal with many courses, and neither of them wanted to stop.

'Do you know the Liver Poets, The Mersey Sound?' Barrie asked. 'You probably don't, it's new.'

Barrie showed Daniel 'Tonight at Noon' by Adrian Henri. Daniel read it slowly, drinking in the contradictions and humour. He felt exultant at this totally new type of poetry, and his spirits soared at the thought of the Fridays to come.

It was time to leave. Barrie could put off his comforting role with his beloved Eleanor no longer and Daniel had to return to Fairmead House.

'See you next week,' said Daniel.

'For more hard labour, you mean?'

'Definitely. Can't wait!'

Daniel walked through the colonnade in his overalls, spattered with clay and paint, looking as if he had been digging all afternoon. As he walked through the alleyway, past the Buttery, he saw De Lacy in his RAF uniform.

'A Jew punished by hard labour. Wonder who thought that one up?' He laughed and ran up the hill to join Pritchard and his other friends.

Daniel was surprised. He heard the jibe, but he felt differently. He had a plan now, and soon he'd be gone from here. He realised the sorrow he'd feel at leaving Barrie, but Israel beckoned. His mood was positive as he trudged back alone up to the crunchy gravel of the Fairmead driveway and more jokes about his mud-spattered dungarees.

As he walked into the hut the next Friday, Barrie was smoking a cigarette, looking out of the filthy window. He flicked the ash and turned to Daniel.

'Could those flimsy legs of yours cycle to Empingham on Sunday?'

'I've biked up to the Eye Brook before. Why'd you ask?'

'For reasons beyond my wildest understanding, the wife wants you to come for lunch.'

Dermot interjected with an overdone accent.

'Oh no, for god's sake no. Don't be letting that Barrie talk in them posh sentences. He'll drive me straight into the reservoir for good.'

Rev. Isaac Watts
The Divinity lesson was over and the boys were running out of the classroom towards their next class. Rev. Watts had been thinking about the Goldberg boy a great deal. He didn't fit the mould and he was suffering. He thought about a recent lesson. Goldberg actually had the courage to proclaim his religion in the face of the barbarous insults that ensued. As usual, he was about to leave the class alone and his maths equipment appeared to be falling out of his pencil case. When the other boys had left, he asked Daniel to wait a minute.

'You're a brave boy, young Goldberg,' he said.

'Brave? How's that?' Daniel replied.

'You're probably the most unhappy boy I've seen in this school. You're derided, insulted, alone and yet you insist on affirming your faith in spite of it all. I'd say that's very brave. It's unusual to have a Jewish boy in this school. I'd like to learn more about your faith.'

'I'm sure you know more about Judaism than I do,' Daniel replied.

'No, that's not what I meant. I want to know about your personal faith, the faith that gives you courage to face what happened in this classroom today, and must happen pretty well all the time here.'

Daniel felt himself blush. He'd always liked Reverend Watts and he was becoming more interested in Christianity – or at least in Jesus and what he said.

'Next Wednesday afternoon, after class, come to the vicarage. Perhaps we could talk a bit?'

'I'd like that,' Daniel said.

Daniel made his way to the vicarage, at the side of the smaller cricket pitch. It was an old building with leaded windows, and a somewhat dishevelled garden.

Rev. Watts was a short man, with a kindly, troubled face. His hair was beginning to go grey, and Daniel had no idea if there was a Mrs Watts or not.

Daniel sat in an armchair and accepted an orange squash.

'I presume you had a bar mitzvah?'

'Yes, of course. I really liked Rabbi Feldman. He told it as it was. He's a Reform rabbi but still quite strict.'

'What does *strict* mean?

'Well, obviously he doesn't eat bacon and I should think he eats kosher food and doesn't drive on Sabbath, but also he didn't take a lot of nonsense from the people in the class. But mainly I'm grateful to him because he talked to me about some psalms.'

'That's lovely to hear, but what have you found helpful?'

'They seem to speak about my life, about how I'm surrounded by people who don't like me and want to cause me harm. They speak about God defending me, supporting me, just ...' he paused, 'being there for me.'

'Yes, I knew you had some inner spirituality. You couldn't withstand the kind of nonsense you put up with day in and day out without something behind you.'

'I'm interested in Jesus,' Daniel said.

'That's fine, but I want you to concentrate on the faith you have – your faith, not my faith. Christianity was born from Judaism. There's enough there for us to talk about and for you to affirm without straying into other faiths.'

'Oh, I'm not thinking of changing my faith. It's just that quite a lot of what Jesus said about the people who are down sounds good.'

Rev. Watts gave a book to Daniel. 'I'd like you to keep this. It's about the psalms and their meaning. I can't think of anyone more deserving.'

'Maybe we could meet again to discuss it,' Daniel said.

'I would've liked that, but I'm retiring. I've had enough of this place with its cadet force and military feeling. I'm going to live near my sister in the Oxfordshire countryside.'

Daniel thought what a shame it was that the only decent man at Oakingham School was leaving, but then he had the book to cherish.

Chapter Eighteen

Saturday Morning

Daniel leant his bike against the wall and opened the garden gate. The short path to the front door was inundated on each side by a riotous deluge of colour. Pink and white roses intertwined and competed to own the walls of the cottage, and the colours merged as they celebrated pride of place above the wooden door. A small pond was festooned with lilies and awash with anemone. A tiny rockery, bathing in the sun, was covered in purples and light blues. Deep red flowers in terracotta pots covered the patio; baskets hung from the low roof. It was like a box of celebratory rockets, where the blue touchpaper had been lit time and time again.

He lifted the large, black, circular door knocker and it hit the wooden door. He was drawn back to look at the garden as he waited.

Eleanor opened the door. She was tall and slim, with brown hair.

She's smiling, thought Daniel, *but her eyes look sad.*

'Come in, Daniel. You're very welcome!'

Welcome, he thought. *What a wonderful word.*

They walked into a hallway. Lavender wafted in waves through the open window.

Eleanor led him into the lounge. It was enveloped by shade. The walls were covered with books and LPs. A red rug was spread across the floor. The furniture was old and homely. His parents' lounge had fancy velvet chairs and onyx tables. This room had a wooden central table covered in magazines and books of all sorts. They weren't arranged, but neither did they seem untidy. In a brief glimpse he sensed this was a special room.

Barrie was on the patio, sitting at a very small metal table, reading a paper. He turned to Daniel and smiled.

'You're welcome to our home, modest though it is.'

'It's beautiful,' he said.

Eleanor came out to the patio and gestured to Daniel to sit down. She placed a glass of lemonade on the table and sat opposite him. She wore a long, flowing cream dress, and her dark brown hair plunged down her back. She spoke deliberately, as if each word mattered to her greatly.

'I've heard a lot about you, Daniel, in a very short time. I feel as though I know you, but I don't. However, I'm hoping I will, if that makes sense.'

'Yes, I'm so grateful–'

She cut him off.

'No! One of our rules is that you're not going to be grateful for anything.'

'Another rule is that you're never going to finish a sentence,' Barrie said.

Eleanor leant on the small table. 'I've so many questions,' she said. 'I'm frightened to ask them all at once.'

'I don't mind,' Daniel replied.

As the sun rose on that summer morning, they began to talk.

Perhaps he had planned it, perhaps it was spontaneous, but Barrie slipped away.

'You're at Oakingham for the rich and famous?'

There was no need to answer, so he let her continue. 'Barrie said he knew it was the wrong school for you within five minutes of meeting you, so why in god's heaven are you still there?'

'That's an easy question to answer, Eleanor. I've no idea.'

'Your parents know you hate it?'

'Until a couple of weeks ago I was calling them every Sunday afternoon, close to tears, telling them I just wanted to leave.'

In the silence of the summer garden, Eleanor sat back and thought:

In the name of Saint Brigid of Kildare, what's the matter with his parents?

It was far too early to ask.

She moved some hair from her forehead and looked at him with a smile that creased her face. Somehow her eyes were still saturated with sadness. Her voice drew him towards her. Here in this beautiful garden, this oasis, this Eden, nobody was trying to taunt him, or hurt him. He just thought, *I like her*, and that was enough.

Eleanor rose from the table and beckoned him into the lounge.

'Do they know where you are?'

'The school think I'm on an extended exeat with my parents. It's been booked for weeks. It's just that mum's been called to Hong Kong, so that's obviously much more important than seeing her son.'

'Don't the school check?'

'They would, but they already had the note from my parents and don't know about the cancellation,' Daniel said.

They were sitting in the lounge now. It was cool and dark.

She eschewed quick, sharp, chat. Her conversation was deliberate and languorous, like a very full velvet cloak being pulled along a summer lawn.

'So, how long should this exeat last?'

'Until tomorrow evening, but I'll be back at the house this evening.'

'Do you have plans tonight?'

'Oh yes, I do. I'll sit in my study and hope nobody comes in to torment me.'

There was a silence. Not awkward, just silence. A clock ticked in the hall. Barrie's car pulled into the drive.

'Please stay for dinner,' Eleanor said. 'We can put your bike in the car and drop you back.'

Barrie came into the lounge. 'Let's have lunch.'

They sat at the dining table, Daniel at the head, Eleanor and Barrie on either side.

'I told Daniel we could talk about art and music, using the theme of loneliness.'

'And he's still here?'

'I haven't missed your sarcasm this morning, Barrie darling. We've had a meaningful conversation. Remember those?'

They both seemed to realise this wasn't appropriate and changed tack. Eleanor put her knife and fork down on the yellow floral plate, and said, 'Let's talk about Edward Hopper.'

'I've never heard of him,' Daniel said.

'Well, after lunch I'll show you a picture that has loneliness coming from it like radio signals. It's called *Nighthawks*.'

'And just so we don't agree a suicide pact, I'll show you something that's happy but still beautiful,' said Barrie. 'It's called *Luncheon at the Boating Party*.'

'What about sport? Do you follow a football team?'

Daniel stopped eating. 'That's part of the problem. I'm just not interested in sport, and worse than that, playing sport is torture.'

They spoke about poetry and some music and art, and then Daniel said, 'Would you mind if I just wandered around this room, and looked at your books and records? I've never seen a room quite like this one.'

'Of course,' Barrie said. 'You do that while the slaves wash up.'

'I'm happy to help with the washing-up!'

Eleanor laughed. 'Surely you know that Barrie hasn't spoken a word without barbed wire in it since he was in the sandpit. Ignore him and take your time.'

A mountain of questions sat in the middle of that room, all of them unasked and unanswered. It didn't occur to Daniel to wonder what Eleanor did for work, or whether it was odd for Barrie to be both a labourer and so cultured. What were their backgrounds? Why were they bickering so often? Most of all, why was Eleanor so sad? In the mists of his mind, some of these questions were there, but they had no form or substance and certainly no voice.

Daniel began to look at the records: Elgar, of course he knew the cello concerto; The Beatles, and Leonard Cohen; Shostakovich, who? Then the poetry books, many of them Irish: Kinsella (who?), Seamus Heaney, W.B. Yeats, Eiléan Ní Chuilleanáin (who again?) A cornucopia of Celtic wonder. Soon, the afternoon sped a wonderful course into evening, and the room surrendered to reds and evening warmth, and more marvellous than anything Daniel could remember, the kind, loving light of lamps on overladen bookshelves.

Endlösung Day minus one
Richard de Lacy thought: *I love that notice about dishonouring the Cadet Force.* His plan had its origin in seven words: *digging trenches and disposing of waste matter.*

In the concentration camps, Jews had been treated like waste matter: they were shot, and their bodies tipped into preprepared ditches. There, their emaciated bodies had piled up on top of each other.

Endlösung was German for 'the Final Solution' – Adolph Eichmann's plan to rid the world of its Jews.

The Upper, Friday 6 pm.
It had been agreed that Barrie would leave the builders' hut unlocked, and Daniel was inside his sanctuary, watching the sun sink slowly over the green fields, enjoying the peace and the calm.

Barrie had gone, and then Dermot put down his coffee and stood up in his filthy clothes.

'Thanks for all that help, then.'

'Don't mention it.'

Dermot closed the door softly. The sun streamed through the filthy window. A last few moments of quiet. The Upper was a peaceful place, provided you weren't playing cricket. Daniel sat, looking out of the window, wondering when he could next visit the Empingham Cottage.

Suddenly, the quiet was shattered, as the door was pushed open so brutally that some of the wood broke and fell into the hut.

Where peace and tranquillity had reigned, now there was noise and shouting.

Like a mudslide through the door, Williams and De Lacy filled the small hut and then punched Goldberg in the stomach.

His enduring recollection was that the remaining events of the day seemed to happen in slow motion and in black and white.

Daniel toppled to the concrete floor and looked wistfully at Dermot's mug and cigarette stubs. His stomach was churning, falling over a waterfall of fear.

What are they doing here? he thought.

De Lacy peered down, his foot on Daniel's stomach.

Try to stand up, push him away! Daniel thought.

Winded, unable to breathe, his mind raced. Gradually his breathing returned and he was faced with Williams' loathsome smirk.

What was Williams doing?

Pinning up Nazi posters.

He summoned up his reserves of vocal energy. 'Get out of here!'

His plea was greeted with loud laughter as De Lacy and Williams began a surreal dance. Two worlds, the holy and the profane, crashed together like express trains in the night. They stopped dancing and turned to him. He didn't hear the words, he felt them.

'*Raus! Schnell! Achtung!*' The language of the camps. '*Die Fahne hoch!*' they repeated, as they dragged Goldberg out of the shed, each holding an arm and swinging him backwards before they threw him onto a pile of rocks. It was the first line of an SS song.

Through the pain, Daniel heard a voice inside him saying: 'Do something!'

De Lacy was stroking his nose. 'Such a treat we have in store for you, young man,' he said, in a mock Yiddish accent.

They grabbed Daniel's arms, wrenched him upright and hurtled him towards the building works.

Williams pushed Goldberg down onto sand near a ditch. 'Read this, Jew-face!' he said.

What's this?

'Read it!'

Yitgadal v'yitkadash sh'mei raba b'alma di-v'ra...

Uncle's funeral, Kaddish!

...chirutei, v'yamlich malchutei b'chayeichon...

His mind was frantic. *What are they doing? Must get up, can't stay here, have to get away, try to stand. They're covering my eyes.*

Terror! Beyond fear, collapsing, dizzy, shaking. Upright? Falling? Shout loudly, tissue in my mouth, choke, spit it out.

Doing nothing! Letting them. My fault! Not stopping them!

Punch or kick them! Why can't I *do* anything?

Williams was talking in a bizarre German accent: 'So, at last, we are back in Belsen! You are not playing the part; you *are* the part! Before you, we did the target practice! *Bang*!'

In a surreal mixture of a Welsh accent and phony German, Williams' words seemed slow and deliberate.

'Freda and Golda and Jacob rolling slowly, dutifully, beautifully, like puppets with no skin, only bones, into the ditch, as the bullet blood seeps down their face ...'

Daniel couldn't see anything. He felt perilously unbalanced.

De Lacy was speaking, as if they were waiting for a swing in the park.

'Now, it's your turn.'

They're taking my clothes off!

'You can't do this! We're not back then, we're *now*!'

'Goldberg, soon you'll be naked, like the effluent of a Jewish whore,' De Lacy spat.

I'm on rocks, tilting over a ditch. It's dark, cold, and I'm naked, tied to poles ...

Like a general anaesthetic, Daniel's conscious mind dissolved into nothingness.

His next memory was far, far, away from that field and all its terror.

The Aftermath

De Lacy and Williams were called to the headmaster's office. Both were expelled, and an escort was provided to ensure they left without delay.

De Lacy's and Williams' fathers seemed very different. Williams' father was disgusted by his son's actions. De Lacy's father smiled throughout the meeting and seemed proud of his son.

Daniel had been taken to the Royal Leicester Infirmary. As he lay utterly traumatised, the white-coated people at the end of his bed appeared blurred and unreal. All his thoughts were fuzzy or incoherent except for this one certainty: he did not want to see his parents. His mother hurried to the hospital, but by the time she arrived, his bed was empty. She found only an exchange of letters with the Israeli embassy and Daniel's note. It was brief and hardly legible: *Gone to Israel. Hope you don't find me.*

Chapter Nineteen

1967 The Israeli Embassy London

Ambassador Ariella was reading the *Daily Sketch* coverage of Israel's victory in the recently ended war. Early in the morning, before her meetings began, she would sit in the brightest room she could find, drink a coffee, bemoan her fate at being in a country which did not know the meaning of the word 'summer', and look through the British press. Her colleagues usually highlighted articles about Israel, but that morning there was no escaping Moshe Dayan's picture, which was emblazoned across many front pages.

She flicked through the inside pages, until an article made her catch her breath and freeze in her chair. A teenage boy, Richard de Lacy, had been expelled from Oakingham, a prestigious English boarding school.

The final paragraph brought her up abruptly. The *Sketch* produced copies of Daniel's correspondence in the days before the attack. Staring out at her from the newspaper was the letter he had sent to her, and her response, both of which had been found on his hospital bed after Daniel had disappeared.

'Crying for help and being bullied! I couldn't know,' she whispered.

She picked up the internal phone.

'I need Debra, Naomi and Gidon in my office, soonest please.'

The story of the teenage Jew left naked on the playing field held sufficient interest to inhabit the inside pages of national newspapers for a single day. Unsurprisingly, it continued to dominate *The Jewish Chronicle*, the bestselling weekly Jewish newspaper.

After the initial shock had abated, and nobody seemed to know whether Daniel had fled to Israel or not, their editorial commented: 'Within the greenhouses of the Establishment, the great public schools, the seeds of anti-Semitism are germinating.'

Albert Friedlander, the progressive rabbi and theologian, wrote an erudite column in the newspaper, entitled: Goldberg's Plight should be our Firebell in the Night.

Michael Leigh, the young Reform rabbi from Edgware, in north London, asked: 'Why, in the same year as their bar mitzvah, would Jewish parents abandon their children in Christian boarding schools?'

Daniel Goldberg's mother had called the embassy and Ariella had agreed to a meeting. They knew of each other, although as far as Ariella could remember, they had never met. Adrienne was renowned for her independent analysis of the Middle East. Bearing in mind her Jewish faith, Ariella was astonished that Adrienne could be so critical of Israel, but having seen her speak, Ariella was in no doubt that Adrienne could defend her position robustly if called to do so.

Clanricarde Gardens, Notting Hill

The Israeli embassy owned three flats in the block, which were useful if accommodation was needed away from their compound. Mossad had installed cameras and microphones, and, as it was a no-through road, it was easy to monitor.

As Adrienne walked towards the flat, she saw two security men with a direct view of the flat from across the road, and one on a balcony. As she approached, the door was opened, and she walked into a hallway. A bike leant up against a wall. It was gloomy. She was accompanied up some stairs. Her escort knocked on a door and a voice called out, 'Come in.'

The room was conventionally furnished. Ariella pointed to the settee. 'Please, sit down.'

Adrienne sat in her chair with a straight back, wearing a twin set, with a diamond jockey brooch on her lapel.

Adrienne was in deep pain. She didn't hide it and yet she felt comfortable with Ariella in a way she hadn't expected. She blew her nose, took some water, and took a deep breath.

'Can I ask … how did Daniel come to contact you?'

'About three weeks ago, your son called us to ask us for our address. That was the very first contact there had been between us. I was shocked when I read what happened to your son, and then, when I saw I had some personal involvement, when I realised the same boy had written to me about wanting to live in Israel, I just couldn't believe it!'

'If there's anything we can do within our remit, any assistance we can give, we will, but I think your contacts are likely to be more useful than mine. One thing I can tell you,' Ariella said, 'my colleagues in Tel Aviv have no record of Daniel entering Israel.'

When Adrienne left Clanricarde Gardens, the busy West London streets seemed blurred. It was as if they had been captured in slow motion, or in an Impressionist picture at night. She had lost her customary self-assurance. As she walked down the steps of Lancaster Gate Station, she had to hold onto the railings to steady herself. She took the Tube to Charing Cross, and, walking through Trafalgar Square, she saw all the familiar buildings, many of which she had visited in her advisory capacity. But now they looked different, and she was hungry for the familiar. When she reached Pall Mall, she walked up the steps of one of the many Gentlemen's Clubs. In common with all the clubs in Pall Mall, it had no sign outside, but it was the Travellers' Club. She would meet her great friend, the Brigadier, and tea on the terrace and his mellifluous voice, might offer just a small vestige of the world she used to know, before her son had gone missing.

Chapter Twenty

Regent's Park, London. Summer 1967

Daniel's father, Howard, had returned from a business trip to America, where he had bought paintings by many artists who had scandalised the traditional art communities. Howard had a deep love for the simplistic loneliness inherent in Edward Hopper's pictures. He had never forgotten the first time he'd seen the picture *Gas*, and it had found an emotional place in Howard's consciousness that would have surprised many an art dealer who had negotiated with him. Edward Hopper had died in his studio in May that year, and Howard had flown to New York for the funeral. Through the years, Jo and Edward Hopper's marriage had been turbulent and Jo had often been demeaned both personally and professionally by her husband.

The Hoppers had kept meticulous, handwritten inventories throughout their lives, showing the pictures that had been sold and the resultant revenue. Edward's widow, Jo, was very ill, and was struggling to keep up with her financial administration. Howard knew how difficult the weeks were following a funeral and was sure his visit would be welcome.

Soon after his arrival at the Hopper apartment, Jo told Howard to go into the great artist's studio. The easel had been empty for some weeks, as Edward's failing health had taken its toll. As Howard walked into the studio, he saw something which caused him to gasp, and then his mouth went dry. He was looking at a painting and he was as sure as he could be that the world had never seen it before.

In 1940, Edward Hopper had painted one of his most controversial pictures. The idea had apparently come to him as he travelled home by train, and he saw glimpses of light, shining from office blocks. The painting, entitled *Office at Night*, reflected many different aspects of the changing role of women, and how that role was perceived by society. An overly voluptuous woman, wearing clothes that were impractical for work, looked at an overworked man seated at a desk. The picture had an eroticism that was subtler than many of the pictures offered by Hopper's contemporaries, and it was this hidden sexuality, as much as the loneliness of the office after hours, that appealed so much to the artistic community. Hopper had drawn very many sketches and prints prior to deciding on the final picture, and many of these had been seen in exhibitions and auction houses.

The picture that Howard was looking at on Edward Hopper's easel had a title on the frame: *Office by Day*. It showed the same man and woman, with bright daylight streaming through the window. The woman was seated in a chair looking at her boss with a shorthand pad in her hand. Their gaze was ambiguous, and Hopper had allowed her skirt to fall away, showing a generous length of her thigh.

On a table, next to the easel, there was a note, and Howard immediately recognised Edward Hopper's familiar writing: *This is for you, Howard, with thanks and best wishes to your wife and son.*

It was clear that the two pictures were a pair, but the world of art was entirely unaware that *Office by Day* existed.

He returned to the lounge where he received an urgent call from London: Daniel had been attacked and was missing.

He dashed to the airport and managed to book an earlier plane on which he had eight hours to think about his role as a father. He thought back to one of the most painful conversations of his life. The day his sister Mandy had called him at work, before Daniel had started at Oakingham.

'Cancel all your other calls and make sure nobody's listening,' she'd said.

This was unusual. Since she'd persuaded him, all those years before, to forget about beautiful Rachael, they'd been close in a 'Goldberg family, fairly unemotional way'. Mandy had married someone who liked to go to synagogue, and they'd started doing Friday night Shabbat prayers. She knew Howard and Adrienne did none of that. It didn't seem to matter. They spoke occasionally, and she had come to see Daniel about once a month in the early days.

She had started by describing the phone call from their mother, Julia, who'd called Mandy the previous day and, with her legendary lack of restraint, had poured out a deluge of bile. Mandy was able to quote her mother's final hurrah: 'Howard would never do that, send his son to boarding school! Since *she* abrogated her responsibility, he's looked after Daniel night and day. This is all Adrienne.'

There was a pause. Then Mandy had whispered: 'Howard, I just want a quiet conversation, and I have no intention of haranguing you.'

'That's a relief,' he'd responded.

'Is she right?' Mandy asked.

'No, she certainly is not. We make joint decisions and Adrienne never abrogated any duties.'

'Howard, I just want to ask you a simple question: Do you really want to send your only son, your gentle Daniel, to some huge, old-fashioned boarding school, far away from home? If you tell me you do, I'll be surprised, but I want to hear it from you.'

As he sat in his business class seat, 35,000 feet above the ground, with four years between that conversation and this inner reflection, he recalled the appalling pain he'd experienced as he'd answered.

'Yes. He's asked to go, we can afford it, and I think it will be excellent for him.'

Howard had been defending his wife, pretending he agreed with her, subsumed in some Oscar-winning performance whereby he extolled the wonders of the English boarding school, while his inner self screamed in protest.

My darling son, why would I send you to Oakingham when I can hug you, see you and nurture you at home?

He had become so accustomed to pleasing Adrienne, wanting her to admire him, that somehow, he'd become a child, fearing her criticism, unable to articulate his wishes. And then he'd stopped trying.

The art world saw him as powerful and strong, and in his professional life he could ascend that throne with no difficulty. It was in the home that the outward display of marital bliss had become less and less genuine. And Daniel had paid the price.

'Cabin Crew, prepare the cabin for landing.'

The burst of reality interrupted his thoughts about the weekly calls from Oakingham and there was no time for further self-analysis about why he'd never allowed Daniel to quit the school he obviously hated.

Now his precious son, the boy he'd dropped at nursery, the little man he'd cherished and who'd made him proud to bursting point, had been attacked.

His need to placate his wife had led to this total disaster, and as the plane screeched and lurched onto the runway, for the first time, he knew for certain he could articulate his anger with Adrienne.

As the taxi crawled through the traffic of West London he wondered where his lovely son might be.

As the early morning taxi pulled up outside his Regent's Park home, he knew he needed to sleep and eat. Adrienne wouldn't be back from her meeting with the Israeli Ambassador until late afternoon.

He pulled his bed covers over his tired body, and sank thankfully into the mattress, he remembered a sentence, but not its origin: 'Hurt becomes agony when guilt becomes shame.'

By teatime Adrienne and Howard were on their balcony. Cumberland Terrace overlooked the beautiful park, and the John Nash terrace allowed a spectacular view of the Royal Park dressed for summer. It was clear that the dynamic between them had changed. They were two people who had effectively been rendered childless. They had been attacked in the press and by Social Services for what was described as their lack of care towards their only son.

Adrienne's take was predictable. He imagined her speaking at a press conference, stylish and assured.

'We are not impervious to these attacks, but neither do we consider them to be fair or reasonable. We have always loved our son, and we decided to give him the best education money could buy. Now, because of an unforeseeable set of circumstances, we are being vilified.'

These thoughts bore not even the slightest resemblance to Howard's searing sorrow.

When he turned to her on their terrace, she heard him speak in a manner that shocked her, and nearly blew off her seat.

'On the plane I wondered which of us was more to blame. I

mean, was it you for putting your career above everything else in your life?'

'Howard, how dare–'

'Oh no, Adrienne, I dare, I can assure you. I've allowed your views to prevail for so long. I've let you talk and talk, and now, our son's missing. He could be anywhere in the world.'

'I hope you're not trying to ...'

'No, I'm not *trying* to say anything. I'm saying it fair and square. If you'd thought about our son a tenth as much as you thought about your flaming career, *none* of this would have happened.'

'You're not going to put this on me, Howard,' she shouted, as she fled from the balcony and went towards her bedroom.

Adrienne's shock at her husband's attack, for it could be described in no other way, engulfed her in the days that followed.

They had been called to a meeting by Leicestershire Social Services for the following day. This and other meetings she attended, the discussions about Daniel, none of those could be experienced as they might have been in her previous life, when Howard loved and supported her, nurtured her, maybe even worshipped her.

It's probably unwise to go into work right now. Unwise? *Diplomatic speak even in her darkest hour?*

I even tried to intellectually analyse Howard's love letter in America. What's the matter with me? Now Daniel's missing. I can't even think those words, they're so impossible to believe. and if that isn't bad enough, Howard's now blaming me for ... well, for everything.

She was in the Regent's Park flat in the morning. Weekday mornings hadn't existed for years. They had been a rush of meetings and decisions, journeys and papers. Now, there was quiet. Truthfully, she didn't seem to be equipped for this kind of disaster. Was anyone? She needed to talk to someone. A man came into her mind's eye.

'No! Not the Brigadier, Adrienne,' she told herself. 'That guilty secret won't help you one jot.'

Then she thought some more and knew the man she needed to speak to. He'd recently lost his wife, knew all about betrayal, liked her a lot, and she felt safe in his company. He was at his Sussex home. She'd put a call through and she'd go and see him.

Birch House, Sussex

The stifling summer weather contrasted so starkly with her previous visit. It had been November 1961 and President de Gaulle had been visiting Harold Macmillan at his home. The classically English Country House library had been warmed by a log fire. She remembered how privileged she had felt to be present at such a meeting where only Macmillan, Philip de Zulueta, the Prime Minister's Private Secretary, and Courcel, de Gaulle's aide, were present, for crucial Cold-War talks. Macmillan had called and asked her if she would come. Nothing would have kept her away! Not even one of Daniel's wretched school concerts. And yes, that is how she'd thought of them. She'd missed so many of Daniel's school events. Anything and everything else had been more important.

And wasn't visiting Harold Macmillan, as he hosted the French President at his home ... *wasn't* that more important?

As she travelled the Sussex roads, she wasn't having an epiphany whereby she suddenly realised her previous conduct had been negligent or even wrong. Her emotions spoke of anger and searing injustice.

How dare Howard suddenly turn on me like that! We made all the decisions together, and hadn't he been pretty damn keen to send Daniel to Oakingham? And don't tell me anyone expected our son to disappear from such a place! If anyone was to blame it was the school!

She had to reconcile, or at least try to understand, Howard's anger, because she was struggling. She loved him and she didn't want their marriage to be in jeopardy, but she wasn't going to be the scapegoat. Howard had also been jetting around the world in the sure and certain knowledge that Daniel was busy at his studies, or on the cricket pitch.

Her journey thus far through the English countryside had resembled her life with Daniel in many ways. Since leaving Godstone she couldn't remember any of the places she had passed. Possibly East Grinstead, but she'd focussed totally on her anger, on the conversation she was about to have, on her mental picture of Howard on their balcony. As the journey had hardly existed, so Daniel's childhood appeared to have disappeared. So immersed was she in her self-justification that she missed yet another opportunity to ask herself the questions that might have avoided the tragedy that was now unfolding.

Not one of those questions crossed her mind, despite the fact that her son was missing.

And some might also have asked why she was travelling to Sussex, instead of sitting by her phone. How could she want to be out of contact at a time like this? And many more would ask, why would she be about to visit a retired prime minister to discuss her marriage and her son?

The answers were not hard to find. Adrienne had written her thesis about the links between psychology and diplomacy.

She thought it was important for diplomats to have a better understanding of human psychology in their dealings with each other.

Now, she had turned that thesis on its head. In deciding upon questions that related to psychology, family love and emotions, she wouldn't trouble the psychiatrists or the new breed of so-called child experts. She had no time for them at all. Instead, she would seek out the intellectually brilliant, to whom she could relate – the diplomats and politicians – because, in her view, they would be sure to shine some light on her present predicament.

If the politician and diplomat was a previous prime minister whose late wife had betrayed him by having a celebrated affair throughout their marriage, so much the better.

As she turned into the driveway of Birch House, she looked at the steps up to the front door, and she was transported back to the frosty day of her first visit, after the French President had called.

Macmillan was on the patio. A white parasol fluttered in the summer breeze; he rose to greet his friend, and they hugged. Soon a Minton tea set appeared and a traditional English tea was arranged on the garden table.

'Adrienne, it's lovely to see you.' He was a sprightly, quite dapper, if overly traditional 73-year-old man. 'What brings you down to Sussex?'

Adrienne related the terrible events of the last week. Macmillan's face registered shock and concern, empathy and thoughtfulness. Everything she had expected.

'And Howard now blames me for all this! I shouldn't have let him go to Oakingham and it's all my fault apparently.'

She finished talking and there was silence. The birds sang, the breeze blew, and Macmillan turned towards her.

Two days later. The Israeli Embassy

Ariella's assistant was opening the post. The hate letter surprised her. It was entitled '20 April Final Solution'. The date was Hitler's birthday. It said: *Don't think Goldberg is safe. The solution must be FINAL.*

She immediately called Ariella, who took the letter and called the police.

'We'll speak to Social Services and send someone round to pick up the letter,' Detective Inspector George said.

Events moved quickly. Adrienne and Howard were informed about the threat. They were also relieved to hear that Daniel had been found.

Howard and Adrienne attended another meeting in Leicester, as did the clinical director of Leicester Royal Infirmary who had looked after Daniel, and Inspector Murray from Leicestershire Constabulary.

Sarah from Social Services said, 'We can tell you today, your son is physically well but psychologically traumatised.'

'Can we see him?' asked Howard.

'Let me explain the situation,' Sarah said. 'Daniel is approaching 16 years of age. Any court will give him some level of say as to where he wants to live. It seems,' she hesitated, 'that when he was at Oakingham he cycled out to see a family who lived in a Rutland village, and they have become very fond of your son.'

'They didn't think to tell the school, or us, about these visits.'

'They did not.' Sarah's tone was matter of fact. 'So, the current situation has multiple facets. The Israeli embassy has received a threat to your son.'

Turning to the police officer, Adrienne asked a question entirely counter to her usual measured process. 'Why don't you just lock up those revolting boys and keep them away from my son?'

'Mrs Goldberg,' Inspector Murray said, 'your reaction is entirely reasonable. However, considerable publicity has been given to this case and it's not at all unusual for groups of extremists to send messages of this sort. There is no evidence whatever that the boys who perpetrated that vile act upon your son had anything whatever to do with this letter.'

Sarah continued. 'So, we now have the responsibility of ensuring your son's safety and welfare.'

Howard was about to say, 'Surely that's his parents' role?', but he could see the riposte to that comment might not be pleasant.

'We're carrying out checks on the Rutland family, and we might recommend Daniel stays with them for two reasons. Firstly, they will be moving away from Rutland to another part of the country, which will provide some safety for him following the threats; and secondly, – and this is rather sensitive –'

Oh, don't let that stop you, thought Adrienne.

At this point, Sarah reached for her papers. 'It's clear to me you're intelligent people and I'd like to read you the legal background for what I'm about to explain, as it's part of the Children Act 1963.

'*Where a local authority satisfy a juvenile court that a child or young person in their care under section 63 of the Children Act 1948 is refractory and the court thinks it expedient to do so, the court may order him to be sent to an approved school or commit him to the care of a person other than that local authority, whether a relative or not, who is willing to undertake the care of him, and where that person consents it, and may also if it thinks it expedient to do so make an order placing the child or young person for a specified period not exceeding three years under the supervision of a probation officer or of some other person appointed for the purpose.'*

As the realisation dawned on him, Howard's horror mounted. 'You're proposing to take Daniel into care?' he said.

'We will need an order to that effect from a judge at a hearing, which you have the right to attend.'

Adrienne sat silently.

'However,' Sarah said, 'there is an alternative route which the Act allows us to pursue. Instead of obtaining an order, which you can contest, we can pursue a consensual programme, under the jurisdiction of the Court, in the interests of your son.'

'And you think you know what is in the interests of my son?' Howard said, thinking how he should have asked his wife that question some years ago.

'It's not about what we think or what we know. It's about our duty in law, to your son,' Sarah said. 'The current situation is that your son is physically safe and mentally frail, traumatised and unable to speak.' She adopted a slightly patronising half-smile. 'He walked out of Leicestershire Royal Infirmary – and yes, there are huge security issues to address there, but that's for another time – and he made his way to the family that I alluded to earlier. This suggests to us and our advisers that he may consider these people to be a place of safety. On its own this would not be sufficient evidence that the family are suitable carers for Daniel within the provisions of the Act. However, if our checks are completed satisfactorily and we and the Court are satisfied that they can provide him with a secure environment, the family might be asked to become Daniel's carers for a maximum period of three years.'

Adrienne felt as if she was listening to a judge passing sentence upon their parenthood. There was a sense of both dread and unreality, and a paradoxical recognition that it was all too real.

Adrienne spoke haltingly, but with obvious emotion. Howard watched her with a mixture of admiration and regret. It was too late for that kind of emotion. Four years ago might have been the time.

'I know it's hard for you to believe this, because it's outside your department's usual experience, but we sent our son into the care of Oakingham School with only the very best intentions, and it's impossible to describe adequately what it feels like sitting here, having someone read us part of an Act of Parliament, so you can take him away from us and place him with a family we know nothing about.'

Sarah was about to interject.

'No, you've had your say for the moment,' Adrienne said emphatically. 'The threat sent to the Israeli embassy seems bizarre to me.' She was clearly thinking as she spoke. 'But Howard and I won't want to contest your decisions if you think they are in his interests – we're not in a fit state to do that any way. But there is one area I would like to know about.'

'Yes, Mrs Goldberg?'

'Can we seek access to Daniel, to see him in his new family, or nearby?'

'That would be up to the Court, but yes, you could seek an order allowing that. There's one thing I would like to say,' Sarah said, 'and perhaps this might surprise you. At Leicestershire Social Services, we don't only deal with poor or working-class people. I say that because you suggested that this case was not within our usual area of working experience. Unfortunately, Mrs Goldberg, the need to protect children has no class boundary, and although I have absolutely no reason to doubt what you say about your reasons for sending Daniel to Oakingham, this is not the first time our department has been asked to deal with the consequences of such a good intention.'

The meeting continued. Howard seemed distant. So alien was the meeting, the austere office, the process and Sarah's reading of the Act that he felt as if he were outside the room looking in. He had no idea what to do or say.

He blamed his wife and his own weakness in equal measure. He had never thought his relationship with Adrienne was in existential danger and yet it would never be the same again.

As they walked around their beautiful flat, into the bathroom, the lounge, the certainty of their feelings had been replaced by a slightly sullen unspoken question that hung in the air: Did he still blame her? Was that balcony conversation an aberration, an outburst caused by shock and misery, or was a love affair to be replaced by a marriage? They were able to pretend that the quiet and despondency was due solely to Daniel's estrangement from their life, but doubt lingered. The unsaid became a virus: festering, reproducing, changing everything it touched. The wide-open spaces of panoramic love had faded from view and in its place the vista was a brown, damp brick wall in need of repair.

A week after the meeting with Howard and Adrienne, Sarah at Leicestershire Social Services received a letter from an unexpected source. She initially had no idea what connection her department could have with the Embassy of Israel. More surprisingly, the letter had been signed by the ambassador in person. Ariella reminded Sarah that Daniel Goldberg had written to her when he was at Oakingham School and, to some extent, she thought her reply had let him down.

Chapter Twenty-One

Eleanor 1968

When Daniel arrived at my door in Empingham that day, one year ago, I saw his face, brought him into the hall, and gave him the kind of hug you might think more appropriate for a child than a boy aged 15. I held him and hugged him, took him into the lounge and found a blanket and sat with him, and hugged him some more. He didn't seem able to speak. Whatever life there had been in his face had drained away. His eyes stared, but not at anything in particular. He clung to me as if he knew for certain that I was the only person who could help him. And he was right. I did know that. I think I'd known from the first day on the patio that one day he would become part of my life. I just had no idea how that might happen. And here he was, apparently so traumatised that he couldn't, or wouldn't, speak.

Another strange thought occurred to me: he was spotlessly clean. On the couch, under the bookshelf, I turned on the lamp, and as I did, he moved and seemed to want to lie in a foetal position, and then he began to suck his thumb.

Daniel didn't remember leaving the hospital, or the journey from hospital to Eleanor's house. He told her later that summer that he must have felt like a homing pigeon; he just knew where he had to go. He didn't remember Eleanor opening the door or lying down on her couch.

As he emerged from a semi-comatose sleep, borne of deep trauma and shock, his blurred sight cleared and there in front of him was the sight he wanted and needed more than any other: Eleanor, smiling with her eyes, leaning down towards him on the settee, cradling his face, hugging him in the warmest embrace of his life. She spoke to him in a soft, lilting voice, words of love and reassurance. It was as if he had just been born, and it was her face he needed to gaze upon.

He had emerged from darkness to light, to the first really loving embrace of his life. It was a rebirth in every sense. Eleanor and Daniel stayed there together, holding each other. Daniel couldn't vocalise any thoughts because he didn't have thoughts, just feelings and instincts.

Barrie had been in Brighton, house-hunting, and Eleanor often wondered what would have happened if she had gone to Sussex with him. It was too painful to contemplate.

That afternoon, as she hugged and comforted Daniel, mutual love passed between them as if by transfusion.

As the light began to fade, the lamp lit up the room. They had no idea that three hours had passed. The phone rang.

'I'm missing you like the Burren misses the sunshine.' Barrie's levity seemed shocking.

'Barrie, Daniel's here, in a terrible state.'

'Put him on the phone. Let's see if I can talk some sense into him.'

'No, Barrie, you're not listening to me. He's traumatised, he can't speak.'

Eleanor's tone of voice seemed to get through.

'I'm coming home, Eleanor, I'll get a taxi from Peterborough. Stay with him.'

Barrie thought about how he could keep Daniel safe. And then he thought about Lucinda.

Barry and Eleanor saw Adrienne on TV. She'd not be getting their nomination for an Oscar.

'We're desperate to find our only son.'

'There's a leprechaun on your shoulder, so there is,' Barrie had said.

'You weren't so desperate to find him when he was in that God-awful phone box, were you?' they asked as they watched the interview.

Social Services and the police reminded Barrie and Eleanor that, 'They are his parents.'

But they also learned that Daniel's right of choice would increase when he became Sixteen.

Eventually, it was agreed by a court that Eleanor and Barrie could look after Daniel, provided that they were subject to regular checks.

Barrie had been considering a second office for his business, which was thriving. He decided that Sussex, with all its prestigious schools, would be ideal, but instead of telling Eleanor, he adopted a slightly different tactic. He was quite certain that Eleanor wanted to move back to Sussex, so he decided to let her believe he'd acceded to her wish, and that despite all the difficulties, they would move to Sussex because her happiness was everything. Eleanor duly played her part and found a cottage in Laughton, near Ringmer.

Eleanor gave notice to her department at Leicester University and left all 'the legals', as she described the process, to Barrie. Everything was now subsumed to her role as Daniel's comforter and healer.

Daniel would not leave Eleanor's side. He slept in the lounge, on the sofa, comforted by an awareness of her presence and by the lamp he had dreamed about under the Oakingham colonnade. In the early days, he spent long periods just staring, as if transfixed, at a picture or an LP cover. Gradually he adopted the foetal position less often. Eleanor wanted to take him out to the patio, where he had felt so secure the morning of his first visit.

'Daniel, I know you don't want to speak right now...'

Then, as if she had found an ancient gold brooch, gently revealed and then lifted during an archaeological dig, she repeated the reassuring words that had touched her during her first Samaritans' phone call.

'...but you and I, we can be silent together for as long as you like.'

She paused, to let her words reach Daniel's inner self.

'One thing I'd like to know,' she said, smiling down at Daniel as he lay on the couch. 'Do you feel safe here? If you do, just blink twice.'

Then came the magical moment, the first direct communication from Daniel since he had arrived at their door. He blinked twice. Daniel rose from the settee for the first time, he stood up, he walked over to Eleanor, knelt down and hugged her as if, in her mother's words, 'In the hugging was the healing'.

'Which of course,' Eleanor later told Barrie, 'so help me Jesus, is the truth. In the hugging is the healing.'

Through that summer of 1967, Dan Maskell reassured Wimbledon Tennis viewers that some traditions just didn't change. Two films gripped cinemagoers, albeit for entirely different reasons; Dustin Hoffman was the 'graduate' discovering the charms of

Mrs Robinson, and Sidney Poitier was quite simply one of the best-looking men Britain had ever seen, in *Guess who's Coming to Dinner*. Flower Power loosened the stiff upper lips a little, and the beaches at Margate were filled with bank holiday revellers.

Gradually, as the Summer of Love brought the spirit of Haight Street to Hampstead, Woodstock to Weybridge and Lucy to her Sky with Diamonds, Eleanor and Barrie watched as Daniel's face relaxed a little, and he spoke more often.

He had no thoughts about his parents. A subconscious mental membrane had hidden them from view.

Regent's Park, London. Sunday
Adrienne and Howard were trying to talk calmly and agreeably in the first-floor lounge of their beautiful house. Their mouths were succeeding but their eyes were not meeting at all.

'We need to understand how he met this family. Something unusual happened.'

'Definitely,' said Adrienne. 'I think I'd like to have a chat with Fraser.' Fraser was Daniel's Housemaster at Oakingham.

'I thought about doing that, but, yes, it might be better if you saw him.'

'I've told them I can't do the conflict resolution workshops, and they've agreed to find someone to deputise for the moment.'

He wanted to say: 'After all I've said, we've said, all the tears, and you're still carrying on about your work!'

Instead, and even this was a step forward for him, he ignored what she'd said.

He mused: 'Must have been a fair bit going on we weren't told.'

Fairmead House, Oakingham

The driveway was festooned with geraniums, as Oakingham and its boarding houses awaited the influx of its parents, alumni and benefactors for Founders' Day. They wouldn't see dusty brown corridors, or lonely bereft boys. They would see smiling faces who'd just won the 880-yard hurdles, or the Thring Prize for designing a working hovercraft. Into this busy preparation came Adrienne Goldberg. She rang the doorbell, and Jeffrey Fraser asked her in, and showed her into his study.

'Terrible business,' he said, as the Labrador under the desk wagged its tail.

'Of course, I knew he was lonely, and I tried to make that clear in my reports, but nobody could've foreseen what happened.'

'Really, Mr Fraser, is that so?'

Fraser sat up in his chair, and Adrienne, using her professional skills, watched as his posture turned defensive.

'Sorry, I'm not sure what you mean,' Fraser said.

'Let me enlighten you. We entrusted Daniel to your care and, lonely or not, your job was to look after him. Despite this, two Nazi-loving housemates seem to have enacted a bizarre imitation of a concentration camp death by leaving our son naked over a ditch. Would you call that *looking after him*?'

'Wait a minute,' Fraser said, trying to restrain his anger.

'Actually, I'd quite like you to just let me finish what I have to say, and then I'll be very pleased to have your views,' she said in a calm and confident voice.

'Let's take it a step at a time. Did you know there were Nazi sympathisers in Fairmead?'

'There are many views held by boys in this school.'

'Mr Fraser, if you are going to obfuscate, the outcome isn't going to be good for either of us. I'm sure you will agree fascism isn't quite the same as vegetarianism or liberalism. It's obnoxious and unacceptable.'

'Yes, I agree,' Fraser said.

'So, I repeat my question. Did you know that these boys held fascist views?'

'I knew there was some level of anti-Semitism, and I'd seen some strange-looking flags and posters in some boys' studies.'

'OK. I think we'll agree that means you did know, and apparently you didn't feel the need to do anything about it.'

'Oh, I did plenty, Mrs Goldberg. I wrote reports every term, trying, in the most diplomatic way I knew how, to get you to take your son away from this school, where everybody apart from you and your husband knew he was unsuited and unhappy.'

'So, we're agreed, there've been failings on both sides,' she said. 'There's one thing I'd like to ask you.'

'Go on.'

'Was there a particular event that led to Daniel being on that cricket pitch that day?'

Fraser sighed, sat up in his chair.

'Yes, there was, and it began when he was discharged from the Cadet Force.'

Twenty minutes later, the conversation concluded, Adrienne decided to leave her car parked in the quad at Fairmead. She walked down the hill and up to the market square, then pulled open the door of the smelly call box, put coins in and called her husband in Regent's Park.

Despite the plunge in their relationship, she couldn't wait to tell him the outcome of her conversation.

Regent's Park

'What did you get from Fraser?'

'Daniel was on that cricket pitch because he was thrown out of the Cadet Force, and he was sent to work with some men who were building an all-weather hockey pitch.'

'I'm glad I spent all that money on fees for my son to be working as a builder.'

'Quite! But that still leaves the question of why he was there after the builders had gone home.'

The previous evening, they had agreed that Leicestershire Social Services must never learn about their enquiries.

'Perhaps a good start might be to establish who the builders were,' Howard said.

'I agree. I've looked in Yellow Pages at builders who might fit the bill, but they're mainly advertising for home extensions and small jobs.'

'Hmm, they were building a new sports pitch, that's quite specialist. Let's keep digging.'

Chapter Twenty-Two

One week later

'Barrie O'Connell Surfaces,' Rita said.

'I wonder if you could help me. This is Fallowdean School near Ipswich. Is it right that you build well-drained sports pitches?'

'Yes, that's our speciality,' Rita said. 'Would you like to speak to someone?'

The call ended abruptly, and Rita was left listening to the dialling tone.

Adrienne replaced the receiver and turned to her husband who was looking at a Sotheby's catalogue.

'There are three candidates, but O'Connell seem the most likely. Their advert shows a picture of a school, and their receptionist says that's their speciality. Can we get the names and addresses of the directors?'

'Companies House will tell us that.'

'Pretty unlikely a director would be digging a sports pitch, don't you think?'

'Not if they're quite small. Anyway, it's worth a shot, and thanks to that ghastly woman from Social Services, we know he cycled to Empingham.'

A letter to Daniel lay on their sideboard, care of Leicestershire Social Services. Neither of them could believe that they had to write to their own son 'care of' anyone.

Laughton, Sussex

'Can I speak to Daniel, please? It's Sarah from Leicestershire Social Services.'

'Of course. Is everything all right?' Eleanor was already panicking.

'It's fine. I just need to ask Daniel something.'

'Daniel! Call for you.'

Daniel came in from the garden

'Hello?'

'Hello, Daniel, nothing to worry about at all. We've received a letter from your parents, which they want us to forward to you. Would you allow us to forward it to you?'

'No,' he said.

'Just tell us when you're ready.'

'I don't even want to think about them right now.'

'We also had another letter that may surprise you.'

'Who from?'

'The Israeli Ambassador. Apparently, you wrote to her from school, and she'd like to meet you.'

Daniel paused. 'Not sure about that, to be honest. I'll talk to Eleanor and Barrie about it.'

'Just let us know,' Sarah said.

The headmaster of the new Ringmer College suggested Daniel should meet a boy called Clifford, who was going to the college in September. Gradually, imperceptibly, Daniel's smile returned.

Hot August Night

Eleanor and Barrie were woken by Daniel's screams.

Eleanor's yearning for a child seemed to have been met in full measure, with sleepless nights thrown in for good measure. She left her marital bed and walked into Daniel's room. The lamp on the side table cast its light on his tortured face. He was covered with sweat.

This was the third successive night that Eleanor had gazed upon this ghostly stare.

'Get out! This is my hut, get out!' he screamed.

'No, you're not stripping me again … no!' The screams rose to a new crescendo.

'No! Not that blindfold, get away from me!' He screamed with terror: incoherent sounds, as if he was being consumed by a burning fever.

'I did nothing, like a lamb to the slaughter, nothing! What pathetic creature does nothing? Well one day–'

She lay next to him, put her arms around his chest and lifted him to her.

'Daniel, darling, you're not in any hut. You're here with Eleanor. You're safe and secure, far, far away from the field.'

His shouting became indecipherable. Porous to her voice, he let her love permeate his mind and dissipate his terror.

Recovery. Summer 1967. Laughton

As the evening drew in, Daniel and Eleanor sat quietly, listening to the breeze. The bond between them was strong, forged as it was in shared sadness.

Daniel loved wandering in their small Sussex garden. Although Eleanor had yet to work her magic, it rejoiced in the colours of lupins, penstemon and pinks.

He still immersed himself in the Psalms, now that they could be enjoyed for their beauty and poetry, rather than as a crutch.

He'd sensed the hidden hand of comfort in the school changing room, and as he sat in this garden, he sensed it still.

One Sunday, when Daniel was writing poems on the garden table, Eleanor and Barrie were preparing lunch as they watched him through the window.

'It's a huge responsibility, isn't it?' she said.

'It is, but you're doing a fine job so far,' Barrie said.

'But I've been thinking about the Jewish part,' Eleanor said.

'Any particular bit of the last 5,000 years or so you'd like to identify?'

'It's not the last 5,000 years, Barrie. It's the next few years here in Sussex.'

'Hmm, I see your point. Go on,' Barrie said.

'You're not allowed to laugh at this.'

'You know I will now you've said that.'

She ignored the comment, as she so often did. 'I'm going to be honest. There's part of me that's enjoying looking after Daniel, the victim, but knowing that means I'm even more keen he shouldn't be a victim for too long.'

'You love your paradoxes, El.'

'I've been doing a bit of research in the library. Seems there's at least three types of Jewish worship going on.'

'Like the Greek Orthodox, the Catholics and the Methodists?'

'Yes, I think so. They seem to dislike each other just as much. I think we should go and meet a few rabbis.'

'Excuse me?' Barrie choked on his apple. 'For a moment there I thought I heard you say something about us meeting rabbis!'

'I did and we're going to do that. But first, there's something I want to do here at home.'

'Oh no, count me out of that circumcision thing!'

'Don't be ridiculous!' She looked at him with his sleeves rolled up, now stirring the gravy. He looked bemused, but she loved him so much his bemusement was almost appealing. 'I'm talking about something called a Friday night Kiddush.'

'What the feck is that?'

'It's a little service you do round the dining-room table on a Friday evening when the sun goes down, and you say a prayer over the wine and the bread.'

'Ah, they stole it from Holy Communion!' Barrie said.

'Think what you just said! Jesus was Jewish, so which do you think came first?'

'Fair point, but what would we do?'

'It may surprise you,' she said, 'to know I went into a Jewish book shop in Brighton.'

'Eleanor O'Connell, previously of the Catholic Kennedy family from Kinsale, now to be found in a Jewish Bookshop,' Barrie joked.

'Tell me, Barrie,' her anger was growing, 'when might you be serious for a few minutes? When you are, maybe we can speak!'

'Sorry!'

'So, in this shop I found a book and it's just been published, called *Jewish Observance in the Home* and it's really helpful.'

After lunch, Barrie and Daniel went to play football.

Eleanor sat in the garden. It was a hot afternoon, but she felt strangely cold. She sat on the metal bench she'd bought and looked out at her garden, fading in the arid summer. A melancholy descended upon her with no obvious origin. It was the unease of confusion. Every part of her life was a tree without roots. She'd married the subject she was supposed to be watching. He thought he'd found love to soothe the terror of the IRA threat, but what had he actually married? *What*? seemed right, not *who*? Was she the woman he thought he'd married, if you took away the IRA? But how could you do that?

Through him, she might stop a terror plot, but she couldn't cope with the love, the fulsome, drenching, wonderful love that she felt for him, and this afternoon, she couldn't deal with the confusion. They both knew about the IRA, but he didn't know what she knew. Amid it all, as she put on a cardigan in the boiling afternoon, there were only two constants, two truths: she loved Barrie and she adored Daniel. After that came horror: the man she loved might one day put the boy she loved in mortal danger. And she was the conduit, the person to blame.

The following Friday evening, Eleanor's dining-room table was covered in a white tablecloth. She had two candlesticks on the sideboard, two platted Challah loaves were covered in a cloth, which had Hebrew words on it, and she had bought a silver cup into which she poured some red wine called Palwin.

Daniel had looked at the book Eleanor had bought.

'Do you know any of the prayers?' she asked.

'Yes, I know the prayer over the wine and the bread.'

So, surrounded by the two people he loved, Daniel stood at the head of the table, placed the yarmulke on his head and recited the prayer.

'It was evening and it was morning, the Sixth Day. The heavens and the earth and all their hosts were completed. God finished on the Seventh Day and He rested on the Seventh Day from all His work which He had done. God blessed the Seventh Day and made it holy, because on it He ceased from all His creative work, which God had created and made.'

Then Daniel said, 'Baruch ata Adonai, mekadesh haShabbat.'

Then he said the blessing over the wine in Hebrew and passed the cup to Eleanor and Barrie.

Daniel said the Hamotzi prayer over the bread. They both drank and then broke the bread, poured salt over it and ate a piece.

'Why are we doing this?' he asked. 'I mean it's nice doing it with you two, I suppose, but why?'

'Because your faith matters to you, and it matters to us,' Eleanor said.

'How'd you know it matters to me?'

'Firstly, you often talk about the Psalms and how they helped you. Secondly, we know you pray, and your poetry's often spiritual. Then there's the small fact you never hid your Judaism in that dreadful school.'

'There's something I'd like to ask you,' Daniel said. 'Leicestershire Social Services told me that they've had a letter from the Ambassador to Israel, who wants to meet me.'

'Didn't realise we were in such distinguished company,' Barrie said.

'I wrote to her from Oakingham, asking if I could live in Israel. Do you think I should meet her?'

'Do you want to?' Eleanor asked.

'I think I do, actually,' Daniel said.

'Then you should,' they said.

St Petersburgh Place West London
The New West End Synagogue, in St. Petersburgh Place, Bayswater, London, was one of the oldest synagogues in the United Kingdom.

Ariella and Daniel were admiring the beauty and splendour of its Victorian interior.

'Why you want to live in Israel? It's rather strange way of leaving a school, I think,' Ariella remarked.

'Ordinary methods hadn't worked, like telling my parents how much I hated it. And before you say anything, I don't want to talk about them.'

'Your Judaism is important to you?'

'It was my companion when I was alone. It helps my night terrors and sometimes, it gives me hope.'

'I'm don't think I've heard a young man speak about it in such a personal way.'

Ariella sat in an outside pew and turned to Daniel who was still standing.

'I want to apologise, Daniel. I took too little notice of your letter'

'I don't see what more you could've done, but I'll accept an apology from an ambassador! I'd love to go to Israel one day.'

'Well, I renew my offer. If we can discuss a date nearer to the time, I'd love to greet you at Lod airport, and if there's anything I can do in the interim, just call my assistant. I've told her to tell me if you call. '

'I'd like to read a book about Israel.'

'That's easy: read *Exodus* by Leon Uris and *Elsewhere Perhaps* by Amos Oz. *Exodus* will feed your Zionist emotions, and Amos's book will give you a better idea about Israel's nascent struggles.'

'Great, I will. And thanks for meeting me.'

Chapter Twenty-Three

New beginnings

On the following Monday, Daniel visited the sixth form college in Ringmer. Social Services had briefed Dr Robinson, the headmaster.

It didn't seem like a school at all. It was new, modern, full of glass and light, not dark buildings and dark alleys.

Dr Robinson met him in the canteen mid-morning. when it was empty except for catering staff preparing lunch. Daniel was just grateful he wasn't in a headmaster's study.

'Can I tell you a bit about this place?' he asked.

'It's nothing like anything I've seen before,' Daniel said.

'From what I've heard that must be a good thing! No, you can forget about school here. This is a college in every sense.'

'Apart from the buildings, what's the difference?'

'The buildings help, Daniel, but the seam that runs through the mine in this school is about the self-esteem of the student. So, let me ask you a few questions about your previous school. Oakingham, wasn't it?'

'Yes.'

'Let's take a subject that you don't find particularly easy.'

'That would be maths,' Daniel said.

'Fine. Did the teachers make you believe that you could actually improve your skills in maths, or did they confirm your own view that you weren't particularly good at it?'

'They reinforced my view that I was dreadful at it, ensured I was humiliated if I asked a question that revealed my lack of understanding, and then let the whole school know how useless I was by putting me in a stream that was something like 4F.'

'Even worse than I thought,' Dr Robinson said.

'What about your boarding houses, where you slept, was there encouragement there, from the housemaster and his team?'

'The role of the House was to reinforce the same concept; for instance, you sat in dining room in the order of success in your entrance exam.'

'That's interesting and useful,' Dr Robinson said.

'And ghastly,' Daniel said.

'Oh definitely,' Dr Robinson said. 'Most definitely. But don't think those attitudes are confined to public schools. They may be at their most extreme there, but many schools believe that educational competition, pupil ranking, and strident streaming will shake out excellence. Since excellence is their only goal, if you aren't excellent then your parents pay a great deal of money in either taxes or school fees for you to be humiliated.'

'Plenty of that,' Daniel said.

Dr Robinson, took a drink of coffee, looked at the workmen decorating the wall. 'I'm interested in the views of an American called John Holt. I don't agree with his move towards home-schooling, but I certainly agree with his views on belief reinforcement.'

'You've lost me now,' Daniel said.

'John Holt has a view that is so obviously correct, and yet it's totally ignored in most educational establishments. If you tell a child they *can* do something, they will believe it, and if you tell a child they *can't* do something they will also believe it. If you couple that with the idea that educational success is individual – that is, it's about the improvement that takes place in the understanding of key concepts within a child – and if you add a layer that says comparisons with other children are only useful in the group sense to detect slow development, then you will have some idea of the ethos that I am trying to bring to this college.'

Daniel was quiet.

'I'm just thinking of all the misery that could have been prevented through the years, in classrooms and on sports fields, if your ideas and Mr Holt's had held sway.'

'Well,' Dr Robinson said as he stood up, 'let's not get downhearted. You're about to spend two years with us, and I have a feeling you're going to have a wonderful time.'

'I'm pretty sure I am,' said Daniel.

Daniel was sitting on his bed, a Mamas and Papas LP on the Dansette record player, and posters on the wall. He lay back and gathered his thoughts. His nights filled him with confusion. He loathed the nightmares that took him back to that field, but the terrors brought Eleanor's visits.

He just knew he loved Eleanor, and she comforted him. If he had any other questions or thoughts, they were like an ancient people looking at the heavens: they had no knowledge of the vast size of the universe, and hence no reason to formulate questions about far away worlds yet to be discovered.

Questions would be asked later about Eleanor's unwillingness to seek psychiatric help for the child placed in her safe-keeping, and certainly about Social Services' failure to offer the follow-ups in Sussex that had been recommended by their Leicestershire colleagues.

Daniel had received no treatment and his thoughts left many issues unresolved. He rarely thought about his parents and yet he harboured a cornucopia of latent thoughts and feelings about them, all unsaid and repressed.

His field of vison and consciousness was restricted to Sussex: his new home, his adopted parents, and now, Ringmer College.

His poetry was beginning to flow, and his prayers were no longer said in desperation but in thanks for his deliverance. He remembered how David's Psalm 69 had offered him comfort. Now he revisited the Psalm, a reminder that the Almighty still watched him, even in better times.

But I prayed to you, O Lord,
in the time of your favour;
in your great love, O God,
you answered me with your sure salvation.
You Rescued me from the mire,
you did not let me sink;
You delivered me from those who hate me.

Chatham House, London. Autumn 1967
In 1919, British and American delegates to the Paris Peace Conference, agreed to establish an Anglo-American Institute of Foreign Affairs to study international issues. This decision led to the formation of what later became the Royal Institute of International Affairs.

Chatham House had been gifted to the Institute and this building, in which Adrienne was about to speak, had been home to three prime ministers.

As Adrienne sat on the stage, she saw many famous foreign-affairs specialists and diplomats in the audience. Her lecture had been well publicised and was much anticipated.

The Foreign Secretary, George Brown, stood at the lectern, ready to introduce her. There were more than a few jokes being whispered in the audience about his propensity to drink too much, but the hall fell silent as he spoke.

'Good morning, ladies and gentlemen. It gives me great pleasure to offer a few words of introduction about our speaker this morning. I say a few, because those gathered here already know her so well that my words will mainly assist our journalist friends with their research. There can rarely be two people who have had greater divergence in their paths to this stage.

When I was trying to put on a posh accent selling furs in John Lewis, Miss Franck, as she was then, was on the way to her first-class honours degree at Girton College Cambridge. When I was causing as much trouble as possible as a trade unionist, Adrienne was studying with Henry Kissinger in America. Since joining this august organisation, Adrienne, as I know she won't mind my calling her, has caused almost as much controversy as I have. Despite much opposition, she ensured the inclusion of an article in the House magazine by the revolutionary Ernesto Che Guevara. She refused to allow her Jewish origins to restrain her from criticising Israel for its refusal to adhere to UN resolution 242. And recently, Adrienne has concentrated on the discipline of conflict resolution. Just think what that could achieve in the House of Commons! I could go on, but, as I'm often told in the other House, you haven't come here to listen to me! Ladies and gentlemen, Adrienne Goldberg.'

Adrienne stood up from her chair on the stage, shook hands with George Brown and replaced him at the podium.

'Thank you, George. This morning I want to discuss two entirely different approaches to conflict resolution. The first approach is associated with Woodrow Wilson and the second is advocated most famously, or possibly infamously by my Harvard friend, Henry Kissinger...'

Adrienne's talk was judged a resounding success.

After she accepted some brief congratulations, she left the building and hailed a taxi in St James's Square.

'Cumberland Terrace, Regent's Park, please.'

'Certainly madam,' said the driver, and turned on his meter.

As the taxi drove down Pall Mall and up St James's into Piccadilly, Adrienne had no time to bathe in the aura of her success. The private detective had called Adrienne the day before, to request a meeting this afternoon.

Howard and Adrienne had finished after-lunch coffee when the doorbell rang. Adrienne, slightly light-headed from anxiety, walked down the stairs and opened the door.

'Please do come in,' she said.

Agnes took Peter Archer's coat and showed him into the lounge.

'I've learned a good deal, and I must warn you that you may find some of what I know concerning,' he started.

'Just tell us the undiluted facts,' Howard said.

'Well, your initial enquiries were helpful, and I now know O'Connell Surfaces did have the contract for the Oakingham hockey pitch. I also learned that their managing director lived in Empingham. Like you, I had doubts about whether an MD would get muddy, but it seems Barrie O'Connell works on a number of the firm's projects himself.

I decided to allow for the possibility that your son had cycled out to Empingham to visit this man.'

Howard and Adrienne were filled with foreboding as he continued.

'Mr O'Connell worked previously at Benenden School and was involved briefly with a staff member, the daughter of a Cabinet minister.'

'Wait a minute,' Howard interjected, 'wasn't that the woman who was killed in a car crash?'

'It was. She died not long after he started seeing her. His trail went dead at that point. He was doing school pitch contracts but there was nothing to show me where he'd lived before he moved to Empingham.

I looked for marriage records in Empingham church, but I didn't want to waste too much time there, because we know they've moved away.'

'True,' Howard said, his mouth slightly pinched with anxiety.

'So, I went to Empingham and picked two or three estate agents.' He cleared his throat. 'I went into the first agent and said I'd been recommended by Barrie O'Connell, but they didn't remember him. Then I walked into the biggest agent, right in the centre of the village, Hardwicke Bennett. When I said the same, the man smiled and asked after Barrie and Eleanor. I replied that I'd not seen them since they moved away, then I hesitated a bit and asked where it was they'd gone, and he told me they'd bought a beautiful cottage at Laughton, near Lewes.'

'You've done well,' Adrienne said. 'It's surreal to be told where our son is by a private detective.'

'Go on, please,' Howard said.

'So, I know where they live and I've seen your son as he cycles to college nearby.'

This was too much even for Adrienne who was normally so composed. She began to cry.

'Thank god you've found him,' she whispered through her tears. 'How does he look?'

'He looks great; happy, smiling and sometimes singing on his bike. The cottage is called Jane Addams Cottage.'

'Who's Jane Addams?' Adrienne asked.

'She was a feminist social worker who tried to stop World War I.'

'Just what you want! Your son living with people who name their cottage after a woman like that!' Howard said.

'Eleanor lectures at a college in Sussex, but actually she's quite well known.'

'She is?' Adrienne said

'She was interviewed some time ago on *World View*. she's a pacifist feminist.'

They looked blank. Neither of them had seen the interview.

'She offered a course with a Republican Irishman, who should probably be under surveillance by the police. Her lectures are rather more measured but ...'

Howard strained to speak. Through a mixture of anger, deep distress and unfamiliarity, he rasped:

'So, Daniel was sent to Oakingham, purportedly to be inculcated with the values of his country,' he paused visibly distressed, glanced at Adrienne who pretended not to notice the accusation, and then continued, 'and he's now living with a pacifist, who lectured with an Irish Republican. Shouldn't Leicestershire Social Services know all this?'

He stood up in exasperation.

'God dammit! that ghastly social worker probably agrees with this woman's views, maybe even thinks they qualify this woman to look after our son. Give him some *re-education*.'

'I don't know,' Archer said, 'but can I just sum up and maybe give you a bit of advice?'

Howard, in a display of emotional confusion, walked over to Adrienne, joined her on the settee and put his arm around her. They were both shocked to the core, and Howard realised seeing Adrienne like that, with all her vulnerability, had made his heart cry.

'Don't do anything quickly,' Archer said. 'Your son's in good spirits, he looks in pretty good shape, he's going to a modern sixth form college.'

'Where he can learn more Trotskyist views no doubt.'

Adrienne said, 'Well, I wouldn't say the Establishment school did much for him, would you, darling?'

That sounded like a concession from Adrienne. Howard smiled inwardly.

'Peter, please go on.'

'He basically looks ok. He's 16 and the lawyer I spoke to anonymously told me a court is highly unlikely to move him against his wishes, especially as he seems to be happy. My advice is bide your time. Send letters to Social Services, let him know you love him and miss him.'

'But surely …' Howard mused aloud, 'surely they should know the woman he's with–'

'We can't let anyone know we've found him,' Adrienne said. 'But we have, and occasionally, perhaps your firm would do some more work for us?'

'Be glad to. We always use different watchers, so they'll notice nothing there. Just be careful,' Archer said, 'and don't go anywhere near Laughton.'

19 Cumberland Terrace, London NW1
Miss Sarah Humphreys
Leicestershire Social Services
Dear Miss Humphreys,
We'd so like to see our son for a short while. We have no idea where he is, or how he is, and no idea if he's read our letters.

Do you think you might be able to organise a brief meeting?

Yours sincerely
Howard and Adrienne Goldberg

Dear Mr and Mrs Goldberg,
Thank you for your letter. Although I understand your natural parental concern, I did explain that unless your son agreed to meet with you and, additionally, we felt it was in his best interests for you to do so, you would otherwise have to apply to the court if you wanted to make such a meeting mandatory for all parties.

While I am not a lawyer, as your son is aged 16, I must at least ask the question as to whether it is likely that you will be successful. I am afraid that I do not think that a court would accede to your request.

Your son is physically fit and seems to be progressing well. I cannot inform you further.

When Daniel reaches the age of 21, a meeting will be entirely at his own discretion, although as you may be aware a recent report recommended that the age of majority be reduced from 21 to 18.

Meanwhile, he has indicated strongly to us that he does not want such a meeting to take place.

I am sorry that I have to give you this news.

Yours sincerely

Sarah Humphreys

Senior Social Worker

Chapter Twenty-Four

Friday, 19 July 1968

Eleanor and Barrie heard screams, coming from Daniel's room.

'Get out of my hut, get out! I'm not going in that ditch, why am I doing nothing?'

Barrie watched as Eleanor left the marital bed, walked out of the door and crossed the hallway. Why was she leaving his bed? Her closeness nourished his night, he cherished their intimacy and now she was gone. On a pragmatic basis, he knew she was comforting Daniel in his trauma, but feelings inhabited a murky world of uncertainty, and as one night followed another, and Barrie awoke alone, he realised he felt envious of the attention she was giving Daniel.

'That's uncharitable, for sure,' he said to himself. 'Grow up, Barrie! The boy needs her love.' But he felt left out, and his questions remained unanswered as the sun rose.

Barrie walked out into the pretty garden with the end of his bacon sandwich in his hand. Daniel, hair down to his shoulders, wearing his new uniform of jeans and T-shirt, was heading for sixth form college for the last day of the first year and the summer barn disco.

'Those girls, they're someone's daughter,' he called out, 'and I'll not be wanting their pa at my door tomorrow morning!'

'I'm a public schoolboy, you know,' Daniel replied. 'We know how to behave!'

'I've seen.' He opened the door to his van.

Daniel called out: 'See you later!'

'*Feicfidh mé ar ball thú*,' Barrie responded.

'Eleanor's told you about that language of yours!' He laughed and opened the bike shed.

As Daniel cycled to Ringmer Sixth-Form College that summer morning, passing farms and fields, he was singing 'Jumpin' Jack Flash' and rejoicing in his own high spirits. Mid-summer heralded the end of his first year with Barrie and Eleanor. The fully dressed trees rustled in the summer breeze and seemed to concur with his thoughts as he sped past them on his bike. Apart from 'the terrors', as he called them, this had been the best year of his life by such a huge margin that he started to laugh and then to cry.

Daniel was always early for college, and he was eager to meet his friends before classes began. They were discussing the upcoming anti-Vietnam War demo in London. Naomi came up the steps. She smiled as she saw Gina and Ros laughing and jumping up and down.

His friend, Clifford said, 'My parents're trying to stop me going, as they reckon there'll be trouble.'

Clifford turned to Daniel. 'Your parents're probably going on the demo too!'

'They are, but not with me.'

'How d'you come to have such lefty parents, but have a voice that's straight out of Eton?'

Daniel didn't answer.

The teacher, 'Old Graham', didn't fit the modern ethos of the college. He seemed to occupy a previous era.

But, Daniel thought, *to be fair, he's trying.*

Derek Graham stood up in his suit and tie, and asked the class of ten, 'In *Sons and Lovers* are the sons urged into life by their reciprocal love of their mother, as Lawrence said?'

'Look,' said Tim who looked like his hair might have sparrows nesting in it, 'if Lawrence said thah, and 'ee wrote it, oo're we to argue?'

Daniel was about to put his hand up, but nobody did that in college.

'It seems to me,' Daniel said, 'the ownership of the book passes from the author to the reader as we read it, so our opinion's just as valid.'

He was used to the comments about his posh speech and his eloquent exposition, but in comparison with his previous treatment, he'd decided not to think about that.

Naomi stood up. She had a habit of standing when she wanted to say something.

'I see where Daniel's going, but there has to be a limit. I mean, some comments have merit and some don't.'

Sarah said, 'And what mark would you give Daniel, Naomi?'

There was good-natured laughter, and the analysis of *Sons and Lovers* continued.

When Daniel cycled home, he didn't notice a Jaguar, parked about halfway on his journey, or the man quietly watching him as he swept by.

Hove University
Eleanor had been called in to see Charles Crawford, her chancellor and her handler.

She sat down in front of his desk. He didn't offer a coffee, he just looked straight at her eyes.

'Not good news.'

Her mouth was dry. She had no idea what he meant.

His velvet voice belied the words.

'Three extremely dangerous people have met in London, and there's been *movement* in Belfast. We're all about to be tested, Eleanor. Do what we say, and you'll have vengeance for Sally, and you'll save hundreds of lives. Falter … and well, let's not think about the consequences of that.'

'We have to move Daniel!' She just blurted it out; it came from her gut, not her thinking mind.

'Don't think about any stupid ideas like that Eleanor,' Crawford said, with a slight twitch in his cheek. 'One change in Daniel's routine and they'll know we're onto them, and you'll all be in the gravest danger.'

She felt physically sick. Perhaps it was fortunate she had no idea of the dominoes she'd knocked over, or the dark impending danger into which Daniel was sleepwalking.

Hill Brow, Hove. 5 pm., Friday

'It's the one night you know we don't go out! And while you live here, that's the rule!'

'So, you hold the purse strings,' Naomi said, 'and you turn the screw! Well, I'm going tonight, I'm not missing the barn disco for your Shabbat!'

'Your Shabbat too, you know! Didn't notice you objecting when the bat mitzvah presents came in.'

'Money again!'

'So, you're Jewish when it comes to going on tour to Israel, but not when it comes to keeping Shabbat.'

Naomi's dad left the lounge.

She went up to her bedroom.

More than anything, she wanted to be sure to go out with a boy who her parents considered *unsuitable*. Luckily, this was very easy! He had to be non-Jewish, and she had her eye on exactly the boy to fill the role.

The Open Barn Disco, near Ringmer

Daniel was on a dance floor, with his arms around Naomi, in an open barn, in the summer, with the moon lighting the straw-covered dance floor. He was loving the smell of her hair, her body leaning into his.

She was holding his hand.

I've no idea what to say, if anything, Daniel thought. His mind raced. *Not sure what to fear. Not seeing her soon enough? Not seeing her after the dance? Wanting to see her this much? What about not fearing anything, just enjoying her lifting her head off your shoulder, kissing your cheek and smiling?*

Naomi held Daniel tightly as she danced, as the music changed to 'This Guy.'

Eleanor loves this, Daniel thought.

Without warning, the slow music was replaced by strident rock. Naomi said. 'Let's go outside.'

They walked out of the barn and into a field, ignoring Tim and Clifford's gestures and Ros and Gina's knowing glances. Sitting on a hay bale, they held hands. Daniel could see Naomi's shining long black hair, her slightly pointed chin and huge smiling eyes. She leant over on that warm summer night, and they kissed.

Safehouse

Evening, July 1968

Eleanor and Barrie had loved the Shostakovich Cello Concerto No. 1 ever since they'd heard Rostropovich play it. When they played the recording to Daniel, they asked him what he thought. The only responses they refused to accept were 'I like it' or 'I don't like it.'

'Okay,' Daniel had said. 'It takes longer to want to listen to it a second time than the Beethoven piano concertos do.'

'Why's that?' Eleanor asked

'Well, with the piano concertos, except perhaps the 4th, you usually get the note you're expecting or wanting next. With this you don't, and there isn't always a melody.'

'Now, that's the kind of comment we're looking for, young man,' said Barrie.

'You're more patronising than my teachers,' Daniel said.

'You noticed,' Eleanor said.

Later that night, as he lay back in his bed, with the light on, Daniel was in a transient state, approaching sleep. He imagined a lake with a smooth, turquoise surface. A mist had settled on the water. Was that a guard post on the bridge? His mother appeared to be taking an oath. It was a makeshift dock, shrouded in mist, and he couldn't make out her facial expression. A phone was ringing and she picked it up.

'No, darling, I'm sure you're at the right place,' she said. 'You'll make friends soon.'

A man stood in a boat, dressed as a court prosecutor with a straw-coloured wig.

'Was that an adequate response, Mrs Goldberg?' he asked.

'It was the only response,' she replied with a firm voice. 'My son was not going to be a quitter. If he'd left, where would he have taken his O levels, and how would it all have looked?'

'Ah yes,' intervened the barrister, 'how would it have looked? And more importantly, it might have disrupted your international relations schedule, and how awful would that have been?'

'Mr Cooper, your flippant sarcasm is unhelpful. I am not responsible for the attack on the cricket pitch.'

Soon, there was another figure in the dock about to take an oath. He was short and thin, with wispy black hair and wearing a Nazi Cap: Williams.

The prosecuting counsel dismissed him.

'You just followed orders from De Lacy; you're not worth cross-examination.'

The mist cleared from the southern riverbank, and behind huge barbed-wire fences, men and women, girls and boys wearing striped pyjamas shouted at the barrister.

'That's what all the Nazis said! That's what did for us! Don't let Williams off the hook so easily!'

But soon their voices became inaudible, and the mist gradually hid them from view.

On the northern riverbank, an assembly of schoolboys appeared.

A man filled the dock with his awesome presence. It was J.C. Hoyle, Oakingham's headmaster.

'Anybody suggesting that this school had anything to do with the little episode on the Upper can sweep the quad clear of pine droppings for a whole term. Boys have to let off steam you know, and this just went rather too far. Of course, if Goldberg wasn't such a weed, and he'd taken boxing lessons seriously, he'd have defended himself with vigour. Now, you revolting boys,' he looked at them with a fearsome stare, 'I want to hear you decline the noun *Rex*. It's fifth declension.'

The boys in the front of the assembly began to look towards the back. An unheard-of event was occurring. One of the teachers had stood up, while Hoyle was in full flow.

Hoyle noticed this display of audacity and recognised the Fairmead housemaster, Fraser.

'Mr Fraser,' he said in a whisper that echoed around the hall, 'it is customary for announcements to await the completion of my address.'

'Headmaster, with respect, you have told the truth, but not the whole truth. Might I ask your leave to offer further evidence of Oakingham's innocence in this matter?'

The sky was darkening over the river and the clouds threatened rain. Standing high above his audience in the chapel pulpit, the headmaster responded to the request.

'Please do, Fraser, please do.'

'I wrote to Goldberg's parents at the end of each term, encouraging them to take him away from this school to which he was obviously so ill suited.'

At that point the congregation cheered wildly and threw their boaters in the air.

The school congregation merged into the mist and the bridge turned into a stage for a Nuremberg Rally. Thousands of invisible storm troopers could be heard, chanting '*Sieg Heil*' and their enthusiasm turned to rapture as a man appeared on a rostrum. Richard de Lacy had a Hitler moustache. As he signalled with his hands, the audience became eerily silent, not a sound could be heard.

'I assaulted that revolting Jew. I am responsible,' he roared.

The audience could not contain themselves and they cheered wildly, and again chanted '*Sieg Heil!*'

Instantly, the Nazi scene disappeared. The river was silent and sombre. The prosecuting counsel was back in his gently swaying boat. A kingfisher dived into the lake. The sky lightened and the clouds raced across the sky.

Suddenly, there was a wide desk on the bridge and behind it was the flag of the State of Israel, and a photograph of the Zionist leader, Theodor Herzl. Standing behind the desk with his shock of unruly silver hair, David Ben-Gurion had arrived at his day of destiny to proclaim the independence of a new state – Israel. Then he turned his attention to Daniel Goldberg.

'The days when Jews allow themselves to hover over a ditch in preparation for death are long gone, Daniel. You betrayed the new Jewish world. We will not be lambs to the slaughter. Far from it. We will fight to our last breath and I give testimony under oath: the only person responsible for the attack on the cricket field was you, Daniel Goldberg. You allowed it to happen and made no attempt to fight back. If you want to be part of the new Eretz Yisrael, the land of Israel, you need to find some grit, young man.'

The counsel spoke to Daniel: 'You wish to address the court?'

'I do,' he said, shivering from the cold. 'De Lacy's testimony is worthless. His joyous assertion of guilt is of no interest whatever. David Ben-Gurion is entirely correct! Only one person was to blame for what happened on the cricket pitch and he has yet to give evidence.'

'Please do tell us, who is that?' the counsel asked.

A roaring sound fell upon the scene, a cinematic god in a biblical epic, and a demonic ventriloquist hijacked Daniel's voice.

'I am responsible! I did nothing.'

Chapter Twenty-Five

Lewes Reform Synagogue

Rabbi Levene sat on a chair in front of his desk, facing Eleanor and Barrie. They told him Daniel's story and his shock and horror filled the room. They felt at ease with the rabbi and liked him immediately.

He quickly understood the complexity of the situation.

'There's no reason Daniel shouldn't embrace his Judaism. And … well, this is going to surprise you.'

'I think we've had the fill of surprises for a lifetime, rabbi, if you don't mind,' Barrie said.

'This isn't a bad surprise.'

'Go on,' said Eleanor.

'Well, I'm sure you've realised this is a very small Shul, synagogue.' Rabbi Levene smiled. 'We're a satellite of the Hove Reform Shul, and their Rabbi Rosenblum and I work closely together. A week or so ago, the treasurer at Hove Shul called me. I've known Peter Klein for very many years, and I like to think we're friends. He said he wanted to have a confidential conversation. He told me his daughter was seeing a boy she was keen on, and they'd met him for the first time. I told him that sounded good and normal. He said he and his wife were a bit mystified. You see the girl's name is Naomi.'

'Oh wow,' said Barrie, 'he's not done anything wrong, Daniel, has he?'

'Not a thing!' Rabbi Levene assured him, 'nothing at all.'

'Thank Jesus for that,' Barrie said.

They all laughed at Barrie's discomfort when he'd realised what he said.

Rabbi Aaron continued. 'They were mystified because Naomi had delighted in the fact that he wasn't Jewish, as she's in that normal rebellious phase of trying to upset her parents as much as possible. But as soon as they met Daniel, they were certain he was Jewish. Now, this is a small community and although it's not impossible to fall beneath the Jewish Radar, it's about as difficult as flying at night and dropping a bouncing bomb, if you know what I mean.

Peter Klein asked me if I knew anything about a pleasant, nice-looking boy called Daniel, and you'll not be surprised to learn, I wasn't able to help him.'

'So where do we go from here?' Barrie asked.

'Slowly and carefully,' Rabbi Aaron said. 'There're many sensitivities to consider. Two young people at the start of a relationship they're enjoying. We don't want to harm that. It goes without saying, you're all welcome to come to our synagogue whenever you choose.

I think you should have a conversation with young Daniel about revealing the truth to Naomi, and I'd like to meet this extraordinary young man,' Rabbi Levene said, and smiled at his Roman Catholic visitors. What an interesting morning it had been!

As the couple parked outside their cottage, a man in a Ford Capri watched their return.

Safehouse

Next Sunday

'You left a place where you were attacked for your Judaism, young man, and now you're safe, where's your Judaism going?' Barrie asked.

Daniel had been thinking about this. He knew Naomi was Jewish, of course, and he assumed she thought he wasn't. He hadn't known how to raise this with Eleanor and Barrie; what could they do?

'Did you have a bar mitzvah, Daniel?'

'Yes, and then on the Monday I went to Oakingham.'

'We've discussed it', Eleanor said, 'and it's one of the few things the two of us agreed on straight away.'

Daniel smiled. 'I'm glad to be the cause of such unity, but what exactly did you agree on?'

'We'd like you to meet the local rabbi,' Barrie said.

Daniel nearly choked on his roast beef.

'So, pick a rabbi? Any rabbi?'

'No, actually we met just the right rabbi on Wednesday.'

'You didn't think to tell me then?'

'No, we didn't,' Barrie said. 'We weren't giving you a choice, and we weren't sending you to a rabbi we'd not met.'

'You've not been through all that bravery, to forget your faith,' Eleanor said.

'Did you hear the one about the Jew who lived with two Catholics, and went to see the rabbi?' Daniel asked.

'We have,' Barrie said, 'and it went very well.'

Daniel walked over to Barrie and put his arms around his chest.

'You're two special people,' he said.

Hill Brow, Hove September 1968
Naomi's parents were in their kitchen.

'If he's not Jewish, I'll fast two days on Yom Kippur,' Tanya said.

'You won't have to. Rabbi Aaron had a quiet word with me last week. He shouldn't have done, as it was indiscreet, but he did.'

'Knew it!' Tanya smiled.

'Let's see what happens when he tells Naomi.'

The following week, Daniel and Naomi were in Naomi's house alone.

'There's something I need to tell you,' Daniel told Naomi.

'You're married? Don't look so serious, Daniel.'

'Actually, it is quite serious. You know I live with Eleanor and Barrie, and you know Barrie's Irish and I'm not.'

'Not hard, that one'

'Well, actually, I'm Jewish.'

Daniel did not expect her response.

'Am I supposed to be surprised by that? Gina and Ros said they thought you were from day one. I was pretty sure too.'

'One day I'll tell you some of the stuff that's happened to me, but right now I've got a really special thing I want to ask you.'

'OK?'

'Will you come to the Reform Shul with me in Lewes on Kol Nidre?'

The evening before the holiest day of the year, Yom Kippur.

'I'd love to, Daniel.'

4 October 1968. Lewes Reform Synagogue

The Jews of Brighton, and indeed the world, agreed that this was a special High Holy Day period. It was just over one year since Israel had won the Six-Day War. For Daniel Goldberg it was the happiest day of his life on the most solemn day in the Jewish calendar.

Eleanor and Barrie had bought him a suit. Rabbi Aaron had taken him to buy a *tallit*, or prayer shawl, and he had a yarmulke to cover his head. He stood in his lounge in Laughton, waiting for the Kleins to pick him up. He'd finished eating his meal and had started the twenty- five hour fast.

Naomi rang the doorbell and Daniel opened the door.

'Oh, don't we look smart,' she said.

Daniel Goldberg, the same Daniel Goldberg who'd cried out in his study, been ridiculed by an entire school and left naked on a ditch, now held hands with his pretty girlfriend Naomi, and walked through the doors of Lewes Synagogue, to be welcomed by the whole community. Naomi and Daniel took their seats halfway back in the small room and Rabbi Aaron began to speak.

'At this hour all Israel stands before God.'

That was almost more than Daniel could take, and he squeezed Naomi's hand tightly. She smiled, and then the choir began the background chant for the most beautiful of Hebrew melodies, *Kol Nidre*.

The small congregation knew they were welcoming a new young member, and Daniel felt their embrace and their love.

Daniel thought back to his dream in which he'd been admonished by Ben Gurion himself.

How could he believe in a compassionate god and a religion requiring such moral rectitude, and yet be so certain that one day, he would avenge his humiliation? As the service, with its call to repentance, progressed, Daniel wondered about revenge and its purpose. What would it look like? Physical injury would assuage nothing. Something very different was required.

Chapter Twenty-Six

Autumn 1969

Daniel was at the end of his first year of study with Rabbi Levene. He had one-to-one sessions every Wednesday evening. Although Hove Synagogue had a formal religious education class, Lewes synagogue was small and did not. Unusually, Daniel was meeting the rabbi on a Sunday morning.

Levene was surprised by, and admired Daniel's unusual interest in studying Judaism, and religion in general. He had a dedication, a yearning to enquire. Did he have faith? Rabbi Levene was reluctant to enquire about that in depth. Daniel's experiences, his *return* to his faith and his thirst for study were all sufficiently unusual to warrant their sessions.

They were talking about the Ten Days of Penitence, the period between the start of Rosh Hashanah, the Jewish New Year, and the end, Yom Kippur, the Day of Atonement.

The idea that the path to penitence opened on Rosh Hashanah and a person's 'fate' was sealed ten days later seemed to fascinate Daniel. Towards the end of the session, Daniel's eyes gazed at the rabbi's books behind his desk and looked at his teacher.

'Can I ask you something very personal and private?'

If Rabbi Levene was surprised by this question, he didn't show it.

'Sometimes, I think of the assault that I suffered on that cricket field as a tiny particle, smaller than an atom, but sort of like the Holocaust,' Daniel said.

'Go on,' Levene said.

'I'd been mocked for being Jewish for a long time, then I was left hanging, naked over a ditch. Of course, I wasn't shot and left to fall in the ditch'

'Thank god for that,' Levene interjected.

'The thing is, I had a weird dream, where all sorts of people were being tried for what happened to me. In the end, David Ben-Gurion turned to me and said it was my fault because I didn't resist and did nothing. That's the problem – I did nothing at all.'

Rabbi Levene shook his head. 'No, Daniel, that's not the problem.'

'You may say that, you may even think it, but I've learned enough psychology to know the importance of perception and I am clear – that *is* the problem.'

Rabbi Levene, leant back in his chair and interlocked his fingers on the desk. He smiled, trying his hardest not to look or sound patronising.

'Let's say I agree that right now, you see that as the problem. I'll also allow your view about resistance being the most important part. But that doesn't mean I have to agree with you that the *problem*, as you call it, is about your wish to hurt yourself even more by blaming yourself, when you're not to blame at all. This is so important to you, which means it's important to me too. But I've got some bereaved people coming in to see me. Could you come to my house this afternoon, about three o'clock?'

Daniel left the rabbi and took the bus to Hill Brow in Hove, to have lunch with Naomi and her family. He'd told Naomi about his dream and his self-analysis, and as he knew she would, she'd vehemently disagreed. They sat in her garden, wearing jumpers for the first time that season, as the autumnal chill began. Naomi's father, Peter, had begun the ritual of burning the leaves. There were very few as yet, but Naomi explained how he loved dealing with the leaves – and if that stopped him asking about her studies, then long live the leaves!

'You know, your dream?' she asked. 'it's not telling you anything useful.'

'Which of us is studying psychology? I thought it was me.'

'I reckon you need to study a bit harder if that's the kind of nonsense you're going to come up with.'

'It's called taking responsibility for your own life,' Daniel said.

'It could be something else,' she mused. 'It could be that you want to blame yourself, you want to punish yourself. You felt helpless. You *were* helpless. That was a horrible way to feel, and now you think you should be punished. Don't ask me why, but it could be.'

Tanya called them in for lunch. They enjoyed bagels and smoked salmon, chopped liver and cream cheese, and then Naomi told her parents that Daniel was going back to see Rabbi Levene.

'You and David are getting quite friendly,' Peter said. 'That's a friendship I approve of!'

'Great way to make sure he never sees the rabbi again,' Tanya said.

'Do I get a say in this?' Daniel asked.

'Of course not!' Peter laughed.

Daniel felt safe in Hill Brow. He loved Naomi and her parents made him feel part of the furniture. That was a good way to feel.

Safehouse

The rabbi's lounge was filled with many books, which covered shelves, small tables and one area of the floor. Many of them had page-markers, and on one table there was a pad with handwritten notes.

The light was fading through the French windows and David put two lamps on. Daniel loved lamps, and while the room had nothing like the effect of the Empingham Cottage, he liked its intellectual chaos.

The rabbi began without any small talk.

'So, which Israeli leaders, which German-Jewish rabbis, which French leaders blame the survivors for the Holocaust? None, Daniel. The catalogue of blame is long, but it's worth going through it, since you've decided to place the blame for your attack – and by association the attacks on so many others – on your shoulders.'

Daniel opened his mouth to speak.

'No, you can't intervene yet. Just listen if you don't mind. First, there are the perpetrators, the leaders of hatred, who gave the orders, encouraged the masses and ensured the death camp ovens were filled with human fuel.

Then there are the other countries, European countries and America, who could have done so much more to help the beleaguered Jews. They definitely share the blame.

There is the thousands of years of history during which Jews have been persecuted vilified and killed, both physically and through literature.

Now, listen to this very carefully Daniel, there are also the people who valued their safety over their religion. Those who hid their faith, or renounced it, or worse still, betrayed their own people.'

The rabbi stood up, walked over to Daniel and looking down at him he asked, 'Which of those describe you? I'll tell you. None of them! None of them at all. You were sent to a Christian boarding school, entirely unsuited to you in every way; a school for sporty people; you were detached from your family, from your religious roots, from familiarity. What did this Daniel who blames himself do? Did he keep quiet about his faith, hide his Jewish light under a bushel, seek friends in the desperate loneliness of the school by denouncing his faith? Not a bit of it.

What you did, young Daniel, was to raise the flag for your faith and bring torment upon yourself. You held fast to the psalms and the prayers, you even prayed in the changing rooms, and you spoke to your God. I can't think of many people who would have had that kind of bravery. So, when this boy who I admire so much, starts talking to me about a dream where David Ben-Gurion blames him, I say: 'No, not a bit of it!' Do we know what the Israeli founding fathers would have said? No, we don't. But I'll tell you what I think. They would have said, 'Stand tall!' Just like you did when enemies surrounded you, when they tried to humiliate you.

There was nothing you could have done on that cricket pitch, nothing!'

The rabbi was close to tears, his emotions flooding to the surface.

'And don't even begin to ask me about all the people who could have helped you, who put you in harm's way. Just don't ask me.'

Rabbi Levene couldn't know the imminent new danger that Daniel faced, or the truth about the supposed 'safe house' in which he now lived. Or the people who, even now, were putting him in harm's way.

That evening, Daniel was alone. Barrie was away working and Eleanor was out. Daniel had no idea where she'd gone. Sitting in the lounge, he continued to think about his time with the rabbi.

Someone must be held responsible for the cricket pitch. Nobody else was doing anything about it two years on, so he had to take it on. But do what?

He'd been thinking about this a great deal. An idea was forming and he had some questions to ask, but his own rabbi had shown he was too close to the problem to allow independent thought. He knew Rabbi Michael Leigh had written the book Eleanor had bought for him, *Jewish Observance in the Home*, and he liked the no-nonsense introduction.

He called Edgware Reform synagogue, explained who he was (his history had apparently turned him into a legend!) and asked if he could make an appointment to see the rabbi.

He took the train to London Victoria, the Northern Line to Edgware, and used a local A to Z to find the synagogue.

'How can I help you if Rabbi Levene can't?' Rabbi Leigh asked his visitor.

'I'd prefer Rabbi Levene didn't know about this visit,' Daniel said.

'I presumed that. Not many teenagers cross the road to meet me, and you've come up from Sussex. So, the floor is yours.'

'You know what happened to me two years ago ...'

'I wrote a piece in *The Jewish Chronicle* about it.'

'Nobody's been held to account for what happened, nobody's been found to be responsible. For quite a while I thought about revenge. I fantasised about all kinds of things I might do.'

'Understandable,' said Rabbi Leigh. 'But fortunate you took that no further.'

'Yes, but I still want some of those people to suffer, psychologically if not physically. I want you to tell me: how can I face my God and my faith if I put my plan into force?'

Chapter Twenty-Seven

As Daniel returned home to Laughton, the man parked in a Ford Granada had decisions to make about his next move.

Dawn. Sunday, 30th August 1970. Isle of Wight Festival
As Daniel and Naomi's friends looked out of their tiny tent, the sight was biblical.

'Depends on your religion,' Gina said, lying near their tent. 'Feeding of the Five Thousand or Moses with the Israelites?'

Clifford was smoking a joint, trying to extend his legs without kicking the people in front. 'Why are you always so fucking serious? Just be with the now, guys, Hendrix and Leonard, and Fairport.'

Clifford's girlfriend, Rosy, had a garland of flowers round her head. She was lying on him as if he was a pillow.

Her brain must be somewhere, thought Daniel, *but it's not in the here and now that's for sure.*

Six hundred thousand people had packed a huge rural area in the Isle of Wight. The islanders were beyond fury about this invasion. Boats had brought the long-haired hippies, with their dreams of peace and love, and eventually it had become bigger than Woodstock the previous year.

Jimi Hendrix had done a set in the middle of the night, but for Naomi it was The Moody Blues who captured the dreamy warm summer of loose-fitting clothes, the carefree of now, and hazy togetherness. As 'Nights in White Satin' was followed by 'The Dream', she wondered if life could get any better.

As night fell, a beautiful woman with a smile that beamed and a voice that came from the angels, sang 'We Shall Overcome' and then 'Let it Be'. Joan Baez rang out across the Isle of Wight and every time she sang the chorus, Naomi turned to Daniel pointed at him and sang 'Let it Be'. Finally, Leonard Cohen sang a version of 'Suzanne' that was dreamier than the recorded version, and the hills and valleys on which the audience lay fell silent.

Naomi and Daniel retreated to their tent, and as Leonard talked of tea in China, and how he wanted to travel with Suzanne, they made love, real love, and held each other with the silence that spoke all the words that either of them could need.

University
February 1971
Naomi was studying at King's College London, in the Strand. The east wind howled as she walked up Kingsway to Holborn, still thinking about her last lecture.

Her family and friends had been astonished when she'd said she wanted to concentrate as soon as possible on Hispanic history. Their comments ranged from 'Why on earth …?' to 'It's obscure!' and 'You'll never get a job with that degree'.

As she continued on her frozen walk, she thought back to the villa in Mallorca. She had been lying on a beach in Puerto Pollensa, two years ago, following the end of the second year of her A levels course. She'd been reading Hugh Thomas' book, *The Spanish Civil War*. A policeman, looking more like an Army officer, had nudged her.

'You shut the book or you leave the beach!' he'd told her.

As he walked away, she was acutely aware that she was not holidaying in a democracy. The front cover had the insignia of both Franco's Falangists and the defeated Republicans. It was illegal to display the Republican flag, hence his proscription.

Towards the end of that summer term, she had been asked to write an essay on the causes of The Spanish Civil War. She had immersed herself in Thomas's rich and fascinating book and produced a long essay looking at both nineteenth century and more recent causes.

As the papers were handed back to the class, her teacher, Chris Robinson, paused.

'Nothing to worry about, Naomi, but I'd like to have word about your essay after the class, if you don't mind.'

As the unwashed, jeans-wearing students left the class with their customary lackadaisical shuffle, Naomi walked to the front of the class.

Robinson brought a chair next to his table.

'Sit down, Naomi.'

'So, what did you think of my essay?'

'It was hard to mark, because it was excellent, but it didn't actually address the question.'

'Excellent without addressing the question? An oxymoron if ever I heard one.'

'True, and that's why I wanted to talk to you. The question asked about the period 1933 to 1936, it didn't ask for a concise history of Spain from 1900!'

'Ah, I see.' She blushed.

'But the truth is I loved it. You write with real verve and your interest, perhaps even excitement about the period well, it's a delight really. Sitting at home reading the same old paragraphs about Nazi dress rehearsals and Socialist and Communist trade unions sent me to sleep. Your essay woke me up!

You're doing Spanish A level as well, aren't you?'

'Yes.'

'Where's the interest from?'

'We go to Spain for our holidays, so I thought it'd be good to speak the language. Then reading about the Civil War sent me back to a different time, before the tourists. Then there's the Jewish connection.'

'Whatever the reason, it's given you a real interest. I want you to think about something. There's a history course at King's in London. One of the lecturers is a friend of mine and he's an expert on Hispanic history. I think Kings' History department would be terrific for you.'

The wind in Holborn chilled her bones; it paid no heed to her coat and scarf. She immersed her thoughts in Spanish history until, just like the gale, her call with Daniel invaded her being. She'd known, or at least feared, for ages, he would say he mightn't be ready to live in halls next year. But this was only February! Why would he want to say that to her? He was preparing the ground for his own failure. Then she thought again. Would he call it a failure, staying around Eleanor for longer, so she could 'soothe his nights'? Meanwhile she'd had many offers that could definitely improve her nights. Was he being unfaithful? Could you call an obsession with an adopted mother ...? Yes, you certainly could! He was prioritising Eleanor over her. What would it take to shake him out of it? If she told him she'd succumbed to George and his version of a nocturnal visit? What if she did? He was so attractive.

She only had to smile at him in the communal kitchen, while he ate yet another meal of baked beans on toast. Hunky Dory would be on the turntable, and they'd be in her single bed by the radiator in no time.

She turned down Portugal Street. LSE students were pouring out of the door, and soon she was in Carey Street, pushing the door of the Seven Stars. Seemed like the history faculty had decamped here that late gloomy afternoon, and Helen, Marion and Tina were sitting at a table opposite two postgrads and George.

'Grab a chair!' they shouted. The pub stank of beer and dope, but the table was enticing, and soon she was part of London student life again.

The Conversation

The Somerset roads were winding and slow. One tractor after another, and at last Barrie thought he could overtake, when a huge livestock lorry came hurtling towards him.

Barrie knew he was not concentrating on his driving. His mind was filled with his current obsession: Why did Daniel still need Eleanor to soothe his nights? It was as if Daniel was perpetuating his trauma, to receive the maternal love his own mother never offered.

Well, thought Barrie, *he's certainly making up for lost time. And what about my needs for a wife in the marital bed?* He didn't like himself for his jealousy, and it had been made worse by Daniel's decision not to live in halls at university. Then there was another lingering concern: Eleanor had not been herself lately. Something was on her mind and he had no idea what it was.

His own sins of omission and commission left him incapable of confronting Eleanor. As he approached Ilchester Manor School and a meeting with yet another headmistress his thoughts were not about the next all-weather lacrosse pitch.

Was it time for 'the conversation'? Any serious conversation with Eleanor made him feel physically sick. The conversation was coming, but it would be very different from anything Barrie had in mind that day in Somerset.

Sussex

It was spring in Sussex again, and Eleanor's memories of her mother came flooding back. The rain fed the streams, the green verges and the copses.

She had been the bereaved daughter, a wife yearning for a child, and then she had lost her baby. Now, a new sadness settled upon her like chilly fog from the hills. It was made more overwhelming by the knowledge that it was entirely self-induced. The new hiatus had brought the walls of safety down upon herself. When the rapids swirl and the hurricanes blow, seek out the certainties of life. But what if there are none to be found?

She loved Daniel and he was doing well in his new life. Her yearning for a baby had been assuaged, yet she was still surrounded by dread and the fear of loss. She seemed destined to bring about her own descent into abject loneliness. In her mind she had created the fantasy that her fall was inexorable and predetermined. She had read and reread the biblical Sacrifice of Isaac, and she could not resolve the crushing question: was she sacrificing herself or Daniel? When she looked at Daniel as he happily started his journey to university, or, as he lay quietly, reading under the lamp in the lounge, she knew her enjoyment had been stolen. One day she would lose his love.

Chapter Twenty-Eight

Bloody Sunday, 30 January 1972

Adrienne was at home with Howard when he took a call from Future World Offices. It was unusual for them to call her on a Sunday.

Howard watched Adrienne's face as the events of that terrible day were relayed to her. Her frown deepened and she looked askance. Although she took the call standing up, as it progressed, she was forced to sit down on a chair next to the telephone table.

'I'll be in the office at six,' she told the caller. She replaced the receiver and turned to face Howard.

'What's happened?' Howard asked, walking over to her as she sat on the chair looking vulnerable and shaky.

'In Derry, Bogside ...' she spoke without clarity or confidence. 'Our troops killed twenty-six unarmed people.' She paused. 'Hospitals are reporting multiple deaths.'

Howard was equally shocked, and long into the evening, they joined thousands of politicians, paramilitaries, and ordinary households, in Ireland and on the British mainland, wondering about the consequences of such a terrible act.

Adrienne was chairing a meeting at Future World in Cavendish Square. She knew the people sitting around the table well. Some bristled at the very idea of a woman as Director of a foreign-affairs organisation, others admired her.

Her old boss, Ted Heath, had become Prime Minister in 1970, and he'd asked her to continue in her role at Future World rather than becoming a Downing Street aide.

'Keep your independence and you'll be invaluable to me, Adrienne. Alec hates everything about your office, so you must be doing something right.' He was referring to Alec Douglas-Home, Heath's Foreign Secretary and recent prime minister. He continued: 'I want to talk to you about Northern Ireland. We've got our men inside Sinn Féin and the Republican movements of course, one quite senior. Pack your psychology and diplomacy into your suitcase and head off to Ulster. See what you come back with.'

She addressed the meeting,

'The only way forward is to negotiate with the main protagonists. Either we do it now, or we'll have to do it much later, after untold suffering.'

The other attendees were shocked.

'You can't negotiate with terrorists.'

'With the greatest of respect–'

'How would that playout in the media?' someone asked.

'It won't,' Adrienne said. 'It will be conducted in the greatest possible secrecy if and when it happens.'

June 1972

Since being expelled from Oakingham for assaulting Daniel, Richard de Lacy had been fanatical about keeping fit. He'd walked long distances with extremely heavy rucksacks. Richard knew Royal Marines and Paras had to walk many miles, carrying at least 21lbs, and that was just the training.

That morning Richard was carrying 28 lbs.

He had applied to join the Paras, and he hoped beyond any other ambition, for a tour in Northern Ireland.

Christmas Day, 1972
The word that kept filling Naomi's mind was 'allegiance'. Daniel had chosen to spend Christmas Day with Barrie and Eleanor. Naomi thought, *It's about being with a person, isn't it?*

She hoped she was wrong, because the person Daniel was with was Eleanor. Barrie too, but she couldn't help thinking Barrie was becoming an irrelevance, or was that just her own obsessional thinking? They could have compromised. It wasn't like they lived far from each other; they could have spent part of the day at one house and the remainder at another. But 'Let's spend Boxing Day together' just didn't do it, however she tried.

As she lay awake in the early hours of Christmas Day, she decided to analyse it as evidentially as she could.

Eleanor had taken Daniel in, looked after him and nurtured him, after a terrible trauma. Of course, he'd be grateful to her. He'd had night terrors. She'd comforted him through nights of trauma.

His own parents had been negligent, no getting away from that, but she'd never heard their side of things. As Christmas Day progressed a plan was forming in her mind. She felt better already.

As Christmas afternoon in Laughton gave way to an early evening, the Christmas tree lights sparkled, and Barrie realised that the IRA were no longer the only threat to his happiness. He loved Daniel, but he thought how complex the situation had become. His concerns about Eleanor's relationship with Daniel were superseded by his fears about the status the IRA had given him as a sleeper. How could he complain about Eleanor's behaviour, when he was hiding a secret like that? Eleanor had been desperate for a child, and now Daniel had walked into their life. Serious conversations could have unintended consequences. Better left alone.

Naomi may have painted an inaccurate picture, but her suffering resembled an arrow penetrating her soul, so intrinsic was it to her sense of self.

Christmas lunch tables, invested with so much love and preparation, either hide or display familial strife. In Hove and a few miles away in Laughton, Barrie and Naomi, around separate Christmas tables, pulled crackers, told silly jokes, and played charades. It was the game that most closely resembled their Christmas Day.

January 1973, Laughton Village
As they left the Roebuck Inn on a freezing Sunday afternoon, Eleanor read a card on the Communal Village noticeboard: Explore Christianity with Rev. Folkes. Wednesdays at 11 am.'

'We've helped Daniel back to his religion, what about ours?' Eleanor asked Barrie.

'Not interested,' Barrie said. 'Just causes trouble all over the world.'

'I've been having different thoughts since Daniel came to us. I might meet Rev. Folkes.'

Barrie could see no harm in it. 'Two religious people in a household of three? Lucky it's not the House of Lords. I'd be outvoted!'

They were both suffering under the yoke of their secrets, but Eleanor wanted to explore her thoughts with a stranger. She'd shrunk her dilemma down to one word: Truth. Was truth in love more important than loyalty to other forces? She was more than aware that it was a little late for such a question, but she needed to talk about it, and Rev. Folkes might be just the man.

What would she ask Rev. Folkes? She couldn't tell him that she was working for the Intelligence Services. How she would have loved to ask, 'I went into this marriage with a lie, but can I change it to a truth?'

He would simply reply 'of course'. But what would happen if she told Barrie about her role with MI5, about the real reason they'd met? She could tell him she knew about his secrets. Would that liberate him? Would his anger with her be greater than his relief at hearing the truth? As the rain pelted the window, and a gust blew over a plant pot in the garden, she decided it wasn't possible to make a decision based on what he might say. What was the right thing to do? Were there any absolutes? The biggest and most unexpected change had been her overwhelming love for Barrie. Despite the secret he hid within his soul, maybe even because of it, she realised that to some extent, her love for him was eclipsing her grief for Sally. The present and the future had reduced the impact of the past.

Was Sally her only reason for helping her country? No. She'd seen the work of the IRA and she'd do whatever she could to stop them causing further carnage. Then the question became pragmatic: would telling Barrie endanger MI5's ability to stop the IRA on the mainland? Once he knew, he couldn't unknow. Meanwhile, it was just the truth: he couldn't tell anyone what he didn't know. And what would telling him do to their relationship?

It was then, as the clock struck two, that Eleanor realised she was asking the wrong questions. They had taken Daniel into a place of safety. A safe house. And yet both of them, silently and separately, had hidden and ignored the truth. This was where the truth became paramount: there was nothing safe about this house. They had betrayed his trust and led him into mortal danger. Selfishly and recklessly, they had experienced the joy of watching him thrive as part of their family, each knowing they were drawing him closer and closer into the IRA threat.

Her question to Rev. Folkes was clear in her mind.

All Saints Church

As she walked down Church Lane towards the church, Eleanor remembered the blackberrying they'd done in the late summer. Now the world had frozen. The hedges were flecked with frost, the puddles topped by ice, and the graveyard was slightly hidden by the winter mist. She walked into the chapel and through into the anteroom where the meeting was due to take place. Rev. Folkes had told her on the phone that he'd like to meet her alone before she joined a group session. He wanted to know more about her faith or even her lack of it.

In his study, covered with bibles and works of scripture, family photos and crosses, Rev Folkes asked her in a gentle voice, 'What brings you to Christ?'

She was taken aback by the stark question. Had she come to Christ?

'Is coming to a church coming to Christ?'

He spoke slowly and thoughtfully.

'Well, that's a huge question, Eleanor, isn't it. You're not a congregant, but I sensed in your call, that Christ's mercy might not go amiss.'

'My question's going to seem very naive. If my marriage, which is sacred to me in every way, is threatening the welfare of a member of my family, if the very safety of that person would be enhanced by my leaving, what would your Christ say about staying or leaving?'

'Jesus loves you in your troubles. When your troubles are deep, he's there beside you. Pray to God about your dilemma. Follow your conscience and remember your vows. You aren't alone. As to the practicalities of your question, I think you know I can't resolve your issues. Here we offer love and solace.'

It was as if Eleanor had not heard his reply.

As she walked back to the cottage, flurries of snow fluttered in the air. It was no surprise to her that Rev. Folkes had failed to solve her dilemma. Leaving the Church, the agony remained.

Chapter Twenty-Nine

Ballysluthra, Northern Ireland, 30th January 1973

On a misty, January morning, a car left Maghera and drove towards the town of Ballysluthra. As the fog settled over the fields, Father O'Connor entered the town, and parked in the car park of St Patrick's Church. It was the anniversary of one of the bloodiest days in modern Irish history – Bloody Sunday. *And there's been too many of those*, he thought.

There had been unrest in many communities leading up to the anniversary, but this was his town, and it was his role to promote the teachings of Jesus Christ to its people.

The contrast between Jesus's teachings and those who claimed to be acting in his name was so stark that Father O'Connor sometimes submitted to the sin of despair. He had been criticised by both sides of the divide, although that gave him a great deal of pleasure. *I must be doing a fair bit right after all*, he mused.

He pushed down the steel door handle of the church door. He resolutely refused to give in to those who said it should be locked. Christ's mercy was available to everyone, whenever they sought it, and so it would remain.

Father Sean O'Connor had joined forces with someone who many would consider his natural enemy: The Reverend William Mawhinney, the Presbyterian Minister at Ballysluthra. Father

Sean saw him as a fellow follower of Christ, even if he worshipped to the tune of a different canon.

Reverend Mawhinney had visited Father O 'Connor a week ago, and they had shared tea in the crypt.

'I've an idea,' Rev. Mawhinney said. 'A short memorial service in the open – neutral so to speak.' They were both aware of the terrible opposition they would face, but they had set their face against division and in the spirit of the real Jesus, they sought peace.

Ballysluthra was a town immersed in the sectarian conflict that had blighted the island of Ireland for centuries, and which had burst onto the international news bulletins in recent years. High walls, with barbed wire scarring the top of the brickwork, separated Nationalist and Unionist housing.

The graffiti on either side of the wall told the sorry story of The Troubles. On the Nationalist side of the wall were murals of Republican fighters in IRA uniform, surrounded by Irish tricolours and the slogans of the paramilitaries. If you approached the same wall from the Protestant roads, you might wonder if you were in the same country, in the same era, given the pro-monarchy slogans supporting the United Kingdom.

Fergal's father was a member of Sinn Féin, the political arm of the Republican movement. He wasn't sure if his father had ever carried a gun or joined the IRA, but that morning he'd seen him pulled from his bed, his sisters woken and screaming, as he was driven away.

Fergal was a normal teenager, who was learning to be a mechanic.

His parents complained continually about their housing, and Fergal was surrounded by fervent nationalists defending their roads against Unionist provocation and dreaming of a united Ireland. Seeing his daddy dragged out of the house, and hearing the screams in neighbouring houses, changed young Fergal for ever.

As darkness fell, and the crowds gathered in the square, Fergal was ready to move on from rocks and stones to petrol bombs.

The sun set, the crowd grew larger and angrier, the Army were in position behind the barbed wire and in the turrets, and Fergal was seething with anger.

Private Richard de Lacy, of 2 Paras, was in his barracks preparing his uniform so his RSM would shout at him a little less than usual. When he'd finished, he walked into a dark corridor, reminiscent of Fairmead House at Oakingham. The notice from the Army Command shocked him, and he became unsteady on his feet.

'Lieutenant Colonel Barnaby Smythe, DSO, MC, has returned to duties in London and the new OC for 2 Para will be Lieutenant Colonel Isaac Levine, VC DSO.'

Agony, sheer agony, thought De Lacy. *Not just because he's a filthy Jew, which he is, but I've told everyone I'll never serve under a Jew; never take commands from a Jew and the filthy fuckers have ruined my Army career before it's hardly begun.* Then a thought struck him. *Was this a joke?* People knew his views on Jews only too well. Had they conspired to humiliate him? No! *This was no joke.*

Soon his comrades in arms started sneering at him as they passed him in the corridor.

'Can you believe they give VCs to Yids?' Sergeant Standish smiled and gave De Lacy a gentle shove.

'A short career, hardly noticeable, what you think, De Lacy?'

'Confining yourself to barracks, are you, De Lacy?'

De Lacy knew his duty: he'd disobey the filthy Jew.

The crowd in the square had grown from hundreds to thousands.

'End Internment!' they shouted, as the evening sky was lit by exploding Molotov cocktails.

Richard de Lacy was in a dark, empty church with a good view of Ballysluthra Square. He finally managed to open a rusty window and standing just out of sight he could watch the seething group of protestors.

The briefing had been clear. The Paras had ruined their reputation on Bloody Sunday. Their commander in Ballysluthra was a decent man. 'Keep the peace and hold your fire.' That was the order.

Fergal was at the back of the square, and Father O'Connor was remonstrating with the men.

'You know better than this. This isn't who you are!'

'It wasn't, Father, until this morning!' said Colin, Fergal's friend 'Now this is exactly who we are.'

De Lacy had a clear view. He held his gun steady.

As the air grew rancid with tear gas, and acrid from the smoke of petrol bombs and burning tyres, a shot rang out and Fergal fell to the ground, bleeding from his chest.

His friends tried to stem the blood, and a doctor used his jacket as a tourniquet.

His cries turned to whispers as the blood spread around his chest, and Father O'Connor leant over him and administered the Last Rites, certain Fergal was going to die.

Two further shots rang out and hit Father O' Connor in the back. The last Rites stopped, as Fergal and the priest lay dying, while their friends took cover.

The atmosphere changed. For a few moments the crowds became subdued. And then the crowds parted like the Red Sea waves, as men in paramilitary uniform, faces covered, armed with rifles, marched up to the incline close to the Catholic estate and one of the men began to speak.

'The Provos will not allow the Brits to detain our men without trial and then murder our people. One of them, a man of peace, a man of God, the other barely a man at all, a teenager. The Brits need a message and we're here to give it to them.'

The crowd roared their approval.

'Either they give us the soldiers who murdered Fergal and Father O'Connor, so we can exact our own justice upon them, or we will show them what a Republican uprising in Ballysluthra looks like!'

Soon the Molotov cocktails flew, cars were set on fire, the crowds marched on the barracks, and the scene grew uglier and more dangerous. The Army returned to its barracks. Through the night and into the smoking dawn, the smell of tear gas hanging in the wind, the tyres still smouldered, torched cars and empty canisters scarred the square. But nothing lessened the fury of the people of Ballysluthra. Their son had been killed and their priest had been butchered in cold blood. The IRA recruited more men that night than they could train.

The following day.
Brigadier Clinton-Dodds was talking to his new CO, Isaac Levine. They had called a meeting of senior officers.

'De Lacy's a nasty piece of shit. Causing loads of trouble. Don't think we want troublemakers like him around, do we? I gather he's got obsessions about Jews too. Might be quite a few here not so keen on the Jews, but there's something about this man I really don't like.'

There were murmurs of agreement around the table.

'Still, we can't accede openly to an IRA ultimatum.'

'Before we go, I've done some digging. De Lacy's father was thrown out of the Army after he gave poor information to his superiors that led to many deaths!'

There was surprise in the room about that news.

The following day, Richard De Lacy was arrested by military police and a lawyer was appointed to represent him at the court martial.

On the day of the planned unity memorial for Bloody Sunday, Rev. Mawhinney put two seats in a field and sat in one. He set up trestle tables in a field, exactly as he and Father O'Connor had planned. The time for the ecumenical service came and went and Rev, Mawhinney sat alone in the field. He said a silent prayer for peace, cleared up, and left the field.

Chapter Thirty

Lewes Synagogue. Late Summer 1973

Daniel was sitting in Rabbi Levene's small office.

The rabbi was talking to a congregant on the telephone. The literary mural behind the rabbi called out to Daniel, urging him to dive into the waters of learning and scholarship. Transformed as he was by a new world of safety, he was excited by the prospect. He had drunk at the fountain of his faith and rather than his thirst being assuaged, it had become insatiable. He wanted to wear his faith and dress in its clothes. He hoped he could become a worthy son of the Holocaust victims. He wanted to understand some of the Yiddish that would connect him to the Jews of the ghetto, and the shtetl. He also wanted to learn Ivrit, modern Hebrew, the language that spoke of renaissance, and so much more importantly to Daniel, of defiance. It was the manifestation of Jewish refusal to allow past ditches to become the future mass graves of expendable Jews. This was the triumphal arch that greeted him, that morning in Sussex.

Daniel the victim had been submerged, so that his previous consciousness could be lost without trace. This was his people; these were the intellectual origins of his religion. Here, in this room he had come to discuss some fundamental questions with a man who had slowly become his friend, his confidant and his rabbi.

'So, young man, this morning I have one question for you from which there is no hiding place.'

He drank some coffee, cupped his chin and put his fingers on his beard. Then he looked straight at Daniel. 'What can you tell me about your relationship with God?'

'It has changed,' Daniel replied.

'Go on.'

'As a child, my image was the stereotypical, all powerful being in heaven. Now I don't seem to give God a physical appearance, and I don't give God a gender either.'

'That statement alone would raise the ire of Orthodox Judaism, so you're doing well so far,' Rabbi Levene said.

Daniel continued. 'God was in that room the first day I met Eleanor and Barrie; he was at the barn when I danced with Naomi and he's in the books behind your desk. But I've started thinking about whether he was in Auschwitz and Dachau too.'

When the discussion was over, Daniel left the synagogue and took a bus to Brighton to spend the afternoon alone.

He walked to a different bus stop and waited for the open-top bus to Rottingdean. His life was crowded, like a street in the rush hour. He never had time to himself. A thought had been forming in his mind. He didn't actually seem to be anybody. He was a boyfriend, a student with the rabbi, he had parents (although he tended not to think about them) and there were the people who were not just the centre of his life, but had become his life. His happiness depended upon Eleanor and to a lesser extent Barrie. As he sat on the bus, he had time to reflect on his recent past.

So much had changed in the last few months. Eleanor and Barrie bickered less, and no longer offered sarcastic retorts to each other. The air was heavy, but as to what made it so, he couldn't say.

Barrie had become withdrawn and morose and, even allowing for his busy work schedule, he seemed to be away more than ever.

Eleanor's pretence that nothing had changed was pathetic. Daniel thought he could trace it back to the day she'd had a meeting with her chancellor. Was her job under threat? He doubted it. She received accolades everywhere for her courses and had been offered lecturing roles at many other universities.

And what of his relationship with her? She was the woman who'd brought him back from the night terrors to better health, introduced him to Rabbi Levene and loved him in a way he'd never enjoyed before. He liked to think he really knew Eleanor, and right now she was suffering. Surprisingly, he didn't think it was about their marriage; after all, that would be the most obvious place to start. They still loved each other deeply and they couldn't avoid showing it, even as they argued or seemed distant from each other.

He could tell Naomi, but that would achieve nothing.

He wandered around Rottingdean for a while, stared at the waves crashing on the rocks. The season was over, the children's laughter a memory, blown away by autumn. The beach was deserted, and it was beginning to rain. He sat on a stone bench beneath a raised, clock-shaped flower bed, now just weeds and brown plants. He felt the familiarity of the rain and an affinity with the emptiness of the forlorn square, and thought back to the colonnade.

His life had been affected by brutal behaviour. What was its origin?

What family regime had turned Richard de Lacy into a Nazi sympathiser; a person who stripped him naked on a cricket pitch? De Lacy's life, probably from an early age, had sent him on a journey to the Oakingham Upper.

Wandering the forlorn streets of autumnal Rottingdean, his mind was awash with questions to which he had no answers. Up to that point his questions had swirled around the Oakingham attack. Who was responsible for the attack on that cricket field? And then, 'What did *responsibility* mean?' Why did these questions matter to him so many years later? But here, in empty Rottingdean, he sought answers from Eleanor and Barrie. And there was only one way to get answers: ask questions. He would ask them individually what was troubling them.

He liked the order of residential areas, the street markings, the driveways, the quietness of a weekday afternoon. A car pulled out, and so quiet was the area, that he heard it as it drove on its way, and the sound diminished into nothingness.

As he waited for the bus that would take him back to Brighton, he thought about his own parents. He hadn't thought about them regularly, but lately he had forced himself to ask painful questions. There was no doubt in his mind that it was his mother who he blamed the most.

After all, he thought, Dad took time off from his job at various times to be with me. Adrienne, as he now called her, had just allowed her career to swallow everything like a whale.

As he returned to Lewes, more immediately, he knew he had to ask Barry and Eleanor what was going on.

Chapter Thirty-One

Monday's Child

1. Neasden, London. August 1973

The three people sitting around a dining table had detonated bombs at Euston and Kings Cross stations, outside the Home Office, at New Scotland Yard and outside the Old Bailey.

'The Neasden Meeting', as it became known, was a plan to raise their activities to a whole new level.

Donoghue started the conversation.

'So, the Mainland Commander has given the order and Noraid has given the funds. We have to hit the Brits so they still remember it a century from now.'

'Do you have a short list?' asked Siobhan.

'I do indeed,' said Donoghue. 'There's only one target on it.'

When Donoghue told the Keegan sisters about the target, the room went quiet.

'That'll do it,' Marion said.

'So it will,' said Donoghue.

'What's the news about Barrie?' asked Donoghue.

'He's living in sleepy Sussex, taken in the Jewish boy and he's building his business,' Siobhan said.

'Well, it's time we woke him from his dreamy suburban slumber. Time we gave him a call and brought him into service. Nobody's to tell him the plan.'

2. Sussex

'O'Connell Surfaces,' Rita answered the phone in her usual efficient voice.

'Could I be speaking to Barrie O'Connell, please?'

'I'll see if he's free. Who's calling?'

'Oh, he'll be free alright, just tell him it's his uncle Brian.'

Barrie froze. The blood seemed to drain from his face and his stomach was taut. This was the moment he'd dreaded. Every waking morning, he had wondered when that call would come.

'Put him through, Rita.'

'Young Barrie, what a pleasure it is to speak to you this sunny autumn morning. How's that young man of yours doing? Daniel? How's he doing, Barrie?'

'What do you want, Brian?'

'What kind of question's that?'

'What do you *want*, Brian?' Barrie repeated.

'Seeing as you're asking, a little reciprocity. We've helped you to your middle-class life in sunny Sussex, now you're gonna help us. North London Tavern, tomorrow morning, 12 Noon. We've just the job for you.'

3. Monday evening
Our Lady of Sorrows, London
Inscription.

Then Jesus said to her, 'I am the resurrection and the life. He who believes in Me will live, even though he dies. For God so loved the world, that he gave his one and only Son, that whoever believes in him should not perish, but have eternal life.'

Barrie sat in an empty church. It was five o' clock on an autumnal afternoon, the period between Solemn Vespers and evening Mass. The high windows showed the reality of a dark sky, and the candles and soft lighting were intended to offer comfort to sinners. But they did not help Barrie. The statue of Jesus on the cross, dressed only in a loincloth, dominated the church, and this afternoon it dominated Barrie's thoughts too. The splendour, spirituality and the solemnity of the church affected him. He would have answered a question about his faith by saying he had none. Yet that afternoon he had come to this place for solace. His central dilemma was this: If Jesus had died for the world, as Christian believers thought, then why should he stay alive, when his very continued existence threatened Daniel and Eleanor and might always do so?

Indeed, everything seemed to point him firmly in the direction of death as the answer, the redemption for those whom he loved. It couldn't be a suicidal death, a death where those around him might wonder if they had somehow contributed to his state of mind. He could already imagine them all, sitting around, guilt-ridden and questioning their souls. It had to be a death caused by another.

Why did he have to die? The skills that had once nourished and provided for Eleanor and Daniel now seemed destined to endanger them indefinitely. While he lived, others might die. Once he was dead, the shadow of Donoghue and the Keegan sisters, of McGuiness and Gerry Adams, would be removed.

Father Kelly entered the church. As so often in recent days, he saw the solitary figure sitting in a pew, with his head in his hands. Father Kelly sidled quietly into the pew next to Barrie.

'What troubles you so deeply?' he whispered, 'You sit here for hours. What troubles you? Jesus loves you. He heals the broken-hearted and binds up their wounds.'

Barrie turned to Father Kelly. 'If as you believe, Jesus died on the cross for us. I know I must die.'

'Jesus didn't die so you should die; he died so you can live!'

'Ah well, that may be true, and for most it probably is, Father, but for me it is not. My Cross is the salvation of the people I love. I can be their resurrection and life, but my living … well, that seems destined to be their death.'

4. Monday Night
Sorrow's Passion

The Autumn night was chilly, the leaves were turning, and the velvet tree symphony could be heard from the Laughton cottage bedroom. The house was empty. Daniel and Naomi were staying at friends for the weekend. Barrie and Eleanor lay on their bed, listening to the languid breeze. Barrie was naked, and Eleanor was just wearing the lace top negligee that Barrie liked so much. As always, before they made love, Eleanor was consumed by her love for him. Holding him, looking at his craggy bearded face, seeing the love in his eyes. She stroked his forehead, his beard, and his neck, and she just enjoyed looking and loving his eyes. They liked to take things very slowly, to caress and hold each other. A street lamp threw light across Eleanor, and Barry gently pulled down the lace top covering her breasts and held them, cupped them, stroked her nipples and kissed them. They loved how aroused they both became, as her nipples hardened, and his tongue roamed over her areole, stopping to look at her and her flushed face. Then he kissed her breasts again and it was then, at that second, that the thought entered his head, the fearsome, terrifying thought about the danger his family was in. Immediately, his erection disappeared, and in an instant Eleanor saw the change in Barrie's face, and she sensed his hardness had dissipated.

Pulling back, they looked at each other, and without a word being exchanged, each was suffused in the sadness and sorrow of the other. Sitting up, holding each other, they let their tears mingle as the well burst. The secrets they hid from each other, and the searing pain it caused, brought forth an outpouring of grief and sorrow, and this at least they could share as they clutched each other in the autumn darkness.

Tuesday's child
1. Morning Plans

Barrie told Eleanor he was travelling to Marlborough College, although her 'people on the ground' told her he wouldn't be going anywhere near the Wiltshire countryside.

Eleanor was relieved she knew a fair bit about Daniel's plans. He was going to London by train to see the rabbinical college and talk to some students about what he could expect. Then he was going to see Rabbi Levene to discuss the visit and enjoy their weekly theological discussion.

Before the day was out, Daniel's faith would be tested to the limit, but not in a cosy room talking to his Rabbi.

2. A weekday morning in sedate Hove

The Neasden Three had ordered their 'followers', Lillie and Aiden, to watch Daniel for some days. They had been surprised to find that a man in a car seemed to be watching Daniel occasionally too, but they just kept watching. As he went to University, as he came home, when he went to see that pretty girl friend of his in affluent Hove, they watched. It was a job they'd done for Irish Republicans for many years, and as Brian O'Donoghue had said, ' If it moves, Lil and Aiden will notice it.'

Leaving the bus in Hove, before his train to London, he decided he had time to go to the best patisserie in the known universe, Zetlands. Lil and Aidan watched Daniel walk up Holland Road with its Regency and Victorian windows, revealing aspidistras, and its white blocks of flats. He turned into Western Road near the manicured Palmeira Square, and walking happily into Zetlands, he bought a Jap cake with a coffee bean on the top, ('the best food on earth'), and then he planned to walk to the bus stop to go to Brighton Station.

Lil and Aidan sat in their unmarked white Ford Transit Van and watched as he came out of the bakery.

With experienced hands and remarkably little fuss, they bundled Daniel into the van.

His shock was total and yet their voices were soft and reassuring. The van was lit inside, and they sat him on a makeshift bench.

He was screaming, 'What're you doing? Who are you?' Frenetic questions, until his voice froze with fear, and he could say no more.

Lil was talking softly to him, from a script agreed with Brian.

'We'll not hurt you and we'll return you safe and sound to your cottage and your girlfriend. We have just to keep you for a while because that man Barrie you live with, well he's not paid us back a large amount of money we loaned him all those years ago.'

'What's that got to do with me?' Daniel rasped.

'Nothing so as you're asking, but we figure he'll pay us quicker if he knows we're holding you as security.'

The van was moving, but there were no windows in the back, so Daniel had no idea where they were headed. For reasons he couldn't explain to himself, he didn't seem scared of these people.

He was shocked beyond measure, and shaking, but this wasn't an invasion of a hut, no Richard de Lacy stripping him and leaving him over a ditch. It held none of those fears.

Lil gave Daniel a mug of coffee which shook as the van rattled and rumbled on its way.

'You'll come to no harm young man.'

'Where are we going?' Daniel managed to ask.

'To London, so we'll be together for couple of hours I'd say.'

3. Belief and Betrayal
11.30 North London Tavern, Kilburn

Daniel was in a room with a tall ceiling, a worn green couch, and some wooden chairs, many needing repair. He was sitting at a long table with a plastic cloth on it. The door was locked and he was far too high up to consider escaping through the window. The windows had been boxed up so he couldn't know what time it was. He had been offered food and water, and nobody had hurt him. It seemed he had to wait until Barrie did something to get him released, but he had no idea whether Lil's comment about a debt was actually true.

It all seemed too extreme. Why would you take somebody hostage? The longer he sat or walked around the room, the more mystified he became. Somebody had been watching him, preparing a van, preparing this room. This wasn't spontaneous. He didn't understand much about business or debt, but he really doubted that ordinary people went to these lengths to ensure a debt repayment.

Thoughts were forming in his mind about what might be happening. They were conjecture, but they led him to think about

Safehouse

Barrie and Eleanor. What did he really know about them? He had never heard about any siblings they might have, or any other family. They had neighbours in for lunch or for one of Barrie's legendary barbeques, but they seemed to live their life in a kind of isolation. He'd lived with them all these years without asking anything about their past. They had rescued him, taken him in. He knew Eleanor had suffered a miscarriage and lost her mother. About Barrie he knew nothing. Yet now he found himself in this room, above a pub, with boxes of Double Diamond and Guinness and Watney's Red Barrel, and tonics. It sounded as if he was here because of Barrie. What part Eleanor had played in all this he had no idea.

Time passed, there were paperbacks to read and he'd just picked up a book called 'Country Girls 'by Edna O'Brien when he heard loud voices below.

One of the voices was Barrie, the other two he didn't recognise.

As fear was about to overwhelm him, he noticed an old bible on the shelf. He turned to his old friend, the Psalms, and he allowed the solace of the words to blend with the presence of his God, the feeling that protection was at hand, and before long this room was providing a clarity about his faith he'd never experienced before.

The shouting was becoming louder.

Psalm 121 1
I lift up my eyes to the hills-- where does my help come from? My help comes from the Lord, the Maker of Heaven and earth. Indeed, he who watches over Israel will neither slumber nor sleep. The sun will not harm you by day, nor the moon by night.

He remembered the prayer he'd read in the Oakingham changing room. It had stayed with him and comforted him so often.

We are loved by an unending love.
We are supported by hands that uplift us
Even in the midst of a fall.
We are loved by an unending love.
Embraced, touched, soothed and counselled.
We are loved by an unending love.
Blessed are you, Beloved One, who loves Your People
Israel.

He closed his eyes, put his hands over his ears, and prayed to the God who loved him.

4. The Pub Kitchen

Barrie was in exalted company – depending of course, as Barrie would have said, on your definition of 'exalted'. Marion and Siobhan Keegan, and Brian Donoghue in one room. What would Special Branch do to get their hands on these three?

Brian Donoghue swept some grey hair away from his face.

'Well, young Barrie, it's an uncommon pleasure to see you this morning.'

'Brian. I didn't necessarily have you down as evil right through, but your gloating at my obvious suffering is making me change my mind.'

Brian Donoghue's face changed in an instant. It was the face of a fighter, certain that he killed in the name of right and morality: that God was on his side.

'Barrie, you've been living a privileged little life in England's

Green and Pleasant Land, while your countrymen across the water are suffering all manner of hardship. Don't talk to me like a self-righteous little prick. If the pleasantries are over, let's get to it. You and your team of cricket-pitch geologists are about to turn your attention to Matters of State.'

As Brian O'Donoghue explained the horrific plan, Barrie's mind wandered, wanting to be anywhere else, aching to hear anything but this.

O'Donoghue finished with, 'You leave the rest to us.'

Barrie had gone white. But the news only got worse.

'We've taken young Daniel into custody, so we have. He's safe and well, and provided you do just exactly what you're told, he'll be returned to you very soon.'

How could he ever tell Eleanor? Panic set in and Barrie felt light-headed.

'Now, wait a minute here,' Barrie said, trying to sound assertive. 'What's Daniel ever done to you?'

'For a fully grown man you're uncanny naive, Barrie, you know that. You and I both know your weakest point is your love for the fine young man that is Daniel. We've also a half a thought your marriage might not be the best right now, depending what you told the beautiful Eleanor about your past. Anyway, the point is, we were never going to leave our bank guarantee, shall we call it, roaming the roads and fields of Sussex, so he could flit off somewhere, were we?'

'Perhaps I can help here, Barrie,' Marion Keegan interrupted. 'I won't hesitate to kill that boy, Daniel, if you don't come across for us. Is that clear?'

As Barrie walked into Kilburn Tube station, he yearned for the mundane and the tedious. Instead, his thoughts were filled with death. For his own mortality, he cared very little.

His dilemma was excruciating. At what point could he betray the IRA? He couldn't allow them to succeed in their murderous endeavour 'But', he asked himself, 'when could he inform the UK authorities, while giving Daniel the best chance of survival?' How could it be that he had even to say such words? What on this earth had he done to the boy?

Truth is, he thought, *I have to tell someone now.*

5. Eleanor's Lunchtime in Laughton

Telephone rings always seem louder when the house is quiet. It was Charles Crawford.

'He's meeting them at the tavern, our man's seen him there this morning. It's imperative you find out what's going on, Eleanor. This is your moment.'

Eleanor had no idea when Barrie would return, and yet she knew from the moment he appeared, their lives would never be the same. Her stomach was tight, her hands trembled. She thought back through the years they had spent together. Could she convince him that her love had been real while her persona had been contrived? Even at this late stage, Barrie's reaction mattered deeply, and yet the truth stood out like a blinding light on a dark night. He would be shattered by her revelation as he saw his certainties disappear into a fog of deceit.

Barrie walked from the train to the nearby bus stop. As he waited, he repeated his first sentence over and over in his mind. 'We have to talk. I have to tell you some things.' He couldn't even mouth the words about Daniel's kidnap. He was about to destroy the woman he loved.

6. *The Confessional Return*

Barrie arrived home in the early evening. He went into the kitchen to find Eleanor sitting at the table. No dinner preparations had been made: the kitchen was spotless. The quiet of the Sussex countryside seemed oppressive.

As Barrie was about to confess all, Eleanor stood up, looked into his eyes and surprised herself with her tone.

'Ok, Barrie, it's time for us to level with each other. You can tell me about the thugs you met in Kilburn this morning and what they want you to do. Then I have to tell you some things about me that will shock you.'

Was this a dream? A nightmare? Barrie couldn't say. How did Eleanor know about Cricklewood? Had she followed him? Why would she do that?

Barrie sat at the head of the kitchen table, his head in his hands.

'There's no time for self-pity,' Eleanor said in a strong voice. 'What's going on, Barrie? I'll help a little. I've known since before the Christmas dance, all those years ago, in the same pub you've just come from. I know the IRA contacted you in Cricklewood. I wasn't meant to fall in love with you, but I did.'

She paused briefly. Barrie looked worn-out. His face was ashen, his shock total.

'There's no time for any of that now. You need to tell me what they've told you to do.'

'They've got Daniel,' he blurted out.

'They've what?'

'They've taken him, to be sure I do what I'm told.'

She was being tested to the core of her soul, but she knew now, more than ever, she needed to stay strong.

'What have they told you to do, Barrie?'

'I've to dig a tunnel from Whitehall into Downing Street, to reach into the Cabinet room.'

'Stay there, Barrie, and don't move an inch.'

She was on the phone to Crawford, but to her emergency number. She gave her code and told the man what she knew.

In no time at all, a new voice took over the call.

'Get him to give you exact descriptions of each of the people, precisely what they said. Then tell him to build the tunnel.'

'They've got Daniel, our boy.'

'That's no surprise. Standard tactics. Get Barrie to do what I say and there's a chance he'll live.'

Barrie was subjected to revelation after revelation. The secrets he'd harboured, laboured under, the terror that had filled his nights – and she had known from the start. It was the reason for them being together.

The change from fearing the reaction of Eleanor, to realising his wife was an agent, no doubt with a handler, left him punch-drunk.

Somewhere in the mist, the shroud of their kitchen conversation, she'd said the words 'I loved you anyway', but he couldn't hear that from someone who wasn't behaving as his wife. How could he know how much was an act and what was real?

She had been his certainty and now there was none.

Eleanor watched Barrie go through all the machinations she'd played out in her mind so many times, and yet, the reality of watching this thoroughly decent man disintegrate, as his life was taken apart like a house being demolished room by room, was worse than she had feared.

'I know what harbouring secrets is like,' Barrie said. 'I just can't believe what you had deep in your soul.'

Eleanor remained standing. She was steadfast and confident, as she responded,

'It started with Sally, that made me realise how much I loved this country, the lengths I'd go to protect it.'

'Never thought of bringing me into that little scheme?'

'Oh, I thought about it each and every day, Barrie. I just couldn't afford the risk that the thugs would learn my real status.'

'You thought I'd tell them?'

'What you don't know, Barrie, you can't tell. And I've a feeling Mr Donoghue and his crew have ways of making people talk.'

Barrie fell silent. The IRA had ruined his life. Maybe he'd be arrested as a terrorist, maybe he'd be shot; he had no idea. That kind of fear he could handle, had been handling to some extent. He had no way to process Daniel's kidnap, or Eleanor's lies.

At twilight, they each stared blankly at the person they used to know and parted.

7. Where is Daniel?

As the light faded, Naomi's family began to worry. Naomi had called some of Daniel's friends. Peter had called Rabbi Levene. It was Tania's call to Leo Baeck College in London that turned worry into alarm. He had missed one of the most important meetings of his life.

The 'phone rang, as if it was an alarm, it filled the darkening room. Naomi picked up the receiver. It was Eleanor.

'What's happened?'

But it wasn't the Eleanor she knew.

'Pray for Daniel's safety. He's been taken.'

'Taken,' she shrieked, 'taken where?'

'I can't tell you any more. The police know about it and if you call them on the number in the envelope under your garage door and give them a code number, they'll tell you to sit tight and do nothing.'

Eleanor rang off, and Naomi dropped the 'phone sobbing and calling out,

'Someone's taken Daniel. '

She hugged her father, tears pouring down her face, contorted with fear and anguish.

'Eleanor was speaking in a voice I've never heard before,' she cried.

'What's happened to him?' her father asked.

'I don't know, Dad!' and through her terrified tears, 'She wouldn't tell me anything.'

She told him about the code.

'Daniel's in danger, and I've no idea where he is.'

Peter was the voice of calm.

'This is what we're going to do. I'm going to call the police and give them your code. Then, I'm going over to Eleanor's house.'

'If you're going, I'm coming too. Don't bother trying to dissuade me.'

'And then,' Peter said, 'tomorrow you and I are going to pay Daniel's parents a visit.'

'What? You don't know Daniel's parents!'

'We know a great deal about his parents!'

'But you never told me!' she exclaimed.

'We just kept the information to ourselves. We thought one day it was bound to be useful.'

Naomi was distraught, and as she spoke between sobs, she asked herself,

'Should I stay here, look for him, go to Laughton, God I don't know. What if he calls, how will I know if I'm in the car?'

Tanya, also weeping, put her arm around her daughter and failing in her attempt to sound reassuring she said, 'I'll stay here in case someone calls. You go with your father.'

8. The Empty Cottage

The headlights picked out the remnants of one of Eleanor's climbers. Naomi used her key to let herself in.

They walked into the lounge and turned on some lights. Barrie's books and records were on the shelves, but Eleanor's had gone.

They looked at each other and walked upstairs, giddy with fear and loss. If they needed confirmation, it was to be found in the master bedroom.

Eleanor's cupboards were empty.

'Let's go,' Peter said. 'There's nothing more to learn here.'

Naomi went downstairs. She could hear the old joy ringing in her ears and visualise it in her soul. Tables of food, the sound of laughter, the foreverness of plans, and a feeling of total safety. Now, it had been shattered, and she knew it would never return.

Chapter Thirty-Two

1. Exodus

She had sacrificed everything for her country. Her marriage to the man she loved beyond words was over; she would probably never see him again.

And what of Daniel, the boy she loved with her entire being? She'd failed him totally, and now she knew she'd never see him again either. Daniel's parents came into her mind. She had no image of them, but of one thing she was certain: they'd want to know how their son had been exposed to the IRA.

There were so many ingredients in the swirling mass of conflicting emotions. She imagined the conversation where she blamed Barrie for allowing Daniel to come into the family, knowing he was putting their joyful young man in grave danger. And yet she knew for certain that she was as much to blame for this sin as Barrie. She had known about Barrie's past, and yet she had offered Daniel a supposedly safe house. She had needed Daniel to love her with all his heart, to be comforted by her, and throughout she had known she was drawing him into a mystical cavern, filled only with fear and danger. And now, part of her was trying to blame the man she loved for Daniel's plight.

As Barrie was caught up in the drama, as Daniel was drawn into it by the IRA, a part of Eleanor had begun to realise that all these relationships were ersatz. She loved Barrie, but they had hidden monumental secrets from each other.

Her own life was in danger. She'd told MI5 about the recent contact between Barrie and the IRA. Her information had been clear, comprehensive and enormously valuable. The IRA must surely suspect her. Her time in Sussex was over.

2. Wednesday's Child
Ogunquit Art, Davies Street, Mayfair

Arabella had been Howard's stalwart assistant for twenty years. She was filing invoices when the telephone rang.

'Ogunquit Art, how can I help you?'

'Good morning,' Peter said. 'You don't know me, but my daughter is going out with Howard Goldberg's son, Daniel. We'd like to speak to Howard urgently.'

Arabella was excited and surprised in equal measure. The first contact from someone in Daniel's life for so many years, and she'd taken the call.

'Mr Goldberg is at home but I'm sure he'd love to hear from you. Could I get him to call you, please?'

Arabella had no way of knowing who this person was. Safer to get Howard to call them.

'Please, do impress the urgency upon him.'

'Oh, I will. You can depend on that.'

When Adrienne took the call from Arabella, she could scarcely believe the words she was hearing.

'The man, Peter, said you should call urgently,' Arabella said excitedly. 'And apparently, Daniel's going out with his daughter.'

'How do we contact him?' Adrienne asked.

'Here's the phone number, it looks like a Brighton number – 0273 ...'

'Howard!' she screamed. It was rare that they were both at home late afternoon on a weekday, but they had booked a golf lesson.

As Howard came downstairs, he saw Adrienne lying on the settee, crying.

At his approach she sat up.

'Arabella just called! It seems Daniel has a girlfriend, and her father wants us to call him urgently.'

Howard was drowning in confusion. Contact from Daniel? Wonderful. He had a girlfriend. Why was the father calling the Davies Street shop? How did he even know about it? But joy! Joy!

Adrienne was usually in control, of herself and others. Now she had no idea what to think. Thoughts of those afternoons in West London while Daniel slept, came into her mind, but now they seemed nostalgic and wonderful as she replaced reality with myth. Perhaps at last she could see her son again and not use that most dreaded of all words, 'estranged'.

Howard sat on the settee by the 'phone and dialled the number, reeling from the information he'd been given.

'Peter Klein.'

'Mr Klein, I'm Daniel's father,' Howard said, glorying in the use of that wonderful word.

'Thank God you've called, Howard. My daughter Naomi is Daniel's girlfriend. We need to see you urgently.'

'Of course! But what's happened? I mean we're overjoyed.'

'Howard, this is no time for celebration. Can we meet you this evening in London?'

Naomi and Peter sat on a Pullman train heading towards Victoria Station. She had been astonished to learn that her father knew a great deal about Daniel's parents.

'But you never told me!' she repeated.

'There wasn't any need to. But now there is, and I'm glad I did my research.'

3. Meeting the Parents

Howard and Adrienne were sitting down, standing up, moving from chair to chair. They had no idea how to cope. Adrienne was thinking. 'This is the first direct contact with Daniel's new life, in six years.'

'No point trying to relax,' Howard said. 'We're not relaxed.'

Adrienne went down the stairs and opened the door herself.

A pretty, chestnut-haired girl stood there looking apprehensive. Her father was a pleasant looking middle-aged man.

They followed Adrienne up the stairs and into the opulent lounge. Naomi had never seen a room with so much art and delicate furniture. There was a desk with slender legs; she later learned it was a secretaire. Occasional tables, statuettes, a sculpture, a single painting of an office (*What a strange subject for a painting*, she thought), where a woman with large breasts, she presumed a secretary, peered at her boss across a desk.

Peter said, 'What I have to tell you is disturbing, but I'm just going to tell you it as it is.'

'That's what we want,' Howard said.

'Daniel's been living with a couple. Barrie's Irish, Eleanor may have Irish connections, but she's from Sussex,' he said, not realising that Howard and Adrienne had discovered this sometime ago.

'Eleanor and Barrie seemed very nice, we became friendly, and Naomi spent many happy times at their cottage in Laughton. It has to be said that Eleanor nurtured and loved Daniel after his traumatic experiences. She encouraged him to explore his Judaism as much as possible and arranged for him to join an excellent local sixth form college where he was very happy.'

'Sounds good so far,' Howard said.

'And it has been good … it *was* good, until it wasn't. Naomi had concerns about Eleanor sheltering Daniel too much, inhibiting his growth, but what happened yesterday, that's altogether different.'

'What happened?' Adrienne asked, looking frightened and anxious in equal measure.

'I received a call from Eleanor,' Naomi said, 'telling me that Daniel was in danger, I should stay by the phone and if someone called and gave the codeword 'Jackdaw' that meant Daniel was safe. She also said if we informed the police, they would give us exactly the same advice. We have and they did.'

Howard was angry and perplexed. 'Where the hell is Daniel, and what's this Eleanor talking about?'

'We don't know,' Peter said. 'My wife's sitting by the phone, but we thought we should come see you and tell you in person.'

Adrienne let Howard ask lots of questions about Eleanor and Barrie, but she was now wondering about the contacts she had and how they could help. If the police knew about Daniel's disappearance, then she might be able to obtain information from the Home Office.

'Look,' Adrienne said, almost moving into professional mode. 'I have lots of Government contacts.'

'Yes,' Peter responded, 'through Future World. I was hoping you might be able to use that avenue.'

Adrienne was astonished. Peter had obviously done his research.

'You know about my work?'

'I wasn't going to let my daughter go out with a boy all this time without knowing about his parents. Daniel and Naomi had no idea I was finding out about you, but I hoped one day we'd meet you. Not in these circumstances of course.'

'Of course,' Adrienne said, feeling constrained, surreal and terrified. 'Let me make some calls. Perhaps you two should return home for now.'

'Yes, we're going straight back. Daniel's very friendly with our rabbi - I'll see if he knows anything.'

'Can I ask,' Adrienne said, 'could you await my enquiries before you tell anyone? Would you mind?'

'No not at all. Just keep us in touch.'

4. Calling the Prime Minister

When they'd gone, Adrienne didn't have to think for one second.

'Ten Downing Street? This is Adrienne Goldberg from Future World. I need to speak to the Prime Minister urgently. Code word Ogunquit.'

'Robert Davidson.' Sir Robert Davidson was Edward Heath's Principal Private Secretary.

'Robert it's Adrienne. I need to talk to the PM.'

'Hello Adrienne, there's an awful kerfuffle going on here, full COBR and all that.'

'I don't suppose it's anything to do with a couple living in East Sussex and my son Daniel who's gone missing?'

There was a pause. 'Hold on a few moments, Adrienne, if you would.'

It was rare indeed for a COBR meeting to be interrupted. Robert Davidson approached the PM and spoke quietly into his ear. He related his conversation with Adrienne.

'Tell Adrienne I'll make an enquiry or two and call her back.'

Davidson left the room and picked up the receiver.

'I interrupted a COBR meeting for you, Adrienne. You might have something, you might not. The PM says he'll make a few calls and call you back.'

In Cumberland Terrace two terrified parents sat looking at each other.

Adrienne said, 'Robert Davidson seemed to think my enquiry about Daniel was worthy of interrupting a COBR meeting.'

'Why's there a COBR meeting?' Howard asked.

'No idea,' Adrienne said.

Chapter Thirty-Three

1. COBR meeting. The Cabinet Office, 70 Whitehall

As usual, the COBR meeting was being chaired by the Prime Minister, Edward Heath. Reginald Maudling, sat to his left, and to his right, were Sir Michael Frobisher, Director General of MI5 and Sir Christopher Smythe Chief of MI6.

General Sir Peter Fox, The Chief of the Defence Staff, commander of the British Military, and Lord Carrington, the deceptively avuncular Secretary of State for Defence, had both been asked to attend.

Edward Heath began to speak.

'We have received intelligence that threatens the stability and security of the United Kingdom. I understand it's come from one of your operatives in Sussex. The country owes her a huge debt.

I have previously briefed Commander Michael Cumberland. The IRA plan to blow up Downing Street, during Cabinet, in three days' time. We have to find Marion and Siobhan Keegan, and Brian Donoghue.

And they've taken a young man hostage. If the plot's exposed, he'll die.'

'Do we know anything about the boy?' asked Cumberland.

'Not sure we can worry about the boy,' General Fox said. 'If the plot isn't stopped, we'll be burying our government!'

The meeting had ended and the PM asked Sir Michael Frobisher, Director General of MI5, to wait.

'Your brave operative, is she of Irish descent?'

'Yes. Her mother served the UK with great distinction as a physicist. She's been working with us for some years.'

'Was your operative living in Sussex?'

'May I ask where this is going, PM?'

'You may, but at this stage I'd just be grateful if you'd answer my questions.'

'Yes, she was.'

'And was she by any chance looking after a young boy called Daniel?'

'Oh my god, there's been a leak,' Frobisher said. 'That's disastrous.'

'There's not been any leak, Michael. Did your people at MI5 know that the young boy was Adrienne Goldberg's son?'

'I honestly don't know how to answer that question, Prime Minister.'

'Try the truth. You'll almost certainly have to answer it in front of a Parliamentary Select Committee in camera, so how about getting some practice now.'

Edward Heath looked askance as Sir Michael Frobisher finally told him the truth.

2. The Gravest Danger

'This is the PM's office, please turn the scrambler on.'

Adrienne complied.

'I've thought about this, and I'm satisfied there's no security risk in telling you what I know. There is, however, a major condition attached. We are in the middle of a huge operation; we need to deal with an existential threat to this country and its government. When I tell you, you can do nothing with the information. In particular, I have to tell you that your son's girlfriend and her parents do not have security clearance for this information. We know they visited your house this afternoon. You and your husband must not divulge this information to anybody. I'm taking a huge leap of faith telling you.'

'I understand that Prime Minister. You have my word, and I think you know what that means.'

'I do,' The Prime Minister said.

'Is Daniel in great danger?'

'The very greatest, I'm sad to say.'

The PM continued. 'Daniel has been kidnapped by the IRA and is being held hostage to ensure the man who has been looking after him carries out a potentially calamitous terrorist outrage. I'll keep you informed when I can, and I will pray for your son's safety.'

'Thank you, Prime Minister. Goodbye.'

Howard finally lost control. He picked up Adrienne, carried her into the bedroom, placed her on the bed and together they held each other as their tears mingled, their fears engulfed them, and they wished with all that was dear to them that they could pretend the IRA had had nothing to do with Daniel, that his life was not in the hands of brutal murderers, that he had never been placed with such a family, and much else besides.

3. Westminster 3.30 pm

Barrie's team wore official-looking uniforms, and everyone ignored them as they dug holes in the Whitehall tarmac.

The area around Parliament Square, including Whitehall, south of the Cenotaph, had all been cordoned off. The square itself was deserted except for police cars and bikes, their flashing lights contrasting against the dark and thunderous skies.

The tunnel diggers came up at noon to a sight they would never forget.

Armed police shouted as each man emerged into the sunlight.

'Face-down, on the grass, hands on your head.'

Three men from Barrie's team had been below ground, and each was put in the back of a police van. The van left the Sanctuary and headed down Victoria Street as part of a large convoy, sirens wailing, blue lights flashing.

Commander Michael Cumberland looked ruefully at the signs announcing the Water Board work. He looked away and ordered munitions experts into the tunnel to check for explosive devices.

A little while later, he received confirmation that the tunnel was safe.

He spoke to one of the bomb disposal men.

'How near to Downing Street do you think they got?'

'Downing Street?' he asked.

'The tunnel's heading for the Cabinet Room,' the commander said.

'Sir, it's going to take a long time for that tunnel to reach the Cabinet.'

'Why so, Major?'

'Because, by my reckoning it's about to reach the Chindit Memorial on the Embankment, Sir.'

He pointed towards Whitehall, in the opposite direction from Downing Street.

Earlier that day two police cars had been driven at speed, southbound on the Edgware Road, heading for the North London Tavern. They knew for certain that both Daniel and Barrie were now in grave danger. The IRA would have kept close watch on Westminster and the presence of Special Branch and the Army, would have told them everything they needed to know: the operation to explode a bomb beneath the Cabinet Room had been betrayed. Now the hunt was on for Donoghue, the Keegan Sisters, Barrie O'Connell and Daniel.

Paddington Green Police Station was the hub of the op, and new orders had the approval of the Home Secretary and the PM.

Soon, all the UK mainline train stations were closed and as each London Tube arrived at the platform, the doors opened and the station staff told the frustrated passengers to leave the train, make their way up the escalators and out of the station.

Ferry and cargo ports were closed: no ships could leave or enter any port area on the British mainland.

Not only were all the airports closed but the world was told that British airspace was 'unavailable to all planes until further notice.'

Chaos ensued. Passengers were stranded, babies were born unattended, weddings were ruined and commuters could only walk home for tea.

'The British mainland has been closed,' the Home Secretary reported to the PM. 'We've given Special Branch the best possible chance of finding the Three.'

As the police convoy approached Carlton Vale, at the west side of affluent St John's Wood, they were just over one mile away from the North London Tavern. The pub had been surrounded by a huge armed police presence.

4. Daniel and his God

He was alone in the room. He had no idea how long had passed since he'd heard Barrie's voice and the argument on the floor below. A woman brought in his meals and left without saying a word, never responding to his questions. Suddenly, a cacophony of dread, a demonic sound coming from the depths of hell, shook his room and the building. Explosions, gun fire, so loud they might have been in the room next door. No faith could shield him from this terror, and he screamed for help, thought of knocking on the door, but he wanted no part in what was happening below. For one second, the thought came into his mind that this was no 'under paid debt'. He had been betrayed and placed in the gravest danger. One or both of his protectors was to blame. Had The Safehouse been filled with lies and deceit? He couldn't know. He was terrified for Barrie, shaking with fear as each explosion rocked the room.

He cowered behind the stacks of beer. Speaking to his God, again realising that this fear was so different to the cricket pitch trauma. And it wasn't just his faith, although that calmed and soothed him. There were no thoughts about Eleanor: it was Naomi he longed to see. He could hear his breathing. He had no sense of time, and no idea what would happen to him.

He thought about his night time 'Tish Call' walks into Oakingham town centre, but 'Dangerman' had disappeared. Sitting behind the tall stacks of beer, awaiting his fate, the person whose face kept coming back to him, whose refusals tormented him, who he blamed more than anyone on earth, was his mother.

5. The Raid.

The officers stormed the pub and found a cellar with its door open. As they lowered their heads to walk through the tunnel into the cellar, they were greeted by a scene of utter carnage. Blood spattered the walls; body parts lay on the floor.

'No heads, just limbs!' the armed policeman shouted.

'I can see that, man,' his commanding officer replied.

Two Hours later. The Home Office
Sir Michael Frobisher, The Home Secretary, Reginald Maudling, Commander Cumberland and MI5 met at the Home Office.

'We've received a statement from The IRA with their usual codes. I will read it to you: "*We came extremely close to blowing up the Cabinet. Next time we will not fail*".'

6. Just Another Ambulance.
Behind the beer stacks, sitting on the wooden floor. Calm seemed to have descended on the building. No screaming, shooting or explosions. Did this mean his ordeal was over? Still shaking, chilled to the bone with fear, he was thinking about the possibilities when he heard the door being unlocked. Were the evil people coming? Who would appear when the door opened? His relief was total as he saw a policewoman, walking slowly towards him. Then he heard the softest of voices.

'You're safe now, Daniel, you can come out'. He ran to the policewoman.

'We're here to look after you, Daniel, no harm will come to you.'

With a voice he didn't recognise, so dry and quiet, he asked, 'Have the evil people gone?'

'They've gone, Daniel.'

Shaking and hardly able to walk, he was led gently downstairs and through the pub. How was Barrie? He had no idea. He was led by the policewoman into a waiting ambulance. The scene outside the pub resembled a film set. Blue flashing lights everywhere, police cars, ambulances, police cordons.   Once inside the ambulance, he sat on the bench, wrapped a blanket around him, and saw a policewoman and an ambulanceman.

'You're safe, Daniel,' the policewoman said gently.

He didn't seem able to collect his thoughts or talk. His mind ranged from the meeting he'd missed at Leo Baeck college; what did Naomi's family think about his disappearance? Did his parents know? A strange feeling of calming blue descended upon him, his frenzied thoughts changed to feelings of thankfulness, and the blanket was warming and soothing.

'We're taking you to hospital just to check you over, and then, and only when you're definitely ready, Sergeant Louise would like to talk to you about what's just happened.'

'If you understand what I've just said, just nod your head.'

He did.

Passers-by just saw another ambulance; sirens blaring, lights flashing, heading towards St Mary's Hospital in Paddington.

Later that evening, his speech returned, and he asked to make a phone call.

The policewoman said that would be fine, and then he answered a few questions about the people who'd kept him captive the last few days.

He wasn't sure how helpful he'd been. He asked if he could take a train to Brighton.

Sergeant Louise smiled at him.

'Daniel, you're not taking a train to anywhere. We'll drive you to Brighton as soon as you're well enough to travel.'

Chapter Thirty-Four

1. He's Free

Naomi had been sitting next to the phone, and she picked it up immediately

'I'm free. They're keeping me in hospital overnight.' Naomi jumped up, screaming with joy, as she ran into her mother's arms.

'He's free!' Naomi almost sang the words. It was as if a river had just reached a waterfall for the first time, and torrents of exuberance burst forth.

2. News about your son

Howard and Adrienne had remained at home since the call with the Prime Minister.

At 3 pm. their direct line rang. It was Sir Robert Davidson.

'We have news about your son. He's safe. Special Branch released him this afternoon and we're taking him to Sussex.'

Adrienne and Howard flew into each other's arms with unbridled joy. Howard called Peter and Tania in Hove, and it was agreed they should await Daniel's return together.

3. No blame attaches.

Howard and Adrienne passed the twin pillars saying 'Brighton' so beloved of holidaymakers, and then there was the dual carriageway bearing multiple signs with numbers that nobody seemed able to explain. Peter had given them directions, and soon Howard headed up the hill towards the windmill, and before long, he turned off the affluent Woodland Drive into Hill Brow.

Adrienne and Howard walked down the steep slope of the garden path and rang the doorbell. Peter greeted them, shook both their hands, and invited them in. Tanya and Naomi were sitting at the breakfast bar. Naomi's joy was total; it was wonderful to see.

Tanya looked at Adrienne. This was the woman, these were the parents, who ignored their son's pleas. Adrienne looked coiffured, as if her hair had just been styled, her make-up perfect. How could she think of such things when her son had been missing? She couldn't like them, but Tanya was generous, and despite everything, she allowed for the possibility that she might feel differently towards Adrienne one day.

'We still don't know what happened,' Peter said. 'We hope Daniel can shed some light on it, about why Eleanor and Barrie have disappeared. But for now, we're just relieved.'

After the shared celebration at Daniel's safety, there was an awkward silence.

Peter said, 'It seems to me we have two choices. We can talk about nothing and hedge around the real conversation, or we can take it head on and really learn about each other.'

Although the choice was an obvious one, the other tea takers were all slightly shocked in their own way by Peter's blunt description of the dilemma.

Adrienne looked at Peter across the table.

'I think we should move gently forward, provided we all feel safe,' he said.

'Did you always want Daniel to go to boarding school?' Peter asked.

'Well,' Howard said, 'when we first met, we talked about education, and how we both believed in excellence, and we'd agreed on private education quite early on. Then when he was about eleven, Daniel asked if he could board at his prep school'.

'Why'd you think he did that?' Tanya asked. 'Seems strange, a boy asking to live away from home.'

It was clear to Adrienne and Howard that Tanya held strong, preconceived notions.

'Before I answer that,' Adrienne said, 'can I say that we obviously understand that, to you, all these events lead back to us. It would be strange if you didn't think we'd neglected our duty as parents and had too little regard for Daniel's unhappiness. If we try to put that right in the centre of the table it'll make things easier, I think.'

Adrienne was using international negotiating skills and adapting them for the conversation in the Hove garden. Give voice to the concerns of the other party, admit nothing, concede nothing, but obtain agreement about obvious concerns.

It was clear that Tanya and Peter were taken aback by what they saw as her honest and frank appraisal of the situation.

Adrienne continued. 'Now to address your specific question … we assumed with so many of his friends boarding, he wanted to feel part of the group,' Adrienne said, 'but I'm going to be honest, I was just so busy working, I didn't have much time to analyse Daniel's decision.'

Howard had his back to a wall with a fading clematis. 'We're not going to understand everything this afternoon, but Peter was right: It's much better to start the conversation.'

Everyone agreed: Howard and Adrienne should not be at the house when Daniel arrived.

4. *Daniel returns to his family*

The unmarked police car stopped at their house. Daniel got out and walked down some steps to the front door. Before he could ring a bell, it was opened, and Naomi was hugging him and crying on his shoulder.

'Thank God, you're safe, just thank God.'

He walked into the kitchen where Peter and Tanya hugged him, and he sat at the breakfast bar with them. Tanya was full of questions.

'Where were you taken? Who by? Did they hurt you?'

Peter intervened.

'Questions are for later. Give the boy some chicken soup in a mug and leave them alone.'

This was the last thing Tanya wanted to do, but she understood.

Later they were alone in Naomi's bedroom.

She had to tell him. Naomi couldn't hide it anymore.

'Daniel, there's something you have to know, and I've only just heard about it.' She looked at his face, into his eyes.

'Barrie's dead, Daniel. He's dead.'

Daniel sat quietly on her bed. He put his face in his hands, and he sobbed.

'Was he caught up in crossfire?'

'Yes, he was.'

'But couldn't they identify him?'

'I just don't know. But he's gone.'

Barrie had been responsible for so much, good and bad. And he was gone. Daniel was overwhelmed with sadness. Grief would come later, but in that bedroom was the powerful distressing sadness that consumed a person when they wished they hadn't heard, wished they could unhear something so final and over.

Naomi loved the lying together, the safety and the closeness, knowing that this was her man, and his sadness was hers too. She sensed she was the only woman in his life now. Neither of them had uttered the name 'Eleanor' but they knew. Naomi thought Daniel would want to pray, and she would pray with him.

He sat up and took Naomi's hand.

'Can you get me a kippah?'

Naomi left the room for a short while and returned. Daniel covered his head and Naomi handed him the *Reform Prayer Book*. There was no point asking any of the others to join them. This was their loss, and they would ask for God's comfort together.

Daniel read.

'Merciful father, be with us as we gather in this house and think of our dear Barrie who has gone forward to life everlasting. We remember all his goodness. May his memory be a blessing.

We thank you for all that was gentle and noble in his life.

In your light we see beyond the frontiers of death to the life that has no end. We shall come together in a home where we shall never part, surrounded by your presence. Amen.'

They stood together, drowning in the sorrow of Barrie's loss, swimming in the love they felt for each other, and yearning for the time when drama would end, and they could just live: to life. L'Chaim.

Daniel returned to the lounge.

'I presume you know about Barrie.'

'Yes, we know. We're so sorry, Daniel, we really are.'

Later, Naomi and Daniel sat in the lounge quietly.

'There's something else I have to tell you: Dad and I met your parents at their home.'

'How did that happen?'

Naomi related the whole story. Daniel's mind was awash with

so many conflicting emotions: the grief of bereavement, the joy of reunion and now 'the whole parent thing', as he described it to himself.

'I need to put that one on the shelf for now,' he told Naomi.

'Of course. But it can't stay there forever, Daniel, and my parents liked them a lot.'

Daniel laughed, without humour. 'Superficially, they're charming. It's the rest that's the problem.'

5. *Later that week*
It had been agreed that Daniel would live at Naomi's house for now.

'Treat our home as your home,' Tanya said. 'Rest while you decide what you're doing next.'

'I'm going to meet Rabbi Leigh and Rabbi Friedlander,' Daniel said.

'Great, have you decided?' Naomi asked.

'I'm going to enrol at Leo Baeck.

About my parents: I blame my mother more than my father.'

Naomi frowned. 'Doesn't seem fair. Surely they made joint decisions'

'I'm talking to you, just you, I'm telling you how I feel. There's no logic or rational thinking here. I'm analysing myself and I know, I blame my mother more.'

'Good bit of self-awareness then. Now you know you have no reason for blaming your mother more, you can work on it.'

6. *Love thy Mother and thy Father*
Peter was at work, and Tanya had gone out. Naomi was in London at an interview. Daniel was sitting on a bar stool in the kitchen at

Hill Brow. He was waiting for his parents to arrive and couldn't work out how he felt. He didn't know if he would have chosen to meet them. He'd been swept into it like an insect under a rug.

Time and again he came back to the disparity between them from his point of view; and did any other point of view matter?

His father wasn't blameless, but he had stopped work to spend time with Daniel, taken him to nursery school. And then there was just the prejudice: the illogical, irrational fact that he had a level of animosity towards his mother that he did not hold against his father. Naomi could point out the lack of justice in his feelings, but what justice had there been in the Fairmead cloakrooms, in the study on his own, in Oakingham on lonely, desolate Sundays?

None.

The doorbell interrupted his intemperate thoughts.

He walked from the kitchen to the front door and opened it.

'Come in,' he heard himself say.

His mother was dressed as if she was attending a conference. Maybe she wished she was at a seminar, instead of being here; maybe she was going to rush off to one, after their chat.

They appeared to have a preprepared script, a seminar paper, perhaps.

'Daniel, we're so, so, sorry, sorry for everything. And we've heard that Barrie died,' Adrienne said.

'You don't know anything about Barrie,' Daniel said, 'so there's no need for you to be sorry about that.'

At this point, a thought entered Daniel's mind. 'What would his religion have him do?' What would the Psalmists say?' The thought sank in a sea of anger.

'We just want to be back in your life again,' Adrienne said.

He sensed desperation from someone unused to the sentiment.

'We know it'll take time,' Howard said, 'but we want to start the journey, and rebuild our family.'

It seemed a reasonable request in all the circumstances. Why should they not have a second chance? They'd been cut off from their son for so many years. Wasn't that punishment enough? Wasn't this the time for mercy?

'I want to know why you refused to take me away from that hell-hole of a school' he said.

Adrienne apparently thought it was time for her international relations skills. 'It's complex and it will take time. We're happy to have the discussion, but it's not going to be a knee-jerk response to a question posed in anger.'

'Maybe I can help then,' Daniel said. 'Taking me away from Oakingham would have been inconvenient in every way. My happiness was sacrificed for your career.'

Howard tried to intervene, 'That's not...'

Now they appeared to be deviating from their script at last.

'You're right,' Adrienne said. 'You're absolutely right, Daniel. What you say is the truth and it can't be denied, so I'm not going to try.'

Daniel was shocked. He hadn't expected that.

'The problem is, I don't forgive you for it. I should. My religion, which means so much to me, tells me I should. Naomi certainly thinks the time for forgiveness has arrived. You've been honest, so I'm going to be honest too. I don't forgive you. And the worst of it is, I'm a psychology student, so I know that the acid of anger corrodes the angry.'

'Oh, we've suffered plenty,' Howard said. 'And what's your religion worth if you can't forgive your parents, who've apologised and been so brutally honest?'

'What's it worth indeed?' Daniel said. 'We've put stuff on the table. We don't have a statement to give the BBC and there's no peace treaty to celebrate. Still, I suppose you could call this 'talks about talks.''

The sarcasm was transparent. The searing anger pierced their heart like a bullet; it didn't require diplomacy skills to see that.

They saw themselves out.

Daniel offered Naomi and her parents an edited version of the meeting with his parents. Naomi would have been beyond furious if she'd known the truth, and Daniel knew it. His parents were hardly going to reveal much, so Daniel felt safe in his untruth with one exception: he was sure The Almighty would judge him harshly, and that mattered to Daniel a great deal.

Nobody knew Eleanor's whereabouts. She had disappeared.

Chapter Thirty-Five

An attempt at peace. August 1973

The unflappable Robert Davidson, the PM's Principal Private Secretary, sat across the desk from the Prime Minister.

The PM said, 'It's a risky strategy admittedly, but after the recent mainland bomb attempt, I'd like to have another crack at an Irish settlement.'

Davidson's equanimity was under considerable strain.

'May I put it to you–?'

Heath interrupted. 'You don't need to. We're about to face one of the most difficult industrial-relations disputes since the General Strike of 1926 and your PM is looking for a diversion in the riskiest manner possible. Was that roughly what you were thinking?'

'Yes, Prime Minister.'

'One of my trusted external advisers tells me the IRA may be ready to talk, and possibly consider a ceasefire. I'd like to convene a conference. Will you get the Northern Ireland boys in here, please?'

Davidson was aghast. Was this really the time for such an attempt? As he was about to call Willie Whitelaw, The Secretary of State for Northern Ireland, he received a call from Future World. The caller told him that Adrienne Goldberg wanted to speak to him. Davidson had enormous respect for Adrienne, and after hearing about Heath's conference proposal, he was looking forward to some common sense.

'Good afternoon, Adrienne, nice to hear from you. How's Daniel?'

'Daniel is progressing well, thank you, Robert. The Prime Minister has asked me to be the chief mediator for his conference proposal. I've accepted it, though I'm quite certain I'll regret it.'

'I rather thought his proposals were, how shall I put it, *embryonic*.'

'Far from it, Sir Robert. We have a pretty star- studded line up. I'm calling to apologise for the breach of protocol. You should have been told earlier. I wanted you to know earlier, but to use Civil Service parlance, we are where we are.'

'Adrienne, I've been in this job far too long to be miffed about protocol. If there's to be a conference, let's do our level best to make it work.'

'I knew you'd say that. McGuiness and Twomey have agreed to attend.'

Davidson was astonished. The two leading commanders of the Provisional IRA had taken part in secret talks the previous year, at Cheyne Walk in London, which had achieved nothing.

'They want another bite at the cherry?' Davidson asked.

'There must be a major reason,' Adrienne said. 'They wouldn't come straight back to us after talks that ended so disastrously, unless ...'

'Unless what?'

'Sir Robert, we just don't know, but we certainly intend to find out. And then there's the even stranger news. When Paisley learned the IRA command were coming, he said he'd come too, and he'd bring someone we don't know.'

'There's logic to Paisley's view. If you're talking to the senior people, you don't need to sell the result higher up the chain. And who's this other person?'

'Gusty McClelland. Apparently a leader in the UVF.'

'You realise what a huge risk this is? These are massively volatile people, with armies that could cause mayhem. Is that what we really want to be doing right now?'

Adrienne's reply was emphatic 'Yes, Sir Robert. It's exactly what we need to be doing right now!'

Bentley Priory, Stanmore Middlesex
Only a military base could afford sufficient security for the risks posed by the attendees. Bentley Priory, Fighter Command HQ during the Battle of Britain, had space for helicopter landings. It was a busy RAF base with security to match.

Adrienne was debriefing the PM, Sir Robert Davidson, and Reginald Maudling. Her team at the talks had included the Northern Ireland Secretary, Willie Whitelaw, Peter Carrington, and, by telephone, her old friend Henry Kissinger.

They were sitting in a lounge in Downing Street. The heavy curtains were drawn, and the room was lit by lamps reminiscent of Harley Street waiting rooms.

'It's going too well. The IRA are going to spring something on us at the last minute. Their *no list* is falling like dominoes. I'm worried.'

'So, if it wasn't going well, you'd be worried, but it *is* going well and you're still worried!' Heath said.

'It's the manner of the *well* that worries me. I'm wondering what their real reason was for agreeing to attend.'

Willie Whitelaw nodded. 'Can we look at the possible options they're looking for?'

'Actually, I'm mainly concerned about their disinterest in the powers being offered to the proposed new all-Irish Council. That should be their big prize, but every time Paisley demands another unionist safeguard, they look disinterested!'

'I agree,' said Carrington. 'They're not here to negotiate. I doubt they'll sign anything.'

Heath, who had been hoping for some optimistic news in the midst of the dark conflict against the miners, looked downcast.

Suddenly he appeared more alert. 'If they're playing us, Adrienne, what do you think they really want?'

'That's what I've been putting my mind to. I've spoken to Henry and McGeorge. The consensus is they're banking on you being desperate for an agreement, so they'll adopt a common tactic: demand something enormous at the very end. But there's something else troubling me here.'

The room was quiet as Adrienne explained her concerns. Each person around the table was relieved to have her expertise, and anxious as to where her analysis might lead.

'In the sessions where they're separated from the Unionists, they bring the conversation round to the failed bomb plot. But the IRA never talk about their own failures, only their strengths.'

'What did they say about it?' asked Heath.

'Seamus Twomey, of all people, the least likely to talk about defeat, said something like, 'The dice are loaded in the mainland war.'

Maudling asked: 'What do you make of that?'

Adrienne was quick in her response. 'They think we've got an informer in their mainland Active Service Unit.'

The meeting ended. Adrienne was exhausted. Daniel and Naomi were having supper at Regent's Park with Howard, and she wished she could be there.

Meanwhile, there was one man above all, whom she trusted

to help through these troubled waters. They had worked together before, and she was as certain as she could be that he would help now. Julian Penrose worked with Phoebe Gilbert in MI5, and Adrienne had befriended both. She called Julian from a call box in Westminster.

'Julian, it's Adrienne.'

'Don't you ever relax?'

'Look, Julian, I need to speak to you. Could we meet in Stein's Salt Beef?'

She knew he couldn't resist some salt beef and latkes, and she was the only person who ever took him to Stein's.

'On my way,' he said.

Kosher cafes were rare in central London, but they were useful. Adrienne had never seen a diplomat or a mandarin at Stein's.

If she wanted to discover something about MI6, the best people to speak to were MI5. They were jealous rivals and personal vendettas were not unknown. Adrienne knew one secret about Julian, and it wasn't available as a bargaining chip. He was a homosexual in a world where it was still stigmatised and career-threatening. Julian had trusted her enough to tell her, though she'd suspected it for some time.

Adrienne began the conversation. 'Thanks for coming, I'll get straight to it. Are Six running an informer in the IRA on the mainland?'

A few days later Julian Penrose called Adrienne.

'I've pulled her file and copied it. You owe me for this.'

'Thanks, Julian, you won't be sorry,' Adrienne replied.

Later, Adrienne sat in her empty lounge and read the file.

MI5 File 1963 (available for wider reading: 1999)

	Reference LV 2/4296/fem
	Dr Eleanor KENNEDY and Dr Michael O'GORMAN Both British Description: Dr Eleanor KENNEDY is, by her own description a pacifist feminist, seeking equality of opportunity for women. She has informed MI5 about concerns she has about a SUBJECT in whom we have had an interest for some months. By assisting us with information about Dr O'GORMAN, and following her mother's path as a patriotic informant, it seems likely that Dr Eleanor KENNEDY could be of considerable help to MI5 and MI6. Dr O'GORMAN is of considerable concern to MI5 and MI6. He has met with IRA Chief of Staff, Cathal Goulding on a number of occasions; he openly advocates the overthrow of Capitalist society, and he discusses what he calls 'Revolutionary Appropriation' whereby individuals or groups join an activist group and seek to use its infrastructure and knowledge base towards an alternative aim. It is clearly possible that Dr O'Gorman may seek to use the IRA so that it turns its attention to the overthrow of regimes which he finds abhorrent, such as that which currently pertains in the UK mainland. Dr O'GORMAN will require surveillance for an unlimited period and consideration could be given to taking him into custody if he travels to Ulster, using the lower arrest thresholds that pertain there.
Date:	1960 Apr 01– 1990 Jan 05
Held by:	Undisclosed
Former reference in its original department:	FJ / 3457/ Intel

Legal status:	Top Secret
	Retained Until 2005
	28 September 2005

Downing Street, The next day

Adrienne was worried. Howard had disappeared. She just hoped it was some art jaunt. She was pretty sure she'd convinced him to leave Eleanor alone, but she just wished he would phone.

She was listening to the Head of Britain's Homeland Security Service talk. Julian Penrose had told her what she'd been suspecting for some time. Eleanor was an MI5 informer who'd warned MI5 about the Whitehall bomb, and men carrying out MI5 orders had rescued Daniel from the North London Tavern cellar before the police arrived. The woman who'd taken her son into her care knew she was bringing Daniel into a dangerous house. How could she have done it?

Frobisher outlined his plan.

'They think we've got a mole, so let's give them one. We think Sean O'Leary will do the job nicely. He's a middle manager in the Provos. We can conjure up supposed lines of communication.'

Later, at her Regent's Park Home, as the evening drew in, Adrienne looked out of her window at the streetlamps. Her husband was missing. She wondered about Eleanor's journey. When did she begin her work for MI5? What stage had she reached when a boy of 15 started visiting her cottage? What could have been her mindset, to offer safety to her son, when she was in the most dangerous situation imaginable, married to a man who'd already been contacted by the IRA? She and Social Services had stopped them seeing their son for all those years.

Questions abounded; answers were scarce.

The IRA must have Eleanor on their list of suspects, knowing Barrie was part of a betrayed plot. What use would she now be to MI5 or MI6? Why not serve her up on a plate to the IRA rather than an IRA activist who'd never informed in his life? Even she realised the nonsense within that train of thought.

Was she capable of any independent, rigorous analysis? No, of course she wasn't. MI5 were prepared to do whatever was necessary to protect their informer, and Eleanor was clearly in real danger. The IRA would be searching for Eleanor across the land, and the Intel services protected their own. As she left her home she wondered, *Where on earth is Howard*?

Chapter Thirty-Six

The Cricket Pitch, The Upper, Oakingham School. Last week of August 1973

Before Daniel began his preparation for rabbinate studies, he decided to travel from Sussex to revisit his Golgotha.

As he walked through the empty colonnade, where the children had yet to return to school, the echoes of his loneliness and desperation called out to him. The classroom block with its windows, where his imagination had run riot. De Lacy's mocking laughter and the fear of the football boot. He walked towards the Buttery, and the outside toilets, now apparently, and thankfully, out of use, and he saw the music room where he had listened to Leonard Cohen. Then, with a mixture of reluctance and determination, he set off up the hill towards Fairmead, past the graveyard. As he reached the top of the hill, he crossed the road, and there was the sign that said, 'THE UPPER'. The notice highlighted a personal dilemma. He had begun to see the attack that he had suffered as his own microcosmic holocaust. He'd never mentioned this to anyone other than Rabbi Levy, and in many ways, he felt ashamed by the comparison. He hadn't been attacked by Alsatian dogs as he was pushed off a train into a blizzard-driven railway siding. He hadn't seen his parents divided into two queues or had his head shaven. He hadn't been starved or tattooed with a number. And yet, Daniel reflected as he walked over the muddy car park onto the field itself, he couldn't choose the resonances in his life. However sacrilegious the comparison might be, privately the sign on the Upper put him in mind of the sign at Auschwitz: *Arbeit macht frei.*

The sun was shining as he walked. The fierce and portentous storm that had afflicted him as he'd trudged towards the hut all those years ago had been replaced by a beautiful autumn afternoon. There were no sports being played, and other than a few staff assembling football and hockey nets, he was alone.

The all-weather hockey pitch had been completed. There was no hut, and Barrie wouldn't greet him with smiling sarcasm. The pain of Barrie's death returned to him as he walked to the back of the field. Arriving at the place that had haunted him for so long, he had to admit to some anti-climax, some disappointment. It was, after all, just a field. There were no mounds of sand, no pipes and no Dermot with his newspaper in his pocket. As he turned and faced the field on which he'd just walked, he saw the spire of the chapel, clouds flying by, and he wondered why he'd come all this way.

He sat on the grass, and he tried to imagine De Lacy and Williams stripping him over the ditch. Nothing came to him. Then he thought about De Lacy. There had been no apology, and probably no remorse.

And then, as a breeze blew the buttercups on The Upper, and diesel smells wafted from a lawnmower, his thoughts turned in a different direction. Like the removal of a cataract, he achieved a new emotional clarity. The pain he felt had its origin not in the humiliation of his assault. He felt his serenity drain away as his stomach tightened, his mouth dried, and he knew he'd travelled to the wrong place. The answers to his questions didn't lie in Oakingham.

His anger continued to rise as he reflected upon the two women who'd failed in their attempts to be the mother figure in his life. There was clearly no point gazing out at a Rutland playing field, thinking about the De Lacys. He walked back to the gate, wondering how to reconcile his clarified thoughts with the upcoming days of penitence.

Belgravia, London

Naomi had started her commute towards one of the most elegant and prestigious embassies in London. The Spanish embassy in Belgravia was housed in a Stucco, detached house designed by Henry E Kendal around 1840. Naomi had learned this and other facts in readiness for her interview. One of the greatest thrills of her life had been the personal call from a senior consul in the embassy.

Speaking in Spanish he had said, 'Naomi, we're so delighted to offer you this role at the embassy. Your excitement about Spain's future under King Juan Carlos, and your knowledge of our country made you shine like the European Cup in Real Madrid's store cupboard!'

As she walked through the door, her excitement was tangible. The country whose culture she had studied for years had now given her an opportunity to play her part in furthering Spanish–UK relationships. And what an exciting time! Britain in the Common Market, and democracy infusing new life into Spain! The job might have been tailor-made for her.

As she walked towards the tube station at Pimlico, she had another reason to be excited. She thought back to the evening when Daniel had returned from Oakingham, and she'd met him at Brighton station as the autumn light was fading.

They took the bus and walked down Church Road towards Palmeira Square. The shops were closed or closing, and after-work drinkers were standing outside the pubs. He'd begun to tell her some of the thoughts and emotions of the day, and then, as they arrived at the floral clock, he'd turned to her, and gone down on one knee.

'My darling Naomi, I love you with all my heart. Will you marry me?'

She hadn't expected it that night, and Hove wasn't necessarily the setting of her dreams, but she had been awash with joy at the proposal and smiled down at him.

'I can't hug you down there! Of course, I'll marry you, Daniel.' And in the middle of Hove the newly engaged couple kissed and hugged.

They took a bus to Hill Brow and told Tanya and Peter. Soon the champagne was flowing, there were hugs, kisses and *mazel tovs*. Neighbours appeared from nowhere and, Daniel being Daniel, there was just a little time for solemn reflection and thanks to God.

After her first day at the embassy, Naomi took the Tube to Regent's Park. She was meeting Daniel at his parent's house, so they could tell them their news.

Adrienne answered the door.

'I've no idea where your father is, Daniel, but both of you come in!'

Adrienne opened the door to Daniel and Naomi. 'We have some news. We've just got engaged!'

'Oh, *mazel tov*! I'm so thrilled, that's such wonderful news. Why didn't you tell me you were coming? I have to go to a meeting. Make yourselves comfortable, I'll not be long, then we can have a celebratory drink.'

When she left Daniel said, 'Of course she has to go to a meeting. Silly of me!'

On a sideboard at the back of the lounge, was a file. Daniel recognised his mother's handwriting on the cover. He opened the file, and its contents astonished him. His mother had certainly been busy researching Eleanor. There appeared to be a copy of an MI5 File.

'What's that you're looking at, darling?' asked Naomi.

'It's my mother's preparation for a conference,' he lied.

MI5 Headquarters, London

Daniel was safe and engaged to Naomi. Howard had still not made contact. Adrienne gratefully returned to work. She had a target, and a determination to attain it. The first, and most important part was the meeting she had arranged that afternoon with Michael Frobisher, DG of MI5.

His desk was covered in the statutory red leather, but they sat face to face in front of it. Teacups were arranged on a table, with some shortbread biscuits.

'I'm struggling,' Adrienne said.

'Anyone would be,' Frobisher said, 'but thankfully Daniel's free.'

'I'm struggling with the idea that you have known all this time that your IRA sleeper was supposedly safeguarding my son, when she was doing no such thing.' She was trying hard not to cry, but her face was changing shape in the effort, and her eyes were welling up. 'How could you do that?'

Frobisher felt his cleanshaven chin. He sat back, deep in thought. Then trying unsuccessfully not to sound patronising, yet still playing the kind uncle, he mused out loud.

'The operation started long before Daniel came on the scene.

Eleanor had been with Barrie since the early 1960s, after he'd been contacted by the IRA.'

'Quite,' Adrienne interrupted. 'Many years before Daniel went to live with them, you knew she was an operative, watching her husband. The most sinister set-up you can think of, and then came Daniel. Maybe take me from there.'

Frobisher leant forward. 'Of course, we knew nothing about the first contacts, the chats in the school hut or the days he cycled out to the Empingham cottage. We knew none of that. It was only after the attack on the cricket pitch, and the joined-up writing came from the strangest source.'

'Do tell me,' Adrienne said full of scepticism and sarcasm.

'The Israeli Ambassador, I forget her name, made enquiries after you met with her. Apparently, Daniel had written to her when he was at school. Anyway, she asked the Foreign Office if they knew anything about Daniel leaving the country, which they didn't, but Government departments were asked to locate Daniel if they could. Health knew he'd been in hospital at Leicester and that led us to Social Services.

Richard Crossman was secretary of State at Social Services, and he told the Home Office that Daniel had become friendly with this family, and finally the pieces came together.

It gave us a dilemma but I'm going to tell you the uncomfortable truth. Intelligence is about dilemmas every day, but it's mainly about protecting the country. The Neasden Three who'd contacted Barrie were some of the most vicious terrorists we've ever faced. The country was in terrible danger. Whether Daniel Goldberg was put at risk, or Adrienne Goldberg denied the truth, was of little interest to us, and it had to be. And by God how right we were! Eleanor proved to be a woman of extraordinary courage.

She was selfless in defending the country she loved, even though her personal relationships were destroyed in the process.'

Adrienne knew when she was beaten. It was all true, every word.

'I'd like to meet her, if that could be arranged.'

'All depends really on whether she wants to meet you and if we can arrange it without jeopardising her safety. She's in terrible danger right now.'

Adrienne left the building feeling despondent. She couldn't disagree with what Frobisher had said.

Chapter Thirty-Seven

Adrienne sat, reading a book, waiting for Eleanor to join her.

In the days leading up to this meeting, she'd thought about how she should handle it. So much for the great international diplomat! She told herself: 'Be clear about the required outcome'. What did she want from Eleanor?

Simon Holmes, at MI5 had called Eleanor a few days ago asked her how she'd feel about meeting Adrienne.

'If that woman wants to meet me, then send her down the road. Providing my security isn't compromised, it'll give me a chance to meet the woman who forgot to love her son.'

'I suspect you'll find it rather more complicated than that,' Holmes had said.

'I rather think I will, Simon. Life's had a complicated turn for a while now, as you may know! And what exactly should I tell this woman?'

'They said you should just be yourself, tell her anything you like. She knows it all anyway. That's all.'

As she sat in her new cottage, Eleanor thought about Adrienne. Apart from the official briefing, she knew remarkably little about her. She'd left Daniel at the school he hated and then refused to take him away. She advised the Foreign Office, or something similar. It seemed that she might have lost her husband too.

Eleanor was driven through the countryside in an unmarked bullet-proof car. Her car stopped in a dusty isolated road. A man opened her door and whisked her into a cottage, with no time to feel the autumn breeze on her face.

Once inside, Eleanor was shown into a small rustic lounge, and there, seated on a settee was Adrienne.

Adrienne thought Eleanor looked like an average suburban woman, queuing to pay in John Lewis. Her eyes were sad, her hair too long for her age. How had this woman caused such mayhem?

Eleanor had seen a picture of Adrienne, but she looked softer than she'd expected, but then her husband had gone AWOL, her child had escaped death by a whisker, and she was now facing the woman who'd watched her son grow from teenager to graduate.

'I'm glad we're meeting,' Adrienne said.

Eleanor noticed she hadn't said, 'It's nice to meet you', but that was hardly surprising.

'I've often wondered about Daniel's mother,' Eleanor said, surprising herself with the warmth of her voice, the lack of animosity.

'Wondered how I kept him at a school he didn't like, gave him too little attention?'

Eleanor was a little taken back by the honesty, the frankness, but it hadn't been said in an argumentative way. Far from it. It had been a gentle question.

'Yes,' said Eleanor. 'But I've also had other thoughts too.'

'I'd like to hear them,' Adrienne said.

'Well, firstly, can I say, we both know that most boys at boarding school don't end up naked over a ditch. Many people were to blame for that. I've mainly wondered about two things, I suppose.'

She paused. The room was silent.

'When he called you from that call box every Sunday, how did you ignore him? That's the first thing. But then I can't imagine how you must have felt for all those years when you didn't know where Daniel was, and you weren't in contact.'

'The second part is easier,' Adrienne said. 'It was a continuous nightmare. I thought about Daniel at work, on the way home, in the middle of the night … constantly.

As to the first part: I didn't ignore him. I heard what he said.' She paused. 'Maybe we've reached a stage where there's no point hiding. We've both made mistakes. We might as well be totally honest.'

'I agree with that,' Eleanor said.

'Well, I didn't ignore him,' she repeated. 'I didn't really know what to do.'

'Why not send him to another school?'

'I can see that seems simple now, but it wasn't. We didn't believe in quitting, and we didn't want our son to be a quitter either. It would've been a big thing to leave a school, and Howard was dead against it too. But there was something else: I've never discussed this with anyone. Daniel told me you had a miscarriage. You'd had one before you first met him. You really wanted a child.'

'That's true,' Eleanor said.

'Well, when I first heard I was pregnant with Daniel, I wasn't happy at all. My career was just taking off, I had so many plans, and having a child certainly wasn't one of them. Even though Howard was doing more of the childcare by the time Daniel went to Oakingham, my son was in a place where he was learning, supposedly being looked after, and where I could get on with my life. I know how bad that sounds, but you know we don't always make unselfish decisions.'

'This isn't going at all how I thought it would,' Eleanor said.

'You thought I'd come here and have a go at you for putting Daniel at risk, and then try to justify all my decisions, and we'd have a huge argument.'

'Something like that,' Eleanor said. 'Sitting opposite a woman who should hate me for so many reasons, I feel safer than I've felt for a while.'

Eleanor allowed her sadness to show. 'I've lost my husband, you've no idea where your husband is. We both serve the country in different ways, and we both love Daniel.'

'I've got questions too,' Adrienne said. 'When Daniel came out to you those afternoons from school, did he–?'

'Replace the child I lost?' Eleanor interjected. 'In a crass kind of male way, I think Barrie hoped that Daniel might take my mind off my miscarriage. He was getting pretty fed up with my depression. But no, not at all. I liked your son. I felt sorry for his unhappiness, and yes, we did have some kind of shared sorrow. Let's put it like this: your son had more empathy for me than Barrie managed. Barrie was trying, but truthfully, he didn't really get it. Your fifteen-year-old son seemed to understand my sorrow. But when he turned up at my door, traumatised ... well, that was different.'

'But when Daniel came to you, how much did you already know about Barrie? No, I'm going to rephrase that. I know you knew, they've told me. So, why did you take Daniel in?'

'A traumatised boy arrives at your door. A boy you've met and felt some empathy for. Would you turn him away? Later, when he recovered, it became more complicated. When he was a victim, needing my love and care, I could justify it all to myself. Truth is, I saw him as a victim long after he'd recovered. I just didn't want him to leave. He'd become the joy in my life, and I ignored Barrie's IRA contacts until it was too late. That's the truth.'

'It's so rare to actually hear somebody tell the truth!'

Eleanor sighed. 'They don't want anyone knowing where I am. I'm pretty high on the IRA wanted list and apparently MI5 have got other uses for me.'

'I hope we meet again,' Adrienne said.

'Likewise; and I hope you have news of your husband.'

Chapter Thirty-Eight

3 September 1973

Adrienne was having dinner In White's Club in St James's as the guest of Brigadier Sir James Ogilvy-Hughes KCMG MC OBE. She'd known 'Jimmy' since she was a teenager and in truth, they were each other's guilty secrets. They'd never crossed a line, never had an affair or even kissed. But they'd always known they were attracted to each other. *It's in the eyes,* Adrienne mused. *We look at each other frankly, we don't avert our gaze, and there aren't any pauses. We can't wait to meet and catch up with all the news and, to be honest, just to be with each other.*

Jimmy was married, not as happily as Adrienne had been, and they'd been out as a four many times. Lady Felicity was rather boring; she talked about fine china in Brook Street shops and lacked humour or spark.

'You said you wanted a favour,' the Brigadier said, as he wiped his face with the linen napkin.

'I've certainly not forgotten or forgiven that bastard Richard de Lacy.'

'I should hope not!' Jimmy said, swallowing some excellent steak and kidney pudding.

She paused. 'Richard de Lacy is awaiting court martial for those appalling murders in Ballysluthra.'

'Yes, I asked to see the papers. He'll get what he deserves.'

'Actually, I'm not convinced he will, if you think prison's enough for that scum.'

'What've you got in mind?' Jimmy asked, with half a glint in his eye.

'I gather he's universally hated in Ulster too. His fellow soldiers, officers, commanders all detest him. You probably don't know, but I've been involved in some very difficult talks with IRA leaders, just to see if they can go somewhere.'

'Can they?'

'That's for another day, Jimmy. The point is, I've been thinking that a show of faith wouldn't go down badly.'

'Now I am intrigued!' said Jimmy, leaning forward, and trying not to reach out for Adrienne's hands.

The peace talks resumed but progress was painfully slow. At the end of one session, Adrienne told MacStioffan and Twomey she'd like to meet them at their secure quarters that evening.

Later that evening, Adrienne was waved through each layer of security, and arrived in the makeshift bar at the erstwhile aircraft hangar.

Macstioffan and Twomey drank Guinness, and Adrienne drank water.

'Ballysluthra,' she said.

'What about it?' Macstioffan asked.

'What do you want more than anything?'

'What we always want: justice. Not Brit justice, our justice.'

'Well, just as an act of good faith...'

'The first since the Famine you mean?'

She ignored the jibe.

'I can tell you that Richard de Lacy will be walking down the road near his barracks tomorrow at 17.15 hours.'

In the days that followed, the press was agreed on one thing: it was no coincidence that De Lacy had escaped and then immediately been kidnapped by the IRA. As to whether anyone was to blame, should be held accountable, or if De Lacy finally got what he deserved there was no consensus.

Three days after his escape, a picture of Richard de Lacy was released by the IRA. His dead body was unrecognisable. His eyes had been gouged out, his ears cut off, and an implement had been inserted into his rectum.

The IRA had their justice and Adrienne felt that, at last, Daniel's assault had been avenged in full measure. Even if her son had no wish for such revenge.

It should have been worrying for Adrienne that Richard de Lacy's fate was entirely disproportionate to the crime of assaulting Daniel on the Upper, but she consoled herself with the thought that he'd murdered clergy in Ballysluthra, and she'd fulfilled her good faith promise to the IRA.

The Twilight Hours

Howard sat in his flat in Grand Avenue, Hove. Adrienne had no idea he'd bought the flat, or that it was fully furnished and filled with artworks.

Howard had another secret Adrienne knew nothing about. Nobody knew. Well, apart from him and Daniel. From the moment Peter Archer had revealed Daniel's location, he'd been secretly watching the Laughton Cottage. He'd used a different car each time, and he'd stayed out of sight. Nothing could keep him away from his son. He'd allowed Adrienne her way in sending Daniel to boarding school, but the reconciliation was going to be done his way and alone. He knew he'd played a much bigger role in Daniel's childhood than had Adrienne: he'd given up his work while she'd immersed herself in hers. He believed Daniel would recognise that difference.

What did all this secrecy, 'duplicity', to name it correctly, say about his marriage?

Truthfully? It was over.

As he sat in the lounge, rejoicing at Daniel's safety, he unwrapped a Havana cigar, poured himself a dry sherry, looked at the white horses on the sea, just visible from the corner window in the lounge, and he thought about his first conversation with Daniel in Sussex.

Five years ago, back in 1968, he had parked in a small road near Ringmer College. He loved watching Daniel ride by in the late afternoon. He had never seen his son look so happy. Sometimes Daniel went into a nearby supermarket with his friends. They laughed and joked, and the contrast between Fraser's reports about his loneliness at Oakingham and this happy frivolity hurt him deeply. One day, as Daniel came out of the shop, he walked to his bike and noticed Howard in the car.

It was an extraordinary moment. Daniel looked astonished but not unhappy or angry. He walked over to Howard's car.

'How come you're here?' Daniel asked incredulously.

'I like seeing you look so happy,' Howard said truthfully.

'How often have you come?'

'Why don't you pop in the car for a second and we can chat.'

And so it was that Daniel had sat next to his father for the first time in many years. As he sat in the leather seats, a feeling of loving familiarity came over him. He was hit by a surprising truth: he was enjoying sitting with his father.

Daniel's friends had cycled off.

'They look like a nice bunch of kids.'

'They're great – mad as hatters!'

There was a long awkward silence. Daniel broke it.

'If you come here occasionally, we can talk. But nothing about my life down here must change, nothing. And nobody must know.'

'Why would I want to change a life that's so good? We've done enough harm already.'

'Speaking of which – I don't want to see my mother.'

He spoke as if she was some distant person, on another world.

'Your mother knows nothing about my trips down here, and neither will she.'

It was as great a deception as an affair; perhaps greater. He had made contact with their son, pretending all the time that no such contact existed. He had colluded with Daniel in maintaining the secret and had tacitly allowed Daniel to put a dividing line between them. Perhaps it was truer to say that Daniel had exposed a divide which had existed for so many years.

Our Lady of Sorrows Church, London
Barrie's coffin was in the nave. It had been received the previous evening, and the Rosary had been said by the resident clergy.

'Any word from Eleanor?' Naomi asked.

'The Lord may know where she is, but I don't, and it's an awful thing when your wife's not at your funeral,' the priest replied.

After the service, they went out into the graveyard, where the roses were fading, and the trees were brown. As the coffin was lowered into the ground, Daniel wept. Barrie had been his friend in need, his only friend in that Godforsaken school, and now he felt the full force of desolate grief.

Meanwhile, Adrienne was again focusing on affairs of the state, rather than the heart.

Harold Wilson now led a minority Government. He and his friend Marcia Falkender called her into Downing Street.

'We know you're friendly with Ted Heath, but we need your expertise.'

'Can I put it as the Americans would?' she asked.

'Feel free,' Marcia said.

'I serve at the pleasure of the Government,' Adrienne said.

'We rather thought you'd say that,' Marcia said.

Chapter Thirty-Nine

Daily Chronicle. News desk. 13 September 1973

Simon watched the older hacks. Their sallow faces spoke of incessant alcohol and smoking. The wall of the office was yellow from nicotine. Helen was typing up her column with the desperation of the aspirant retiree. The new Wilson Government was struggling to pass any legislation and inflation was still through the roof.

The ringing of Simon's desk phone shook him from his torpor.

'Some joker for you,' Nancy from the switchboard announced.

'Great!' groaned Simon.

'I have new information on the Cabinet bombing plot. And just to verify I'm not a timewaster, I can prove they were digging the tunnel in the wrong direction.'

Later, Simon greeted 'Crucible' at the Newsdesk reception. The caller had insisted on the codename.

They sat in an office more akin to a cupboard: a desk, two chairs and a tape recorder.

'Firstly, you may not be aware of the link between the Jewish boy who was beaten up on a cricket pitch seven years ago and the Westminster bombing plot,' Crucible said.

'No, I'm not,' Simon said.

'When the boy was left traumatised after being beaten up by a crazy anti-Semite, he went to live with a family he'd previously befriended near the school. Leicestershire Social Services agreed he could live there under supervision.'

Simon assumed they'd get to the bomb plot sometime during the afternoon.

'The boy's name was Daniel, so let's call him that.'

'OK.'

'Daniel's case at Social Services was led by a woman called Sarah. She told Daniel's parents that they couldn't have access to their son, because he didn't want to see them.'

'Not surprising from what I remember of the case; they'd left him in some isolated hell of a school.'

Crucible continued, 'Sarah didn't know a vital piece of information: the husband of the new, supposedly safe family, was an IRA sleeper, who went on to take charge of digging the tunnel in Whitehall.'

'You have evidence of this link?'

'As much as you like. And I've got Letters from Social Services to the new family, as well as a letter from Social Services passing on a request for the Israeli Ambassador to meet Daniel.'

Simon was struggling to keep up, but he knew this could be a career-changing story.

'Then there's the Neasden Three,' Crucible said.

'They were killed by the police, weren't they?'

'Well, they were killed, but as to who killed them, that's for later in the story. While Sarah at Leicester Social Services was lecturing the parents about their negligence, she was sending Daniel into a house under IRA threat. But the really important part of the story is about who knew what and when.'

'And what's your angle on this? Why are you here telling me all this?'

'You're not going to know that, and before I tell you anymore, you and your editor are going to promise me ...' Crucible paused '... that even in the most extreme situation, you will never reveal your source.'

The front page caused a storm:

Jewish Victim Sent to IRA Hell House!

The story implicated Leicester Social Services, who refused to comment. Sussex Social Services said it was Leicester's case. Why would there be a link between the school assault and the Westminster plot? The letters flooded into the *Chronicle*.

It was the second interview that blew the lid off.

Simon sat in his editor's office. He liked Frank Lancaster and respected his abilities, borne of long service. Frank's office was a definite promotion from the cupboard.

Crucible sat in an office chair.

'Ok, what I'm about to tell you has implications for the country, the safety of its vulnerable children, and the Intelligence Services.'

Neither of the listeners were sceptical. They'd received all the evidence promised by Crucible, and their newspaper had sold in huge numbers.

'The Intelligence Services knew that Daniel was in a house that was unsafe, that the husband was an IRA sleeper, and they knew he was in danger.'

Frank was on the phone, on his big, messy desk.

'Get Hughes in here now!'

James Hughes was the in-house lawyer. He arrived and took a seat.

'Hit us with it,' Frank said, in a failed attempt at sounding hip.

'Both MI5 and MI6 knew the IRA sleeper was the husband in that house.'

'Why didn't they arrest him then?' Simon asked.

'They were playing the long game – very long actually. '

'They hoped he'd lead them to the big cheeses?' Frank ventured.

'They did a bit more than hope,' Crucible said.

The room was quiet except for the sound of typewriters in the adjacent office.

Crucible continued. 'It's hard to believe, but the woman who was married to the IRA sleeper was working for MI5. She knew he was an IRA sleeper.'

Frank interrupted. 'Knew when she took the boy in? Surely not!'

'Absolutely! She'd known since 1963.'

'You're kidding!' Simon and Frank said in unison. Hughes was in danger of swallowing the biro.

'MI5 have a file on this woman. Her name is Eleanor. You can't keep the file, but I can show it to you.'

Crucible took out a sheet of paper and read Eleanor's file. Simon was thinking about his career and what a great story this was. Frank, to his own disbelief, as an old hack, found himself caught up in the emotion of the revelations.

Crucible was still talking.

'The file can't be seen by anyone before 1999, but I've got it, you've seen it and you can confirm you know the reference. It is …'

'You got any other evidence she was working for MI5?'

'Ask a man called Julian Penrose, he works for MI5. Just tell him you'll reveal his sexual proclivities if he doesn't confirm Eleanor was working for them.'

'Blimey, you're all heart, aren't you?' Simon said.

'Then don't meet him. Take it from me, it started in a pub, the North London Tavern, back in '63.'

As Crucible revealed chapter and verse in great detail, Frank and Simon knew they had a huge story on their hands. The question was: could they run with it?

James Hughes spoke in a slightly plodding baritone voice.

'Let's be honest, Frank. You're going to run with this regardless, so just pass me the rubber stamp.'

There was rarely much love between editors and lawyers.

When Crucible left, and Frank was alone, he knew there was one call he had to make. The *Chronicle* was in financial trouble, like so many Fleet Street papers.

Lord Fairfax was in his parliamentary office, about to vote in the chamber.

'Harvey, it's Frank. Ignoring yesterday's sell-out run ...'

'You might ignore it, I'm not,' Lord Fairfax sounded tipsy.

'Anyway, the next part of the story's explosive, but it could get us prosecuted.'

'Give me the worst'

When Frank had finished speaking, and the Division bell was ringing in the Lords, Fairfax paused.

'Lord Wellesley, the Duke of Wellington. Good afternoon, Frank.'

The phone went down, the line cleared, and Frank smiled. Wellington had said, 'Publish and be damned'.

So, they would.

MI5 Offices, Crucible Story: Day One
The *Chronicle* story had put Frobisher at MI5 and Kershaw at MI6 into apoplectic anger. Who'd given this story to the Chronicle? And who knew that level of detail?

Senior personnel from Special Branch, MI5 and MI6 arrived in the Chronicle's Fleet Street Offices.

Frank Lancaster greeted them in his office. 'We've been expecting you!'

'By the time we've finished, you might not be smiling, Mr Lancaster,' said one of the raincoated spooks.

'Oh, I don't know about that. I've consulted with every editor on this fine street, and for once we're united: you try to intimidate us, take us to court or censor us, you'll be dealing with the entire national newspaper industry.'

'Mr Lancaster, my name is Davydd Williams, I'm the senior legal officer at MI5 and I have no intention of intimidating anyone!'

'Ah, that'll be why four of you marched into this building unannounced.'

'Standard procedure, Mr Lancaster, that's all. Now this is really simple. National security requires that you tell us the source for this story. We can't allow this sort of thing; we've got a country to protect!'

'So have I, Mr Williams, so have I, and I'm just hoping I do a better job than you people have been doing the last few years. Now please get out of here.'

'Who gave you the story?' Williams asked.

'You'll need the waterboarding and the thumb screw together, for that one I'm afraid!' Frank smiled and lit a Hamlet cigar. 'Happiness is knowing you're in the right!'

'Harvey Fairfax doesn't have pockets big enough for this,' one of the raincoats said.

'Lucky we've got the *Telegraph, Mail, Express, Sketch, Times, Sunday* ...'

'Okay, we get the picture. We'll see you in court. I hope you're proud of breaching UK security like this.'

'Actually I am. How're you guys feeling about letting that young boy, Daniel, live in an IRA cesspit you knew all about?'

The raincoats walked out of the building, and Frank hit the phones.

That afternoon, Michael Frobisher called Adrienne.

'Time for us to have another chat,' he said.

'I was about to call you. Before you ask me, *no*, I was not the source!'

'Sorry, Adrienne, but we don't see how it can be anyone else. I mean, who else knows that much about it?'

'Sir Michael, I suggest we meet in a secure place so you can apologise unreservedly for calling a long-term servant of this country a liar!'

Adrienne took a taxi into MI5's office. Frobisher was there, his deputy, a senior man from Special Branch, and a man she presumed to be a lawyer.

'This is Sir Terence Bentley, from Lovetts' solicitors,' Frobisher explained.

'And this is Fraser Cameron from Clifford Turner,' Adrienne said as a tall grey man walked into the room. 'Now perhaps you'd like to tell me exactly what I'm accused of, and what evidence you have.'

'It's not that kind of meeting,' Frobisher said.

'I think it is,' Adrienne said. 'You have your lawyer here, you've accused me of being a liar on the phone, and you think I breached national security. All of those things are entirely untrue.'

Major Bentley had a wool grey pin stripe, and a voice to match.

'Mrs Goldberg, we all hold you in the highest esteem. We just want to understand who else would have had motive to name and shame Leicestershire and Sussex Social Services. Who else knew about the link between your son and the now deceased IRA sleeper?'

'I've been wondering that myself, all night,' Adrienne said.

Fraser Cameron stood up. 'You have no evidence against Mrs Goldberg. You're making accusations that are most unpleasant. Please contact me when you have something substantial to discuss. Mrs Goldberg, I suggest we leave.'

The Crucible Story: Day Two

MI5 Agent Was Married To IRA Sleeper Looking After Daniel!

Harold Wilson called a COBR meeting.

It was agreed that Adrienne must be taken off all security-sensitive roles. Nobody was searching for evidence, because there were only two people outside MI5 and MI6 who knew Eleanor had been watching Barrie since 1963. Eleanor was one and Adrienne was the other. Very few people knew where Eleanor was, and she seemed an unlikely source for the story. Most people agreed that Adrienne had taken revenge on Social Services whom she hated.

Adrienne returned to Regent's Park having been stripped of every role she had ever nurtured or loved. She was *persona non grata* and not even Henry Kissinger could help her. In any event, he was shocked by the developments in the UK.

Adrienne was totally innocent. She had nothing to do with the story. Everything appeared to show an intimate knowledge of her role: every nuance, and slight was guaranteed to ensure that she was implicated.

She had called Frank Lancaster so many times at the *Chronicle*, but he wasn't returning her calls. In days gone by, he would have been begging for information from her.

Crucible Story Day Three

Crucible had just finished speaking to Frank Lancaster at the *Daily Chronicle*. There would be a few more sins to forgive at Yom Kippur, but at last, his mother knew about the agony of injustice, rejection, and more than anything – not being heard.

It was about time.

Chapter Forty

Looking at the family group, gathered in that small synagogue, an observer would have seen nothing remarkable. Daniel, Naomi and her parents. What could be more natural? Yet each of them, in their own way, was thinking about their journey to this place of worship, on this most solemn evening.

Naomi and Daniel clasped hands together as the beautiful song rang out, as it did throughout the world. When the rabbi said Daniel's favourite words, 'At this hour all Israel stands before God', Daniel knew that this Yom Kippur would require him to face up to his faith, to allow his recent sins of commission to collide with his love of God. He had ruined his mother's career and found no mercy for her when she had almost begged for a reconciliation. How could a man like that deserve to become a rabbi? How could he even sit in this holy place on the Day of all Days, naked before the Almighty? Yet wasn't this the very purpose of the day? He could use the time of reflection to determine his new direction, to see if he could find a place in his soul to forgive his mother.

His thoughts turned to his father. What did it say about his father that he had been prepared to encourage secret meetings with Daniel, further dividing a family already in deep crisis?

As the Kol Nidre service moved towards its sonorous end,

he realised that the next day, Yom Kippur, he would have to face up to his own responsibilities instead of playing God, literally, in apportioning blame between his family.

At this hour it was Daniel who stood before his God.

Cumberland Terrace, Regent's Park, Adrienne

Jewish families everywhere would be going to synagogue. Parents would be exhorting their children to get dressed and not to forget their head coverings. The orthodox would walk, the progressives would drive, and all would arrive for this most solemn day of prayer, to face their God.

Knowing this, imagining this, made Adrienne's solitude black. The deep well of loneliness was beckoning her, drawing her in, and she was succumbing in full measure. She could even see the people walking to Great Portland Street Synagogue from her balcony. She sat, in her silent lounge, and reflected on the crushing events of her life.

When she'd learned she was pregnant, all those years ago, her turmoil had deep roots far beyond her interrupted career.

In her lounge, that Yom Kippur morning, she took herself back to the days when her own parents had made her feel as if she was nothing more than a nuisance. As her school reports became more glowing, so their relationship deteriorated. Who needed a bright bookish child? Her parents played sports every weekend. Her mother played hockey and netball, and her father played golf and football. The house was often quiet, so she had thrown herself lovingly into her studies. When parents came to collect her school friends from birthday parties, she had watched the children run out to hug their parents and jump happily into their cars. Adrienne had felt no such glee. They never beat her, or starved her, but she had suffered an emotional deficit where love should have been, and she had always been determined that she would never inflict such a fate on any child of hers.

Her pregnancy had required her to face up to her past, and she had felt terror and foreboding at the thought of the awesome responsibility ahead.

As she failed to bond with the little infant in the cot, it seemed her worst fears had been realised. Mothers were supposed to adore their children; to hug and play with them, to make silly noises as they changed them or lifted them out of the bath. As nobody had explained to her that these feelings of detachment were common and said nothing about her likely ability to be a good parent later, she'd assumed that this was just the start of the downward spiral of poor parenting that, more than anything, she had dreaded.

Neither academic brilliance nor diplomatic aplomb on the world stage required the basic level of emotional intelligence which would have told her that it was spending time with her son, devoting days just to him, being there to play with him and to greet him, to listen to him and to hug him that were the requirements of a loving mother.

Nobody would understand how her paralysing fear of being a disinterested mother had led to the paradoxical mistakes in Daniel's upbringing.

Now, as she fasted, as the morning wound around, the fissures in her family crushed her spirit and she sobbed alone in her luxurious flat.

Daniel

The hectic morning prayers in synagogue were over. As parents left to give their children lunch, a spiritual somnolence descended on the Yom Kippur day. Where the hall had been crowded to bursting point, with latecomers having to stand at the back and sides, now there were many empty seats. Older men sat quietly listening to the tale of Jonah, or not listening. Thinking about their lives and loves, their victories and failings. Teenagers could be heard in the synagogue garden, indulging in the slightly less spiritual pursuits of flirting and laughing with their friends.

Naomi, Peter and Tanya had left. Daniel had the time and space to reflect alone.

Why hadn't he told Naomi about his meetings with his father? He had been worried that the collision of his old world with his happy new world, the blurring of the boundaries, might somehow change his idyllic life in Sussex. In fact, seeing his father occasionally without telling anyone had made his new life easy. He had been in touch with his father while loving his new life. Once Naomi, Eleanor, Barrie or anyone else knew, the entire dynamic would have changed. That was his truth, but telling Naomi now meant admitting the deceit and how might that change their relationship.

As he sat and prayed, his mind was made up. He would tell Naomi everything and face the consequences.

Well, not quite everything. Crucible would be a revelation too far.

This decision made, he turned his attention to the two other women in his life. He had no idea where Eleanor was. It was clear that she was far more complex than she appeared. To some extent she had endangered his life, but irrationally, he had few inner dilemmas about her. She had nurtured him back to health, and he was grateful. She had given him the home which had enabled him to meet Naomi, and she had encouraged his Judaism. He had much to thank her for, even if questions remained. He thought little about the life-threatening danger to which she'd exposed him.

Just before the memorial service began, as people began to file back into the hall, Daniel asked forgiveness from his God, and decided that he would try to reconcile with his mother.

Howard

Yom Kippur had never been special. He'd usually worked through it if it fell on a weekday. He was due to meet an art dealer in the Brighton Lanes and a good lunch was a certain accoutrement to their discussions.

Howard had experienced no guilt about his many meetings with Daniel. He didn't think Adrienne deserved any apologies, or revelations, and he wasn't about to offer any.

The time would come when he must tell Tanya, Peter and Naomi about his flat in Hove, but he was enjoying the idea that Adrienne had no idea where he was.

Howard remembered how he had encouraged Adrienne. He'd even taken a prolonged sabbatical to facilitate her return to work. His sister had been annoyingly right: he had been dragged along with Adrienne's avalanche. Adrienne had wanted Daniel out of the way at boarding school, so he'd outwardly justified a decision that inwardly broke his heart. It had all been an act. He had drowned in the waters of Adrienne's ambition. Instead of empowering them both, their love had eviscerated his sense of self. He hated himself for his weakness. He hated her for having no interest in his views, and for the resultant effect on Daniel.

Missing was his sense of responsibility for his own actions, for his own weakness.

Now, he was looking forward to a new future. He had inherited many paintings created by Edward Hopper's wife, Jo. Edward had ignored her talent, but Howard planned to tell the public about the secret art of Jo Hopper and make some money in the process.

Daniel and Naomi, Peter and Tanya
On the early evening of Yom Kippur, the service was suddenly interrupted. Peter Klein had received a message from a Steward that he was wanted in the Beth Midrash Hall. When he returned, he looked solemn and fearful. Daniel and Naomi were puzzled as he walked up the steps of the Bimah, the raised platform which held the sacred scrolls, from which Rabbi Levene was currently leading the service. Peter spoke into the rabbi's ear.

Peter faced the synagogue.

'This afternoon we have heard some grave news. Israel has been invaded on at least two of its borders, and fasting soldiers are being hurried to the Front.'

The congregation were stunned and tearful.

'Before we resume the usual service, as we surely shall, I think we'd all like to sing the Israeli National Anthem.'

As Naomi lay in bed that night she was thinking about Israel, but mostly she was trying to understand the late-night conversation with Daniel. It seemed to have Catholic undertones. He had kept things from her, but now he wanted to tell all. Provided he never kept anything from her again, would she forgive him? She'd been deeply shocked about the meetings with his father. It was hard to believe that for all those years, he'd been seeing Howard. He'd been unable to confide in her, worried others would know. But why? Didn't he think she could keep a secret? From that angle it seemed unforgiveable. And how would she know if he repeated his behaviour?

But then, he had found the courage to tell her the truth and to admit his mistakes and she loved him the more for telling her the truth.

Safehouse

Which still left the problem of Adrienne. How were they to deal with Daniel's almost visceral hatred for her? There were many more conversations to have; but then, she supposed, that was what marriage was about, conversation and communication in a loving framework.

Eleanor

She knew it was Yom Kippur. When she lived in the Laughton Cottage, she had put the major Jewish festivals in her diary. She wondered how Daniel would spend it. She had been cut off from the boy she loved, and the pain was deep, but she had pride too. She had brought him back to life and strength and sent him back into the wild. He had forged a wonderful relationship with Naomi and her parents, and her MI5 contact, Sam, had told her he'd been seen at his parents' flat.

She had taken Daniel into her house in the certain knowledge that hers could never be a safe house. He had been a whisper away from being killed by the IRA, and both she and Barrie were responsible.

As she thought about never seeing Daniel again, she knew it was no more than she deserved.

Adrienne

Late in the afternoon she listened to the BBC, and she heard about the attack on Israel. Just a week or so ago she would have been rushed into Downing Street, perhaps even flown to Washington. Her phone remained silent.

Israel

In the extreme heat of the Negev Desert, a hut stood alongside building works. The Israeli flag flew next to the hut, and irrigation work that would help Israel and its neighbour, Jordan, was bearing fruit, quite literally. A tall, bearded man emerged, filthy, from the hut and spoke to one of his geologists. His Hebrew was appalling, made much worse by his Irish accent.

He sat under an olive tree and read the letter.

Dear Chaim,

I know how glad you'll be when I tell you that your protégé recently married his fiancée in Ramat Gan. They said a memorial prayer for you, told everyone how much they loved and missed you, and went off to start married life. Thanks to your 'death', they need never worry again about being held hostage by the IRA, and here in Israel, we are thankful that your skills are being put to good use in the service of your new country.

I hear through the breeze that fills the olive trees you've met a lovely lady. I couldn't be happier.

Lots of love,

Ariella

Epilogue 1

Cumberland Terrace, Regent's Park

Adrienne found it hard to believe Daniel's revelations. He'd been seeing Howard all through those long years. He'd admitted his hatred for his mother and told her he couldn't be a rabbi without trying to resolve his family issues. He wanted to forge a new relationship with her: one that acknowledged both of their failings.

Her joy at this reconciliation with her son was in danger of drowning in the sea of hatred she now felt for Howard. It was the ultimate betrayal, and she would never forgive him, wherever he was.

In the past twenty-four hours, she had also thought a great deal about her betrayal at the hands of the press story. Late in the afternoon, the previous day, it had occurred to her that there was someone other than Howard who'd had access to Eleanor's MI5 file on her sideboard. She'd left Naomi and Daniel alone for a couple of hours in the flat.

She decided she didn't want to know the truth.

White's Club, St James's London

As her meal with Jimmy ended, and they both drank port, their hands slid to the middle of the table, and they grasped each other.

'Don't you think it's time, darling Adrienne?'

'I certainly do, long overdue,' Adrienne replied.

They held hands as they left the grand dining room, and they climbed the wide stairs to the first floor. The pictures of prime ministers and royalty, previous members of the club, seemed to nod their consent as they walked towards the bedroom that Jimmy had booked.

Soon they were in a loving embrace, and Adrienne could forget about Howard and Daniel as Jimmy's surprisingly tender caresses and kisses, combined with her long- lasting love for him, sent her out to sea on a wave of want.

Epilogue 2

Somewhere in the United Kingdom. October 1974
It was an isolated spot: the nearest town was more than ten miles away.

Eleanor walked around her garden, pulling weeds, and thought about many of the people who'd come into her life over the last few years. As the afternoon sun put her fading flowers in the shade, she thought about Daniel. Did he hate her? Did he wonder where she was? Did he even think of her at all?

Then she thought about her extraordinary meeting the previous day with elderly Sam Reynolds, her original MI5 contact.

He'd met her in the village near her home, and as the local folk and a few remaining tourists enjoyed scones and jam, he smiled and gave her an envelope. His life had taken its toll on his face. It was craggy, with deep lines and furrows. His eyebrows were thick and his hair white. She looked at the official-looking envelope.

'Open it at home.'

She'd taken the bus home, and as she walked back from the bus stop, down a small isolated lane, her cottage came into view. She looked at the front garden and thought of the improvements she could make. Then she went into the kitchen and sat on a bar stool.

She opened the letter. It was headed with the Royal Coat of Arms.

Eleanor trembled as she read the typewritten page.

Sandringham, Norfolk
On behalf of the United Kingdom and all its inhabitants,
I want to thank you for your recent service. Prince Philip
joins me in this expression of our sincere gratitude for
your courage and patriotism.

Elizabeth R

It was a handwritten signature.

As she sat next to the wobbly table where Daniel had enjoyed his lemonade all those years ago, she looked at her watch. Her guest should be here soon.

A few minutes later, the doorbell went. Eleanor walked to the door and opened it.

'You're very welcome to my home.'

Adrienne walked through the house and sat at the wobbly table.

Two women who'd both lost their husbands, who loved the same young man, and who'd both sacrificed their family life because they loved their country, enjoyed the last rays of sun.

Adrienne's ejection from her role in Government and her public humiliation had delighted the UK Intelligence Services. The Government's loss would be their undercover gain. And what a woman to have on their side.

'The Israeli embassy told me Ariella's engaged,' Eleanor said.

'That's lovely,' Adrienne said.

Eleanor filled some flutes with champagne.

Something Daniel had once said came into her mind. She raised her glass.

'Do you know the one about the Catholic spy, the Jewish diplomat from Regent's Park and the Israeli politician? Well, here's to us all. We'll choose the people we support, bring hellfire and damnation on those we don't, and if we're successful, nobody'll have a clue what we're up to.'

As the final rays of Autumn sunshine faded, and the wind blew the fallen leaves, they toasted each other.

Their impact on world events would be incalculable in years to come. But for now, they sat around a table in Eleanor's garden and talked about the boy who'd changed their lives for ever.

THE END

Author's Note

Editors, and others who have helped me, have asked me about the portrayal of anti-Semitism in the fictional Oakingham School.

Sadly, I have had to tell them, and hence you, that at the actual school I attended I experienced everything that Daniel went through except the physical assaults. There was a study full of Nazi regalia and there were pupils who hero worshipped Hitler. Both were tolerated by the school staff. The other anti-Semitic behaviour was exactly as portrayed.

I was thrown out of the Cadet Force, but sadly I was never greeted by Barrie or Dermot in their hut.

I did cycle to Empingham, but I never enjoyed Eleanor's garden, lemonade or solace.

I am more than aware of two important factors:

Many people loved boarding school, even in the 1960s, and especially those who were good at sport.

Boarding school today bears no resemblance to the austerity that Daniel suffered at Oakingham.

The Rabbis and Clergy mentioned in this book.
The late Rabbi Dr Michael Leigh graced the bimah / pulpit of Edgware and District Reform Synagogue for very many years. We had many conversations and the comment I attribute to him in

the book, about boarding schools, was made directly to me.

I was privileged to be taught a module on European Jewish history at Warwick University by the late Rabbi Dr Albert Friedlander.   Again, we discussed many matters and his extraordinary humanity lit up our sessions

Lewes Reform synagogue, to my knowledge, does not exist and Daniel's mentor, Rabbi Levene, is a fictional character.

All the Christian clergy are fictional.

Schools and Pupils

All the pupils mentioned in the book are entirely fictional and none are based on any real character. Oakingham School in Rutland exists only in my imagination...

About the Author

This is James Adley's first novel. He has been a financial adviser for four decades. He lives in North London with his wife, Jude, who is very much a part of his writing team. He has two children, three step-children and four grandchildren, who keep him very busy when he is not writing.

The Belief and Betrayal Series

Events and people interconnect across the twentieth century. Secrets lies and betrayals. In England, Ireland, Palestine and Germany, the consequences of Gloria's venomous hatred ripple through the generations.

People who will go to any lengths to destroy their country and those who risk their lives to stop them.

And each of them confronts their faith – Christianity, Judaism or just their conscience – as their lives fail to live up to their prayers.

Each book is a story in its own right, but the tentacles of perverse hatred and a searing search for justice, pervade them all.

Coming next: Book Two in the Belief and Betrayal Series – 'Gloria'